DEAD DROP

A ROGUE WARRIOR THRILLER

IAN LOOME

INKUBATOR
BOOKS

Published by Inkubator Books
www.inkubatorbooks.com

Copyright © 2024 by Ian Loome

Ian Loome has asserted his right to be identified as the author of this work.

ISBN (eBook): 978-1-83756-298-5
ISBN (Paperback): 978-1-83756-299-2
ISBN (Hardback): 978-1-83756-300-5

DEAD DROP is a work of fiction. People, places, events, and situations are the product of the author's imagination. Any resemblance to actual persons, living or dead is entirely coincidental.

No part of this book may be reproduced, stored in any retrieval system, or transmitted by any means without the prior written permission of the publisher.

1

MEMPHIS, TENNESSEE

The gym was ancient, a relic above an old furniture store, from the era before flat-screen TVs and digital experiences. It reeked of labor, sweat and blood, permanently part of the atmosphere.

Bob mounted the last two steps and drank the place in. It seemed dimly lit despite plenty of low-hanging fixtures, the front windows smudged with dirt, uncleaned for years, and the late afternoon sun barely seeping through.

It had been a long time, more than a decade, but little had changed, as if frozen in time. The benches inside the front entrance looked like splinter factories. The walls were lined with old fight posters, "Jersey" Jerry Park v. Larry Tate, ten rounds; Sugar Ray Leonard v. Donny Lalonde, a starburst of text proclaiming "The Ultimate Comeback."

Some of the posters were newer; most were old, many in black and white, dating back to the Second World War, the era when the fights were the kings of Friday night; when a man with furious fists could captivate a starstruck nation, folks from the oldest senior to the youngest kid gathering around the radio or TV.

He looked to his left, around the corner and front desk. A weedy young man in a string vest sat on a stool, looking bored.

The gym proper occupied most of the upper floor. Heavy bags hung from chains in each corner. Towards the entrance, a row of weight benches and racks sat just ahead of doors to offices and the locker room.

In the ring, nearer the back wall, a kid in black trunks and black gloves moved across the blue canvas in a lithe shuffle, bouncing on the balls of his feet.

The guy he was fighting was bigger, older, probably more experienced.

They closed at the center, where the passing of years had worn the branding logo off the surface.

The older man moved in confidently, guard shifting around as he looked for an opening. But the kid was tagging his opponent as if he stood still. A stinging jab, a bob to one side to slip a punch, two more jabs, sweat flying. Two muscular figures crashing together, one driven back.

Bob crossed the atrium to the locker room. The gym was loud; weight machines clanked; leather gloves slapped leather gloves in the ring. The men ringside laughed at something, gesturing at the sparring partner, whose expression had shifted to genuine concern for his own safety.

Bob retrieved a key from his inside pocket. He'd had it for years, never really expecting to need it. Life on the street had been voluntary; running hadn't been his choice. But he'd run short of cash in New Orleans. Hiding from the CIA wasn't going to be cheap, and the go bag he'd stashed at the gym fifteen years earlier was a security blanket.

New Orleans had been a hell of a mess, coming just a few months after fleeing Chicago. Three weeks cooling his heels in Jackson, Mississippi, had preceded Memphis, a chance to let the heat die down after his near miss with the police.

He knew he'd have to call his Louisiana friends, Pastor Don Green and his wife, Wanda, before long. He needed to be sure they were handling the clergyman's recovery okay.

The locker room was clean, rows along each wall. But it smelled of damp, sweaty gym socks. Bob wrinkled his nose. After parts of a decade living on the streets of Chicago, that was saying something.

There were about two dozen lockers, unchanged with the passing of years. The gym was legendary, more than a half century old, home to several champion fighters. The key was short, with a crimson head, the number 14 engraved into it. Bob walked over to the lockers to his right, following them to the fourteenth. It was nondescript, gunmetal gray like the rest, a short wooden bench ahead of it.

He reached out with the key.

"You mind telling us where you got that?"

He withdrew his hand and put it back into his pocket. The FN 5.7 sat in his other pocket, its weight familiar and comforting. His attempts at avoiding violence since Chicago had been largely futile, thanks to his duplicitous former boss, CIA deputy director Andrew Kennedy, who had hired men to kill him once already. A group of New Orleans criminals had compounded his troubles.

He liked knowing that if violence flared again, he had an appropriately serious response.

"A friend left it to me," Bob said as he turned. "Not that it's any of your business."

The guys from ringside.

The three men were beefy themselves, the broken noses and cauliflower ears suggesting they'd boxed a few rounds. But they were older, middle-aged.

"Yeah? Smart mouth on this guy, Henry." The lead slab of beef had a wavy permanent hairdo and gold rings, his white dress shirt open two buttons at the neck, sleeves up. He looked like an extra from *The Sopranos* after a few months of free buffet access.

"See, this is our gym, my friend…"

"Funny, I thought this gym belonged to Norm O'Hearn. Pretty famously so, actually…"

"He owns half. We own half. So that makes it our business. And we're getting real tired of thieves sneaking in here and ripping off lockers. So answer the fucking question before we give you a reason to remember your manners."

"You used to be a fighter?" Bob asked.

"My good looks gave it away?" He pointed to Bob and turned to his friend Henry. "This guy must be one dumb motherfucker, because he answered my question with another question, which is a good way in his situation for a fella to get hisself punched in the head."

Bob looked him up and down with studious attention.

"Southpaw with a losing record. Never got your shot. I'm guessing you threw a few along the way, too," Bob said. "Let me guess: you started off well, a couple of big wins, got your confidence up. Your manager handled you well, let you fight palookas for a few months until he thought you deserved a shot. Then some actual contender cleaned your clock like he was tossing out old lunch meat."

That hit a nerve. The beefcake tipped his head to one

side, like a dog studying a particularly ballsy cat, then flexed both fists.

"That it? You just... you know... old lunch meat?"

"You're not doing yourself any favors, fella," he muttered.

"I think maybe this guy needs a lesson, Chuck," Henry suggested, crossing his equally beefy arms.

Defuse this. It's childish.

The inner voice being sensible for a change. Nice.

Bob held up both hands, one dangling the key. "See? Locker key. If I was here to steal... So, no need for anyone to get into a fight."

"We saw the key," Chuck said. "The question is what you're doing with it. Because we ain't never seen you in here. Never."

He took a few steps forward.

"You sure you want to do this, Chuck?" Bob said. "I mean, no disrespect, but you're a hundred pounds or more past fighting weight, and I have no real desire to hurt you."

See, that was a stupid way to put it, Bobby. True, but stupid. Now you've hurt his pride.

His attempt at tact had backfired. Chuck strode towards him. "I'm going to show you what it means to—"

He got within two feet of Bob, the left jab thrown twice, snapping the big man's head back.

Chuck shook his head to clear it, a hand flying up to his nose, a trickle of blood coming away. He started forward again, furious. "You sonuva—"

Bob hit him again, snapping his head back with the jab once, twice, three times, Chuck stumbling into his friend Henry's arms. "Big guy, we really don't have to do this," Bob said.

"Motherfucker!" Chuck steamed towards him, eyes

blazing with rage. He threw two surprisingly quick punches, a cross, a roundhouse left, Bob ducking and weaving his way out of harm.

Another cross sailed past him, and he shifted his weight to the ball of his front foot, leaning in to head butt his target in the bridge of the nose.

It cracked, audibly, Chuck stumbling backwards again. This time, Bob followed up, stepping into a hard right cross to the chin that rocked the man. Chuck tried to turn back towards Bob, but the roundhouse left caught him square.

Chuck's legs gave up like wet pasta; he slumped to the ground, dazed.

His friend Henry began to take a step forward. Bob held up both hands. "Gentlemen... really, do we have to do this again? You get hurt, I get hurt... what does anyone gain?"

Henry wasn't having it. "You hit my friend, you've got to go down," he said matter-of-factly. He dropped into a fighting stance.

"Cross-arm Archie Moore defense," Bob said dryly. "Neato."

Fighting guys of this caliber was tiresome. They were trained to within an inch of their lives, but they weren't talented, and they were old, and they were slow.

"Forty-seven professional fights, thirty-four wins, thirty-one by knockout," Henry said as he inched closer. "Chuckie's a good guy, but he never was much in the ring. Me? I'm the real deal. I fought Boom Boom Mancini in his prime, asshole..."

"Congratulations. I assume he knocked your ass out in fairly rapid fashion."

"Sonuvabitch!" Henry threw a couple of quick jabs, Bob letting them bounce off his forearms. He saw the roundhouse right coming early and stepped away from it. He left his weight on his back foot, resisting the natural temptation to step back in on his opponent. As he'd expected, an uppercut flew in from Henry's right hand, Bob still too far away for it to connect.

A few feet away, Chuck groaned pitifully and began to crawl towards the door.

"Five-punch straight-cross combo, if I recall correctly," Bob said. "Pretty well thrown, too. Slower than a tap drip in December, but... you're trying, I'll give you that. I know what you're going to throw before you throw it, Henry. That means this isn't going to end well for you."

"Yeah? How do you fig—" Henry didn't get a chance to finish the sentence, Bob's foot coming up with blinding speed, catching him flush in the crotch. The former fighter's eyes bugged out, his hands going instinctively to his groin. Bob stepped in close and pivoted on his left heel, slamming his elbow into the man's jaw.

Henry's eyes swam around as he went over, balance gone, his big body crashing to the tile floor.

Bob turned to the third man. He had a round face, like a pie plate, a look of panic setting in. His hand shot inside his coat.

It came out gripping a pistol.

Missing his wedding ring. Tan lines say his watch, too. Glock 17, twenty-two ounces of fun, good trigger discipline, too slow. Bob's left hand shot out, grasping the pistol by the barrel. He yanked hard, pulling it from the man's grasp.

He popped the magazine and tossed it to one side, then threw the Glock over his shoulder. "You want to use that on me, you shouldn't hesitate. Now you're going to have to go past me and get it."

The thug's eyes widened again; he turned to run out of the locker room. Chuck was already gone, Henry crawling in that direction.

The owner, Norm O'Hearn, passed them as he entered the locker room. He was elderly, short and stocky, with a face like bunched-up dough, his nose obviously broken multiple times. He had a young fighter next to him.

He looked irked.

"Well... that was a disappointing display."

"Not from where I'm standing. I've been out of commission for years, but I handled that pretty good, I think..."

"You about done?" Norm asked. "You could've just explained yourself to them..."

"I didn't really get a chance. And prior to that... it was nobody's business."

The kid nodded Bob's way. "You want me to kick his ass, Norm?"

Norm patted the kid on the back. "Nah. Nah, that's okay, Kenny. Bob and I go way back. You go finish sparring, okay?"

The kid left the room, looking warily over his shoulder.

Norm held out a hand to shake, and Bob reciprocated. Then Norm shoved his hands into his trouser pockets, in the way older guys sometimes do when they're a little sheepish and embarrassed. "He's... he's a good kid. His mother's quite the tiger, makes sure he's home and out of trouble when he's not training."

"Uh-huh. Look, about the locker..." Bob began.

"It's been a long time. Nobody's heard word one about you in a decade. I figured you'd left me too much money, but after this long, it mostly just covered the rental. Which, with as little as we charge for a monthly locker, is pretty nuts."

"Your business associates... they went from zero to ten

pretty quick," Bob said. "Are they all former fighters of yours?"

"Eh? Lord no!" Norm said. "No... Henry was here for a few months early in his career. But that was twenty-five years ago. They're just a little on edge, is all, because of the thefts."

"Oh. Good. I had a momentary thought the guy might be deluded enough to think he's still got pro speed in his forties."

"You seem to be doing okay."

"Eh... it's a bit different. My training was lifelong, more rigorous than anything normal. And I spent a decade pretty much hoboing it, so..."

"Living hard. Keeps you lean, if you can protect against the cold and damp..."

"It was tough sometimes. But... old news," Bob said. "That's in my past." He nodded back towards the door. "Those guys own a piece of your young fighter?"

Nick nodded. "I manage him for my piece."

"They said they own half the gym."

"They probably like to think so. But they're all... well, let's say 'involved' in the business. On behalf of their employers. Promotions and security and such. Some investment."

"They're mobbed up."

Norm shrugged. "The fight game hasn't changed a whole lot in my seventy-four years," he said. "So... where've you been for a decade, Bob? Last I heard, you were just passing through on furlough from the military or something, some secret dealie..."

Or something. "Yeah... I retired. Then things went... badly for a few years."

"If I recall correct, you had a young lady you were going back to see..."

"Yeah." Bob sighed, probably louder than he'd intended. "Maggie died, unfortunately, not long after that. Car accident."

"Ah... Geez. I'm sorry, Bob, really I am..."

"It's okay. I mean... it's one of those things that's never okay..."

"I get that. My best buddy since we was little died in 'Nam. I mean, it's not the same, I'm sure, but... yeah. That was a half century ago, and I still think about him on the regular."

"I try to just focus on what was special about it, just remember her that way."

Norm nodded over his shoulder. "Look... about the locker. You mind sharing what's so important inside it that you held on to it this long?"

"No time like the present." Bob walked over and unlocked the metal door, the spring-loaded latch clicking back as he opened it. He handed the padlock to Norm.

Norm looked confused. "It's..."

"... completely empty. Yeah, that's the impression it's supposed to present, just in case things changed and someone opened it prematurely."

The locker was divided into a main compartment with a hook attached to its back wall, as well as a small top shelf. The shelf and compartment were both bare.

He reached in and under the shelf, feeling the bottom of its cool metal surface.

There.

The key was attached to the bottom of the shelf. He'd used black electrical tape to ensure the glue didn't give with time. On its head the letters "FMB" were etched on one side, the number 2226 on the other.

Bob held it up. "Feel like taking a trip down the street?"

The older man had a sort of light in his eyes, like he'd been hit with an intriguing puzzle for the first time in a while. "So you stashed something secret in a safe-deposit box, then hid the key here."

"It made sense. Someone gets a key off me and it's the safety-deposit box key, I lose my stash. But this place has been here for over fifty years, so I figured it was safe, and the locker key is anonymous, basically untraceable back to a lock."

"That's... some serious caution."

"I had some bad people paying me the wrong kind of attention; if they managed to wreck my day-to-day life, I needed a place to retreat to. I figured with your cement head and good looks, you weren't going nowhere."

"Oh, charming. Marg loves my broken schnozz."

"Huh! You're still married. That's good. Do I get to meet the long-suffering Mrs. O'Hearn this trip? Back when I was working out here..."

"You mean back when you were turning down my offers to train you as a fighter..."

"Because clearly I needed the help."

"Good point. Like you said, I got a cement head sometimes. You unretiring? You know, doing whatever that secret government trouble was you were doing?"

"Not exactly. Speaking of trouble... who was the third dude? The guy with Henry and Chuck?"

"Morris. He's Chuck's... I dunno, bodyguard? Bouncer? Paid buddy? Something like that."

"Did you talk to him about the missing stuff?"

Norm squinted sideways at him. "Morris? He's been coming to this gym for nearly twenty years."

"So he can't also be a sneak thief? Sometimes, people can surprise you."

"How do you figure?"

"His ring," Bob said. "He had a wedding ring on his left hand. It left a tan line, which suggests he only recently removed it."

"He got divorced six months ago. So?"

"So he left it on for a while, judging by the tan line, which was recent. Then there's the wider tan line on the same wrist."

"Huh."

The older man had something in mind. "His watch?" Bob suggested.

"Yeah... he has a gold Rolex. Had it for years. He loves that watch."

"But he wasn't wearing it today. I noticed when they entered the room, he was scratching his elbow repeatedly, like he couldn't shake an itch. He did it as well when he was over by the ring, watching the fight."

The elderly trainer was trying to put it together, but the pieces weren't fitting. His impression of "Morris" was interfering with his judgment, Bob figured. "He's pawning his jewelry; he's itching at weird times; you're missing things that I'm guessing could be easily sold…"

Norm's mouth dropped open slightly. "He's got a drug problem."

Bob shrugged. "Just a hunch. You'd have to ask him, I guess. When a 'bro' like that changes his ways that quickly, something's usually up. Now…" They began to stroll towards the door.

"Now?" Norm asked as they left the locker room.

"Now I need to get to the bank. I need money, Norm. I wish I could tell you this trip is about stopping by for old times' sake, but..."

"I gotcha, I gotcha," Norm offered. "The branch is still three minutes east of here."

He nodded towards the front counter and the spindle-thin man with greasy brown hair. "Pat, I'm heading out for the day. Make sure you wipe down the universal today, okay? I don't want no more bitching from guys about the bench being damp."

Behind the counter, Pat used a raised index finger to salute as the two old friends took the stairs down to street level together.

IT HAD BEEN another thankless day. Another day of picking up disgusting old towels, hosing down the showers, cleaning the pooled sweat out of the ring.

Pat hated working at the club, but he had a long criminal record, and no one else was hiring. There were, however, just three hours left in the day. He could go home, put his feet up and spark a bowl of crystal meth.

The fight had been something else: short, furious and unexpected, both in occurrence and outcome.

He couldn't see what most of it was about with three gorillas blocking the locker room door.

Or... briefly blocking the locker room door, anyway.

He'd made sure to avoid eye contact with Chuck and Henry when they'd fled, tails between their legs. They were bad guys, old-school gangsters who wouldn't hesitate to take their frustrations out on a smaller man.

A few seconds later, Norm had entered, then strolled out of the room, chatting with some dude Pat had never seen before. He hadn't caught the front end of the conversation.

"Now I need to get to the bank. I need money, Norm…" he heard the man say. Then the guy had turned his head slightly, and Pat missed the rest.

But maybe he'd heard enough.

What had his friend Alexi said? *Find me hard motherfucker, Patty. Some fighter who needs the money. Find me hard man, and I give you reward.*

Pat waited until Norm was gone and he heard the sound of the heavy front door clunking shut. He leaned over the counter and checked around both corners to ensure no one was listening.

He took out his phone. If he was lucky, Alexi was at the diner he'd been frequenting for the better part of a week, ever since a fallout with his boss. The call rang for less than five seconds before being answered.

"What?! I just talk to you yesterday. I am lying low, yes?" Alexi's Russian accent hadn't dimmed in the decade he'd been in Memphis.

"Where you at?"

"I am down the street at Yvgeny's diner. Until June-Marie comes back with car, I cannot go anywhere. Too much risk Victor see me, or one of his people."

"You need muscle still? Because a dude was just in the fight club I work at, and he laid some kind of beating on three wise-guys. Single-handed and all. And he said he needed money." A little embellishment couldn't hurt. "It was brutal. He was like Mike Tyson, if he was a tall, white guy in his forties."

"Huh. You hear where he's going?"

"The bank a block from where you're sitting right now. That's why I'm calling. He should be walking past any minute, with Norm O'Hearn."

"Who?"

"The old stocky guy who owns the gym around the corner."

"Huh. Good! Good, good. Okay, I go..."

"Hey! You said you'd give me a reward..." Pat reminded him, careful not to make it sound like a demand. Alexi was not a warm individual.

"Huh. Reward. Yes, yes. Next time we talk, okay?"

"Yeah, but..."

But the Russian had already hung up the call.

THEY GOT to the bank just as the front door was being locked. The woman doing so was sympathetic, but unable to help.

Bob sighed. "So that's what I get for leaving this until late in the day. We'll have to come back tomorrow."

The woman looked slightly embarrassed. "Tomorrow is Sunday. We're not open."

Bob tried not to let his head sink at all. "Okay. The day after tomorrow."

Norm was smiling as they walked down the steps to the street. "So... you're going to stay until Monday?" Norm wondered as they watched the busy downtown afternoon traffic.

"I guess so, yeah."

"You got somewhere to hang your hat?"

Bob shook his head. "I'll find a cheap motel, something discreet..."

Norm looked up at him like he was mental. "We go back twenty years. You aren't staying in a damn motel." He took out his phone, then waited for a call to ring through. "Sweetie... yeah, it's me. Look, make up the spare room, would ya? We're going to have company for a few nights."

They followed the sidewalk back towards the gym.

They passed the wide front window of a coffee shop, neither man noticing the sudden attention paid them by the man in the corner booth.

2

Alexi Pushkin had been on the run for days.

His accounts were frozen, and he was wanted on police warrants for drug trafficking and assault. His south Memphis apartment was being watched.

All of that paled compared to what his criminal associates planned to do to him — if they ever caught him, of course.

He sat in the corner booth of the café, wolfing down a double cheeseburger like it was his last supper. The large side of fries went down just as quickly.

He'd been on the move often, trying to duck Victor's men. Between his feet, an old tennis bag with "Head" written on the side held the nearly $20,000 he'd stolen before he'd fled.

Eventually, he'd realized from being repeatedly found that they'd tagged his car with a GPS tracker, and had abandoned it on the city's western outskirts. He'd spent chunks of each day since at the diner, owned by an old friend from Russia who'd managed to stay out of the game.

Now he needed to find a new place to stay, something low-key, in a suburb where Victor's organization wouldn't have eyes. June-Marie was already working on that for him.

All you need is break, Alexi, for things to bounce your way. All you need is sign things will...

He froze in mid-thought as the two men walked by the picture window.

One of them was familiar immediately. He'd seen the short, elderly man at the gym when he stopped by to get money from the junkie, Pat. *Mr. Norm O'Hearn.*

The other took a moment to recognize.

Bozhe moi! It cannot be...

He had not seen that face in twenty years, not since the most terrifying night of his life.

March 3, 2002,
Al-Mazrae, a village near Bait Karim
IRAQ

THE OPEN-BACKED Ural-4320 transport truck rattled and shook as it cruised along the rutted, bumpy dirt road.

Two men were in the cab. Seven more sat in the rear cargo bed on a long metal bench, its opposite filled with gear.

The men, dressed in nondescript desert fatigues unmarked by any affiliation, were slumped, weary, covered in sand and dust. Their AK-47 rifles were propped between their feet.

The night was beginning to cool. Alexi Pushkin sat at the end of the bench and studied his colleagues. Like them, he was a mercenary, a member of the Ferak Group, a "private" military contractor that took its orders secretly from the Russian government. Most were former Russian military, accustomed to the fight and with few job prospects at home.

Pushkin knew he was not cut out for any of it, not anymore. Fighting the insurgent forces had been fierce, including two weeks in a suburb of Tikrit when they'd had little supply or support.

It wasn't the violence that frightened him; it was the statistics. Alexi had no qualms about hurting others. In fact, he felt very little for anyone but himself. His father had been equally cold-blooded, perhaps more so, goading his boys into brawls regularly to toughen them up.

But Alexi knew the odds of surviving multiple firefights and that, eventually, his number would be up.

Sweeping villages for resources — cash, weapons, supplies — had been infinitely preferable to fighting on the front lines.

He had no idea why they were there, why anyone in Moscow cared about the Iraq conflict. He just cared that they were well paid.

The village of Al-Mazrae had been particularly enjoyable; they had decent livestock holdings, which meant the men had been able to spit roast an entire lamb or goat on each trip back. The village had been easy pickings.

The villagers were frightened, untrained, accustomed to being treated badly by local army, militia and rebels. They'd remained behind the closed doors of clapboard huts, or huddled in the shadows, watching the men treat their town like a brothel on a weekend furlough.

To be certain they'd face no opposition, the Russians had shot a deputy chieftain and raped his daughter.

They'd also found about a metric ton of hashish in a storage pit. That was worth a lot of money in the west, and Alexi wanted his cut.

They left Kasparov behind and moved on to the next village to keep the hash and weapons in view until they could, on their way back to base, pick most or all of it up. Their truck had enough room for the job.

The truck turned the last corner, the dirt road rising up a small hill to the village's plateau. At the top of the hill, twenty yards before the village entrance, its brakes squealed as it ground to a halt.

Why are we stopping?

The diesel engine chugged throatily as it idled. One of his colleagues stood and tried to peer over the top of the cab. Then he walked up to it and banged on the back window. "What's going on?" he called out.

Alexi heard the driver's side door open. He craned his neck over the side and watched as the sergeant who'd been at the wheel got out.

"What's the holdup?" Alexi called out.

But the driver just waved a hand back at him dismissively and headed for the front of the vehicle.

"What's going on?" Alexi asked the corporal who'd banged on the cab. "Can you see?"

The corporal ignored him and hopped over the high-sided trailer and onto the soft ground.

Alexi could hear the men jabbering in animated fashion, but the engine noise was making it hard to understand their conversation.

The soldier to his right lost his patience. "I'm going to find out..." He opened the back gate to the trailer and climbed down, then began walking towards the front of the truck.

The man next to him joined him.

A moment later, a second man got out of the cab.

Major Kusnetsov, taking charge.

Alexi didn't move. They were under orders to stay in the truck until they reached their destination. It was probably just a goat in the road or something stupid like that. The others were risking reprimand.

"Aren't you curious, Alexi?"

Yuri, the soldier next to him, looked anxious. But they'd done everything together since they were kids, including joining up. Yuri always waited to see what he wanted to do, because Yuri appreciated that Alexi was the smarter of the two.

Alexi jerked his head towards the scene ahead of the truck. "Go, if you're so fascinated! Me, I'm staying right here until ordered otherwise."

"Why?"

"Don't be stupid, Yuri! You know what Kuznetsov is like about discipline! He's probably reading those guys the riot act as we speak. This area is deeply contested, too, with snipers around. It could be a trap…"

"You are too cautious. I'll go see, report back!"

Yuri scarpered off the truck, followed almost immediately by the one remaining colleague.

They are foolish. This is against protocol. Kuznetsov should order them all back to their seats.

But Alexi knew they were probably right. It was just his nerves.

You've been here too long, that's all.

He could hear voices being raised over the growl of the motor. Something was going on; that much was obvious.

Fine. Whatever this is must be pretty damned important...

He got up, walked to the back end of the truck and jumped down. Alexi peered around the vehicle's rear left corner.

The others were standing in front of the truck, partially surrounding something he couldn't make out. Alexi inched closer until he reached the back of the pack of men and peered over another's shoulder.

It was Kasparov.

He was tied to an office chair, chin on chest, his beard matted with blood. He'd been bound with the same thin barbed wire the locals used on cattle enclosures, the metal cutting into his skin through his clothes. He had gaping gunshot wounds to the chest that looked a day or two old.

His eyes were wide open, gazing ahead lifelessly. Flies had settled on his eyelids and buzzed noisily around his body, perhaps initially drawn by moisture.

A folded note was hanging around his neck from a thin piece of filament.

No one reached down to open it.

Eventually, Major Kuznetsov pulled his combat knife from its sheath. He used the tip to open the note without touching the wire it hung from, each man well aware that booby-trapping bodies was common among the insurgents.

"It's in English," he said. "Russians, go home before you join him. Why fight for Saddam? He means nothing to you! Your friend's death was brutal. Imagine how his family will feel, knowing he is gone, knowing they will never see him again. Do you wish your wives and daughters to cry nightly? Leave now. You are warned."

He put the knife back in its sheath. "Is anyone frightened by this?"

The men shook their heads sullenly. They were violent, accustomed to brutal death.

"Do we cower before these savages? Or do we enter this village and exact revenge for our comrade?"

"*DA!*" the half-dozen men agreed in unison.

All but Alexi. He'd had a bad feeling about the mission before, but now? They were taking the warning too lightly.

He slowly retreated to the back of the truck, away from the group, instinct telling him it couldn't be as simple as the vengeful pack believed. No one had ever suggested to Alexi that he was a smart or gifted man. But he'd always had a strong survival instinct, and the situation seemed off.

"Kill who you like, take any women you want," Kuznetsov announced. "But leave the elders for me. We'll deal with them one by one, see how much they hold back intel when listening to their loved ones scream. In the meantime... Gregor, Yuri... once we're clear, untie him and cover the body. Keep a watch for wires. The rest of us will go settle this. We'll give him a decent burial once we've dealt with them."

The major worked the bolt on his AK. "Let's move."

He took one step towards the village gates, and the top of his head exploded, the *thwip* sound of the second bullet thudding into his body coming a moment before the light *pop* of the rifle's discharge.

Kuznetsov dropped to his knees, the light dancing in his eyes for a few moments before his heart stopped. He pitched over, face-first, and slammed into the dirt.

"SNIPER!" someone screamed. "DOWN, DOWN!"

The men all dropped in place, flattening themselves on the ground.

Based on the sound, a good way off, Alexi thought. The top of the major's head had flown backwards, suggesting the shooter was on the other side of the village somewhere, likely elevated. Alexi crouched low by the rear tire, using it for cover.

They were completely unprotected except for the truck. The nearest village hut was fifty yards away. But with a competent sniper and decent hardware, it might as well have been fifty miles.

The prone men were sitting ducks, trying to flatten themselves to the ground, crawling away, whimpering, praying for help. Bullets thumped into them, just separated by the time it would take to adjust aim. Vladi Lirianov, a corporal Alexi barely knew, realized what was happening. "Oh God!" he cried, as he tried to find his feet and run, his rifle raised as he turned to search for a target a split second before a bullet blew the back of his skull off.

A few others recognized their plight and tried to scramble clear on all fours. But the sniper was lethally accurate, the wind minimal. Bodies slumped to the dirt, one after another.

Yuri must have also realized what was happening, as he rose quickly and sprinted towards the truck.

The shot caught him about six feet later, before he could get past the left front wheel. It was a large-caliber bullet, something with major muzzle velocity, as it caught him in the shoulder and spun him around, the soldier tripping and falling ahead. He moved to rise, the second shot going through him, his body falling facedown.

Alexi curled into a ball, trying to make himself small. He

tried to squeeze under the truck's rear end, behind the oversized double tire.

It was suddenly starkly silent other than the gentle breeze picking up a few moments too late to affect the sniper's aim and help his comrades.

He could feel his breathing laboring, becoming more ragged, panic setting in, the panting sound drowning everything else out.

He closed his eyes tight. *Yuri! He got Yuri!*

Fear ran through him, mixed with hot anger, confusion.

Please, God, do not let me die here.

If he rose and ran for it, he would be gunned down. That he did not doubt. But if he stayed there, the shooter would eventually come and check to ensure he had no survivors.

Could he ambush him, perhaps?

No. He would have counted the men in the truck. His expertise was obvious, his accuracy unerring. This was not a man who left strays or made mistakes. *If you show yourself, he will kill you before you get a chance to defend yourself.*

He wondered how far off the man was. The report had sounded faint. A kilometer? It seemed possible. The way Yuri's body had spun in mid-stride, it was a big bullet, perhaps even from a BAR .50. Those shells could punch through light armor.

In the open, I have no chance. At least here, he might miss me, or just leave thinking I've already escaped.

But... how long? How long do I wait before I am just waiting to be the next?

The villagers had big hearts but were poorly trained, making them easy victims on their first visit. They would fight if it was a matter of life and death. But few, if any, had the kind of sniper training required to put down eight men from a half mile away. That required specialization, as did the use of a high-end sniper rifle.

So... this was not an Iraqi. This was a foreigner, working for the rebels trying to overthrow Saddam. Or it was a government or private contractor.

The note had been clever. Booby traps on bodies were so common they would've expected it. The sniper had probably written a few more words than necessary, just to keep a commanding officer in the open for long enough to do the deed. Kuznetsov had been bold, brash in his willingness to step to the fore.

It had cost him his life.

With few locals able to pull off long-distance kills, they had not been expecting a ranged attack.

He heard something, he thought. It was faint, just a light scratching sound coming from somewhere due north. He peeked around the side of the wide tire.

Yuri!

He was still alive and was crawling, slowly, along the ground on the driver's side. He managed the strength to look up and met Alexi's stare. Sweat was beading along Yuri's brow, straw-gold hair matted down from his cap, which had flown off. His gaze held a glimmer of hope, and his eyes glistened in the dim moonlight, soft, accepting. A moment of recognition and warmth, captured for a split second. Even though he was bleeding out, he smiled gently at the sight of his closest friend.

The bullet thudded into the back of Yuri's skull, slamming him face-forward into the dirt.

The crack of the rifle was almost simultaneous this time.

Alexi froze.

He's relocated, closer. He's coming to finish us.

He did not have time to mourn, he knew. Alexi scrambled back around to the other side of the tire and pulled his knees in tight, holding them, his fear growing.

Yuri! He killed Yuri...

Yuri is dead. He felt a profound emptiness, sorrow overwhelming him in the moment, the image of the younger man's face frozen in that last moment of love and recognition.

He thought about running, just sprinting away, moving as fast as he could. But Yuri's death had drained his hope. He did not even feel the strength needed to be angry.

It was another thirty seconds before he heard the slight rustle of feet in the dirt.

Do not even look.

The rustling stopped. A gunshot echoed in the still of the night. A moment later, another.

He's making sure.

One of the other men had clearly been playing dead, and he rose to his feet quickly from the pile of corpses, attempting to sprint clear.

The pistol sounded twice more, the man's body crashing to the ground.

The sound of boots shuffling through the sand drew nearer, the man's steps following the left side of the truck.

Alexi checked his left shoulder from under the truck. He saw the man's boots step over Yuri's corpse.

Alexi could not hide his fear, breath coming out in ragged pants, his body rocking slightly, waiting for the inevitable sting of the bullet.

"Whoever's under the truck... you can stop worrying."

The voice was American.

"I counted seven of you in the back, two in the cab. The

other eight are all dead. That means we have one straggler, probably the last guy off."

Don't make a sound. Don't even breathe.

Alexi tried to control his nerves, the involuntary shudder that was making his teeth nearly chatter.

"If I wanted to kill you, I could toss a grenade under there and either blow you up or flush you out. But I need you alive."

Something flew under the truck, tinkling metal-on-metal, landing just ahead of his left foot. He threw up his arms in an automatic attempt to protect himself from the explosion.

But there was none, just the continued, droning chug of the diesel engine.

He looked down at the two objects. The Zippo lighter was brass. The key chain was streaked with blood.

"Those belong to the major. You can use them as proof. I need you to take them back to your base. I want you to give combined Russian and loyalist forces there a message: the villages here are off-limits. The civilians here are under my protection. It doesn't matter how many you bring; it doesn't matter how well armed they are, or how skilled. They won't even see me, just like today. Do you understand? Say *da* if you do…"

"*DA! Da…*" Alexi offered. "I see nothing."

"In a moment, you ARE going to see something. You're going to get up and walk to the driver's door of the truck. When you get in, you're going to see exactly what I did to your friends. That's the image I want you to take back to them. If you diverge from my instructions, if you look up at me, if you attempt to draw a weapon or to run, I will kill you. Understood?"

"*Da*... I mean yes. Understood."

"Okay. Get up."

Alexi retrieved the keys and lighter. He wiped the blood on his khaki trousers and rolled out from under the truck.

The man was standing less than five feet away, to his nine o'clock. "Remember, eyes on the ground," the sniper said.

Alexi climbed into the cab hurriedly, without looking up. He worked the double clutch. He threw the truck into reverse and backed up ten feet, then turned the wheel left, the back end swinging around so the truck could turn.

A moment later it was heading north.

He looked back in his rearview mirror as soon as the truck had forward momentum. The man's face was clearly visible under the single bulb by the village gate. He had angular cheekbones, a squarish jaw, dark hair and darker eyes.

To Alexi, he might as well have been the devil himself.

His gaze flitted back to the mirror every few seconds until he was certain the man was out of sight.

MEMPHIS, Tennessee

ALEXI HELD the empty fork aloft, stunned and frozen.

It was him. It had to be.

That was a face he knew he would never forget, not even after twenty years.

He could still see the man's image, frozen in time and perfectly framed by the oversized wing mirror of that Russian transport truck.

The massacre had been the first in a series of losses for the Ferak Group. Speculation had quickly arisen that the Americans had a specialist in the region, a man given a bounty for each Russian scalp he took.

None of that had mattered much to Alexi, who had been dishonorably discharged from the unit. They would rather, they had made it clear, that he died with his comrades. Anything else was just cowardice or, worse, betrayal.

He had been smart, however, keeping his money overseas. He had kept extra paperwork in Europe, too, a false identity as "Alex Brillstein," an Israeli accountant. He'd used that to move to Memphis, where a sizable Russian diaspora had taken him in.

It seemed so long ago, now.

His English had been so poor, his prospects dim. The money had almost run out.

But eventually, he'd found a mentor in the local criminal underworld who would vouch for him, Victor Malyuchenko. Victor had a father with influence in Moscow and powerful gangster friends in New York. Malyuchenko's crew ran underage prostitutes, drugs and protection rackets across Memphis.

It had been going brilliantly until she'd become an issue.

June-Marie.

He looked back out the window, but the pair had strolled out of sight.

He got up and threw his napkin on the table, along with a ten-dollar bill from the stolen wallet. He headed for the door.

Outside, the sidewalk foot traffic was light, though Overton Park Avenue was packed with drivers, folk out doing their weekend shopping.

He could see the men twenty yards ahead and kept his distance, his old training coming back into play. He knew he needed to watch his own six, and he used store windows to make sure nobody was tailing him.

The last thing he needed was for Victor to find him just then.

He'd just seen his sign, his message.

It is him. It has to be.

He remembered the tall man's face. He hadn't seen it in nearly twenty years aside from the occasional appearance in a nightmare.

Twenty years. Had it really been that long?

He pushed his way past a couple of elderly tourists in white trousers and golf shirts, holding up a hand to apologize, and resumed his pursuit.

His fear of death on that day had been considerable, overwhelming. He'd had occasional panic attacks for several years after leaving the Middle East.

But eventually, he'd come to see it all as a sign, pushing him towards life in America and making his fortune.

On first view, the fear had flooded back. But a few minutes of consideration had changed his perspective. He was no longer a frightened ex-soldier in a strange land. This man was here, on his turf, in his town.

And I need a killer.

3
___

Norm O'Hearn and his wife, Margie, owned a tiny two-bedroom on the south side, in Evergreen. It was eight hundred square feet, a box with dark blue siding and tar shingles, with a white picket fence and a postage-stamp front yard.

It wasn't fancy, and their furniture dated to the early seventies, wood tone offset by mustard and bright green cushions. The kitchen was a small galley, with a counter on either side of the room. The spare room had just enough space for a twin bed and a closet along the other wall; it was half the size of the tiny master bedroom.

But Bob understood the appeal.

There were just the two of them; cancer had prevented Margie from having kids, Norm said.

The backyard also made up for any shortcomings in the house; it was a long, private garden, with hedges on either side. They both had a green thumb, it seemed.

Evening was settling in. They stood side by side on the

rear deck, Norm rocking slightly on his heels, the pride obvious in his expression.

"Margie planted the roses along the back left there — that's where they get the most sun. She's responsible for most of this, really," Norm said enthusiastically. He had an open bottle of Miller High Life in one hand and reached down to retrieve another from the cooler next to his deck chair. The porch was screened off, to hold back the mosquitoes. "I'm mostly just handling the vegetables, which are in those containers against the back fence."

Norm popped the cap on the second bottle and handed it to Bob without asking.

"Oh. Damn..." Bob said. "I forgot to mention, I don't drink..."

"I'll take it." Margie strode out from the back door, a tea towel in hand. "Dishes done." She grabbed the beer from Norm and settled in the hanging wicker chair at the end of the small coffee table. "You're not a fan of the drink, then, Bob?"

"I'm not, no. Had a problem with it for a long time."

"Well... just as well, then," she said, her expression mildly disappointed. "I generally distrust nondrinkers, but I'll make an exception."

Margie had broad shoulders and thick forearms, like her husband. Bob figured she hadn't brooked any shit since the Carter administration. "You make a hell of a potpie, by the way," he said. "Haven't had one that good since my grandma's when I was a boy."

"Uh-huh... well, I'm mighty pleased y'all enjoyed it. I do love to cook. I especially love it when people don't drown my food in hot sauce..."

"Nectar of the gods," Norm insisted.

"Norm's condiment taste notwithstanding, he's always been a real fine judge of character," Margie said. "We moved out here from Queens back in '74 — I'm from here but met Norm there while I was in nursing school. We've had a bunch of Norm's prospects stay here until they could find their feet. Lots of young fighters who are like family to us now, and we still hear from years later. But... I must admit, you're a little older than most of his usual strays."

"Yeah... I'm just on the road for a while."

"Settling old scores?" She had an inquisitive sort of gaze, with deep, penetrating blue eyes behind her cat's-eye spectacles.

"Oh, heck... hopefully not, no. More or less trying to keep my nose clean and my head down."

Norm downed the last of his bottle of beer and set it down, then fished a cigarette out of the pack on the table. Margie sighed theatrically as he lit it.

"So, I do got to ask you the obvious question," Norm said. He cleared his throat from the smoke, hacking slightly. "One day, I'll quit these damn things, I swear..."

"Well, sure you will... coz they'll kill you stone dead," Margie muttered.

"Lay off, Margie, geez... Anyhow, I've got to ask you the obvious question, which is how you learned to fight like that. I maybe should've asked back in the day, when you turned me down despite what I might fairly call a pretty decent track record. I mean... I was a trainer for fifty-two years, and that was the most mechanically perfect jab I think I've ever seen, short of a week working on Marvin Hagler's crew back in the eighties."

Bob blushed. "Yeah... that's nice of you to say, there, Norm, but I've been out of serious training a long time..."

"Nah... that was muscle memory right there, kid. That was doing something thousands of times, the right way, until it's grooved and smooth as silk undies. I notice you also managed to duck and weave around the question. You learn that in the military, too?"

Margie rolled her eyes. "Yeah, like I didn't hear enough about that crap from the colonel. Bob, you want a tea or something? A little orange pekoe with some milk maybe?"

He nodded. "Sure. The colonel?"

Margie walked out.

"Margie's old man was a lieutenant colonel in the Army. They moved around a lot. Real ballbuster, the colonel, God rest his soul."

From the other end of the hall, Margie's voice echoed back. "God didn't have nothing to do with that man, believe me."

"It was a different time," Norm said meekly.

"Don't make any excuses for him, now, Normie," she called back. "Is he making excuses for that mean old bastard, Bob? Don't listen to him. My old man was a piece of work, and y'all know it's true."

"She's not wrong," Norm said. "He did love his family, though."

"He loved being in charge," Margie said as she returned from the hall. "His yell was so sudden and powerful, it could just about make me break down and cry."

Bob frowned. "Not a pretty picture, making your kid cry."

She sighed a little as her mind drifted back. "I take a certain pleasure in the notion of an afterlife. Makes me feel like all the troubles in this world might lead to something bigger and better. But when he comes to mind, briefly, none of those debates matter; because if there is an afterlife, that old bastard is burning in Hell. And if there isn't, he ain't nothing at all."

"Please! It all sounds pretty familiar," Bob said. "My old man was... tough. He made old leather seem dainty. Real serious and quiet, most of the time. But he'd fought in 'Nam, so he'd had a rough time of it."

"You army too, like Norm?" She headed towards the kitchen again.

Bob shook his head. "Marines," he called after her. There was no point bringing up his post-Forces career with the CIA. That was a world they did not need to know about.

"I've met a few," Norm said. "None of them could fight like that, though. That was the mixed martial arts, I take it? I mean, the boxing was fine, but the whole elbow-strike thing..."

"Something like that," Bob said. "My father taught me karate as a kid, then introduced me to Jeet Kune Do, which was sort of a precursor to mixed martial arts. Then, over the years and with the Marines, I picked up expertise in some other styles. It's... well..."

He was having trouble expressing it pleasantly. It wasn't a comfortable idea.

"Spit it out, kid," Norm said. "I've seen that look before, on the fighters who know they've got something but don't want to brag. That's it, right?"

"It's natural to me," Bob said. "Or, at least, the learning of it is. The muscle memory, the replicating what I see. It's the only real talent I've got."

"That's some talent, though, as these things go. Are you autistic or something? Like, a savant-type dealie?"

Bob wiggled his head back and forth. "Eh... they were never really certain what was up with me, and my old man was never too interested in finding out. You know how things were back then."

"Sure."

"But it was something odd, no doubt. Didn't apply to things other than physical action. I couldn't read a math book and just know math or anything like that. But sports and fighting? They were different."

"That good, huh?" Norm had a slightly cynical edge to it, like maybe he'd heard it from a few young fighters who eventually failed. "You ever try anything but combat?"

"When I was a kid, I briefly got interested in baseball. I played two Little League games at fourteen, went eight-for-eight at the plate, hit five home runs. This was near Detroit, mind, so scouts immediately heard about it and started bugging my old man. But... he didn't like any of that, me out there socializing with other kids my age. He thought getting close to anyone other than family was a weakness."

Norm sighed a little. "Yeah. Yeah, that was often the way..."

Margie returned and handed Bob his tea.

Bob took a sip. "If my father had taken me to the ball diamond on the weekends instead of dumping me in the woods with a hunting knife, a book of matches and a hearty pat on the back... I don't know, maybe I'd be a retired major leaguer now."

"But instead, he taught you not to be a dreamer, to fight, because that's what the tough ones from our generations did," Norm offered. "We did what our fathers did, which was learn how to fight and be prepared for it. My old man, he was first-generation Irish American, living in Queens in the forties. Tough? That man could walk through brick."

Margie sat down and retrieved her half-finished beer

from the coffee table. "So, Norm mentioned the fight at the club."

"She thinks you're right about Morris, too."

She pointed the bottleneck at Bob. "You nailed that one. I told Norm a month ago — though I expect he wasn't paying attention, as always — that Morris had light fingers. He was at the funeral for Cheryl Amos's late husband, Neil — Cheryl and me, we used to work together — anyhow, he was at Neil's funeral, and two of the silver candlesticks from the chapel went missing right after he was in the visitation room. And wouldn't you know, they charged that to Cheryl's bill, which did not seem right..."

"While you're visiting the bank on Monday, I'll be having a little word with Morris," Norm said. "That won't be a whole lot of fun, if you're right."

"And tomorrow? What's your Sunday looking like, Bob? You going to join me at church... or Norm at the church of beer and football?"

"I'm going to contact some friends up north, do some laundry and then, beer excepting, probably join Norm in watching some football. I have to admit... I'm not what you'd call a deeply religious person."

She shrugged. "Me neither, I just like the songs and the people. But you fellas do you, as the kids like to say. In the meantime, you can use my dryer if you want to save money, but the washer's busted. We're getting her fixed next Thursday."

Bob frowned. He hadn't done a wash in weeks, and his tiny selection of clothes was getting rank. "Do you have a laundromat somewhere nearby?"

"Sure enough, about six blocks away," Margie said. "Y'all can borrow my little beater. I wouldn't leave your stuff there, though, unless you want it stolen. They've got a TV and magazines and such, and there's a little coffee shop next door."

"After that, maybe we can get out, and I can show you the town a little," Norm suggested. "Feel like a tour?"

That wasn't a good idea. Bob knew it was likely his former CIA boss Andrew Kennedy still had freelancers hunting for him.

"I'll probably take a rain check on anything too active past laundry," he said. "Day of rest, and all."

4

June-Marie Kepler sat behind the wheel of the rusting red '91 Dodge Shadow and watched the man in the laundromat.

The front windows were partially painted over with advertising, so she'd occasionally lose sight of him behind the *B* in "Clean and Bright."

He hadn't moved in an hour, her view only interrupted by the blur of the odd passing car. She'd followed him, as Alexi had instructed, when he'd driven an equally old and rusting Ford Focus from the old man's home in Evergreen. It hadn't been easy. Traffic was surprisingly busy for a Sunday, and she'd had to cut in and out of lanes. June-Marie wasn't a confident driver.

It was hot. She wore a halter top and short shorts, but she was sweating from the lack of air conditioning in the car.

She hated the Dodge, with its scalding vinyl seats and the old-fashioned tape deck. Who owned tapes? But Alexi insisted it was a "secret weapon," on account of the sixteen-valve, two-hundred-horsepower engine.

It didn't make up for the absence of air conditioning, that was for damn sure. When she'd finally made it and had her own money, June-Marie vowed, she was going to buy a sports car, maybe even a convertible. And when it was too hot to have the roof down, she'd turn the AC up to max and forget what it was ever like to swelter in the Memphis heat.

"Just follow him," Alexi had demanded. "Victor does not know you took off, yes? He thinks you are at church. So find out where this guy goes. Find out what he is doing here."

It sounded easy enough, in theory. But in practice, the man was going nowhere. He'd driven down the street about five or ten blocks, turned a few blocks south, parked and gone inside.

He'd carried a small bag inside, exchanged bills for some change at the counter, then loaded up a washer and sat down.

She took out her phone and dialed Alexi. "Hey."

"What's he doing?"

"Laundry."

"Eh?"

"I'm serious. He's just gone to a laundromat near the house on Garland you followed him to yesterday. He's been here for fifteen minutes already, and he hasn't moved. He's just sitting there, watching it spin. He went next door for thirty seconds and got a coffee, then came back."

The line was quiet for just long enough to make June-Marie wonder if the call had dropped. "Alexi? Baby, you still there?"

"Hmm... yeah, just thinking, honey pie."

"About what?"

"About how to get him out of there and somewhere we can talk. He is dangerous guy, so somewhere public..."

"Well... what about the laundromat?" she suggested. "I mean... dude doesn't seem to be going anywhere."

"Not public enough. We need restaurant or something."

"There's Crosstown Brewing Company, about five minutes from here. That's the place I waited tables before dancing. They've got a real nice patio, shade from a big awning and such. Y'all would really like it."

"No, it must be indoors. I cannot risk anyone spotting me and calling Victor."

That required no explanation. He'd been pilfering from the tribute kicked upstairs to Victor by dealers around the city. It was only maybe ten grand, as far as she knew, but it was more than enough to sign his death warrant.

And as far as Victor knew, June-Marie had quit Alexi a year earlier. She was the boss's girl now.

"Okay then. There's a Cora's near there, too, on Poplar. Big, lots of booths. But... how do we get him over there?"

"That is easy part," Alexi promised. "You're going to take him a note."

Alexi ended the call. He stared at the home across the road from behind the wheel of the old Toyota station wagon.

He'd solved his mobility crisis by "borrowing" the car from the same unfortunate vacation renter who had "loaned" them his home; the man was hogtied in the basement, out of their way until Victor had been dealt with.

The front door opened, and a short, stocky older man in shorts stepped out for a moment. He lit a cigarette and looked up and down the street.

It was the same senior he'd seen with the American, the

old man from the club, Norm. He'd watched a woman leave just before June-Marie called. A wife?

Well-timed. It is like he came out to greet me.

Alexi got out of the car and slammed the door. He drew the Smith & Wesson Model 19 revolver from his waistband as he crossed the street. He strode towards the man and raised the pistol on route.

The man froze at the sight of him striding up the front walk.

"You! You come with me now, or I shoot you in the face!" Alexi declared.

The senior regained his composure. He studied Alexi for a moment. He took another puff off the cigarette. "Nope," Norm said.

"What? Are you stupid?" Alexi demanded. "You see gun, right?"

"Sonny... I've seen plenty of guns in seventy years. But I'm old and tired, and I figure if you want me to go with you, you've either got the wrong guy, or I'm just leverage of some sort for someone else. Either way, I'm not going nowhere."

Alexi strode ahead quickly, up the steps, until he was standing directly ahead of Norm. He raised the pistol and pressed the barrel against the older man's forehead. "Stupid! You want bullet in brain?"

Norm looked past the gun to its holder. "You're not impressing me, son. You're just embarrassing yourself."

The old man is crazy, Alexi thought. *He does not care... or he values his freedom too much.* It made no sense.

Frustrated, Alexi smashed the side of the pistol into Norm's temple, the old man stumbling a step sideways.

"You think I give a shit how calm you are? You want to die, stupid!?"

Norm straightened up. He remained stoic, but his eyes had narrowed, a slight worry setting in, anxiety at what was to come.

So he is human enough to be a little scared, at least. Good. I can work with this. "I see your wife leave house earlier. Maybe we wait here for her if you do not want to come quiet."

Norm clenched both fists and turned to face him directly. "You don't even think about touching her, you dirty piece of shit…"

Alexi hit him again. The old man stumbled sideways, dropping to one knee. "Get up," the Russian ordered. "Walk ahead of me. Take passenger side at car so I can cover you, then slide behind wheel and drive. We go now. Soon, I go meet your friend, make deal. Then your life will be easy again."

BOB WATCHED his laundry rotate in the washer.

It made sense to do something else, to find a cheap paperback or watch some TV. Anything to take his mind off the events of the prior month.

But he knew he couldn't focus on anything that wasn't a priority. It was a mental trick, a discipline he'd developed in childhood at his father's prompting. As long as he knew there were bigger concerns at hand, taking time off was out of the question.

It wasn't healthy.

At least, that was what Nurse Dawn had insisted. His Chicago-based friend worked in a community clinic, not a shrink's office. But she'd been through enough trauma to know people couldn't stay in productive mode all of the time. They had to take time for themselves.

But what does that even mean? he wondered as the laundry spun. *Who the hell am I now?*

When he was a Marine, the decisions had been made for him. When he was in Team Seven, he'd risen to Alpha and helped plan their missions — but there was never any doubt what and who they were.

But he'd never been a "civilian," not as an adult. He wasn't sure it was even possible anymore. As long as Kennedy and his lapdog Eddie Stone wanted him dead, he would be forced to remain on the run. Homes would be limited to temporary accommodation, as low-profile as possible. Jobs would be part-time work, mostly labor.

He'd hoped to stay in Jackson for a while. It was wholly unfamiliar turf, but that also meant no chance of running into old headaches. But with a third week in a hostel approaching, he'd called his friend Nick in Washington to try to access funds from an emergency bank account, which he'd thought undiscovered by the agency. Nick had discovered it was frozen.

That meant heading to Memphis and his stashed go bag. That meant staying on the run.

There was no "normal" in his future.

Motion in the corner of his eye caught his attention. The laundromat front door jingled as it swung open. It was a young, blonde woman. She was pretty, with angular cheekbones, and tanned deeply. She was skimpily dressed in a halter and short shorts, sandals with leg strappings — purely local and, judging by her size and gait, no threat.

As she got closer, he noticed she had dark eyebrows, the platinum hairdo from a bottle. She had a tattoo on her ankle of a crow with a rose in its beak.

She tilted her head to one side slightly as she looked him over, like an anxious host greeting a new arrival.

"Yeah... hi!" she said, cupping one hand to wave nervously. "My friend wanted me to pass something to you."

Am I getting offered a phone number? Bob briefly thought. He hadn't thought about women beyond some quick self-gratification in years. It had always seemed wrong after losing Maggie, a betrayal. Plus, the girl looked half his age, at most.

She leaned forward and nervously handed him a folded slip of paper. "Okay... I've got to go..." she said, backing away towards the door. "Alexi just asked me to pass a message..." She turned quickly and disappeared out the door.

Alexi? What the hell was that about?

Bob opened the slip of paper.

I know who you are. I saw what you did at Al-Mazrae. I need a favor. It would be wise to comply, or a friend of yours may suffer the consequences. The Cora's at Poplar and North Watkins, 2 p.m. Come alone. Back booth or closest to it. I will wear a Detroit Red Wings ball cap.

How bizarre.

Al-Mazrae. That was so long ago. It felt like a lifetime, like it had been a different person, sharing his memories.

Bob knew it could be one of the villagers, or it could be the one Russian merc he'd left standing. She'd said Alexi, which sounded Russian.

Curiosity was quickly getting the better of him. Either

way, someone who knew his past life was keeping tabs on him. That was a problem waiting to happen.

The Red Wings had cachet in Russia for decades due to the Larionov-Fetisov days, when Russians first entered the National Hockey League. *If I had to put money down... I figure this is the guy who was under the truck.*

Instinct suggested his best bet was to show up at the meeting, find somewhere quiet and then bury the guy. But he was trying to change his ways, avoid hurting anyone unless it was to protect someone weaker.

Goddamn it.

The last thing he needed in Memphis was old Team Seven business rearing its head.

Al-Mazrae had been a solo job, from his time as a roving sniper. He'd gone in with one purpose, to lessen the impact foreign mercenaries were having on the tide of the civil war, bolstering the forces challenging the Hussein loyalists.

It had been just one of a dozen villages, the contingent of a half-dozen or so Russian mercs as arrogant as the others, assuming the impoverished locals offered no threat. They'd rolled up to that town as if they had superpowers, no recon or initial engagement, no weapons readied.

Picking them off from three hundred meters away, as they stood under the village's only streetlight, had been as perfunctory as mowing a lawn. He'd taken no enjoyment in it, only the grim satisfaction of a task accomplished with no SNAFUs.

Bob looked down at the note again. Across from him, the washer spun down, rolling slowly to a stop.

He needs a favor. So it's blackmail of some sort. But Bob had no connection to that village, to the chieftain the Russians had murdered.

What does this person possibly think they have on me? And who could he possibly know that I know?

He rose and opened the washer, transferring his small collection of clothing to the adjacent dryer. It would take about another hour. Bob checked his watch; it was almost one. That seemed about right.

Time for a late breakfast.

5

The man in the Detroit Red Wings cap looked older, but that could have been due to a hard life.

His nose had been broken several times; a wicked scar ran partway across his forehead. His rust-tone facial hair was wispy and unkempt, as if he'd spent days traveling.

He didn't smile or show any real visible reaction when Bob walked in and approached the table. "You're Alexi?"

"I am."

As he sat down, Bob noticed the smaller man flinch away slightly.

"That bad?" Bob suggested.

"Eh?"

"The nightmares about Iraq. I freaked you out so badly you flinch in my presence?"

Alexi looked away briefly, as if irritated by the suggestion. He nodded to the woman two tables over. "It is not that. She just put hot sauce on eggs." His accent was heavy, still.

"Fucking Memphis, man. Everyone here think you must disguise flavor of all foods with sauce that burns your guts. It's loony tunes." He sniffed. "Besides... that was long time ago. You seem different here. Less... frightening."

"You haven't gotten to know me yet," Bob said. "Let me guess: you were the dude under the truck."

The Russian nodded. "You put such a scare into the Feraks that Moscow had to double their pay to get them back into the field."

"You're welcome," Bob said.

"You did not spare me out of generosity. You spared me..." Alexi stopped talking as the server arrived. "Just coffee."

"Tea, orange pekoe, milk," Bob said.

The waitress left.

"You spared me," Alexi continued, "because it made sense tactically to use your kills there to scare others who might follow. It was a calculated decision..."

"True."

"And now it shall bite you in the ass." The Russian reached down as he said it, lifting a small glass vial from the chain around his neck and kissing it before setting it back under his shirt.

"Because..."

"That mission cost me my career with the Ferak Group. It ruined my reputation in Moscow, making lucrative private security work impossible to come by. It also cost me someone important, someone I care for."

"And it gave you nightmares." Bob smiled thinly as he said it. He wanted the man to know he was pleased he'd introduced terror into his life. It was best if he recognized whom he was dealing with and gave up whatever he was pursuing quickly.

The Russian snorted at that, as if disgusted. "You are proud of what you did."

"I've never taken any joy in killing anyone. But satisfaction at saving others? I don't have too much of a problem with the collateral cost to you and your ilk."

"My 'ilk'?"

"Your kind."

"As if you were better. As if you were some knight in armor…"

The waitress returned. Both men fell silent for a moment as she set down their drinks. When she'd gone, Bob leaned across the table slightly, his voice stern but quiet.

"I fought for my country and its values, not the highest bidder. It may have been naïve, but at least it was still righteous. People like you are why people like me had to exist in the first place. Now… state your business before I lose my temper and decide to end this meeting prematurely."

Alexi looked around, as if clocking their surroundings, moms with kids out for a pancake brunch, old couples laughing and chatting across tables, young waitresses in peach dresses. "No, I don't think so. I think guy who leave me alive at the scene, he is not same guy who endanger all these restaurant patrons. He is guy who care more about the people in village, what they think of him, than end games and results. I do not think you will do shit to me. Besides… what is your name?"

"You can call me Bob."

"Besides, Bob, you *are* going to do job for me. Once it is done, everything is copacetic."

"Copa-what?" Bob frowned.

"Copacetic. Is first word in English that I learned as young boy, from old Shirley Temple movie, where she tap-dance with old black man."

"I think its use has passed."

"Huh. For real? Then makes sense I never heard it much. Okay, then I say hunky-dory. You kill Victor Malyuchenko, everything is hunky-dory. And I give you something back in return, something you value greatly."

That took some balls. "Why would I help you? I'm still contemplating whether I have to kill you to make sure you don't pester me anymore. What do I gain?"

The Russian's expression shifted completely, from agitated to ice cold in a heartbeat. "You will do so because you wish to help your friend." He took his phone out of his pocket and passed it across the table. "While you were busy washing your undergarments, I was visiting Norman O'Hearn."

Bob studied the image on the phone's tiny screen. Norm was tied to a chair, gagged. The room appeared featureless, just a tiny transom window near the ceiling line, suggesting it was a basement.

Bob shook his head gently. "Not smart."

"You kill Victor, I set him free."

From his tone, Alexi clearly thought "Victor" was famous, or maybe infamous. "Who?"

"You kid, right? He runs biggest crew in Memphis."

From his research during the New Orleans situation, it seemed clear organized crime had changed; it wasn't like the old days, where everything was split along ethnic or cultural lines. Criminals lumped together wherever and however they could to make a buck.

If he was the city's biggest gangster, he probably had his fingers in a bit of everything. That meant he was already under surveillance by the police or feds. That would be another complication.

"You want his business?" Bob asked.

"I want him gone. If that opens up new opportunities... well, I do whatever he asked for ten years. I had to be his right hand. I deserve break."

"Why now? Why aren't you working for him anymore?"

Alexi looked away quickly, probably the closest he got to expressing shame, Bob figured. "He is a fool and madman. He fell for my girl, June-Marie, and wanted her to become his new girl, away from wife's prying eyes. So he push me out, replace me with his pet dog, Jerry Perry."

Bob didn't buy that was all of it, not for a second.

He'd known enough criminals over his years with the Team to know that the coldest fish operated on a selfish hierarchy of needs — but one that began and ended, usually, with money. A boss wasn't getting rid of his right-hand man unless there was money involved.

But for now, it sufficed.

"And if I agree... where and when?"

Alexi reached down beside him and pulled a plain brown manila folder out of his backpack. "Here." He slid it across the table. "This is everything I know about him, including phone numbers for him and key staff, security codes for mansion. He rarely leaves house, but when he do, is usually for business. His number two, Jerry Perry, keep him on strict schedule. Meetings come to him, so there is no electronic trail that can help you."

"Protection?"

"Is in file. He has pair of bodyguards with him at all

times, both former US Special Forces. He has two more guards in house, three more on grounds including man at the gate. He has handful of other men he can call on. Then there are smaller gangs who pay tribute up to him and can be called on if needed."

"Exposure?"

"When he gets in and out of his limo."

Bob leaned back in his chair. He picked up the cup of tea and sipped, contemplating everything he'd been told.

"So?" Alexi demanded.

Bob looked up at Alexi, maintaining his own stoicism. "You realize if you hurt even a hair on Norm's head, the way in which you die will haunt the very Earth itself. I'll take so long, you'll beg me to end your life."

There was a flinch, the briefest look away that suggested Alexi believed he was telling the truth. Then the Russian steeled himself. "We all do what we must," he said.

"All of this over the girl?" Bob said. "I have a hard time accepting that."

"I do not care," Alexi said. "We hate each other, Mr. Bob, but we will work together. Because if you are not successful, I will kill your friend."

"And if I succeed…"

"I will release him. And… you get to be a hero."

"How do you figure?"

"You get to save June-Marie. Believe me, she does not want to be with Victor. He is cruel, sadistic man. And we are very much in love." The middle-aged Russian frowned, looking forlorn again for a moment. He withdrew the glass vial necklace from his shirt again and rubbed it for a moment. "I… did not wish to do this. When I saw you, it brought back terrible memories of loss and pain. But I love her; and he will kill her."

"Or you'll kill Norm O'Hearn, a nice guy I barely know," Bob said. "If you're lying about her, you're in the wrong profession, Alexi, because Hollywood is calling. But that doesn't forgive the route you took. You don't get a pass for this. And if you harm a hair on that old man's head..."

"Save her, and that will not happen."

"Yeah... about that: she didn't look too much like she needed saving," Bob said. Inside, he cursed his own curiosity. The girl hadn't looked much older than nineteen or twenty. Being involved with either of the Russians was a guarantee she faced a difficult future.

"She is... bubbly. Fun. She is not... how would you say... a deep thinker. So much of life is passing her by as she tries to handle whatever moment she is in. So... you need to get her away from him, or I am not responsible for what happens. Play hero again, like in Al-Mazrae. I am sure after you killed all my friends, the savages in that village sing praise to your name. So... now, you save June-Marie."

He had the wrong idea about Iraq, Bob knew. It hadn't been like that at all.

Head in the game. She's not your problem. Concentrate on saving Norm, first.

Bob took out his phone and held it out to him. "Enter a number I can get you at."

The Russian did as asked. "If I see this number, I can assume it is you, yes?"

"You can. But phones come and go these days. I'll give you a three-ring hang-up if you don't answer right away, then call immediately back."

"*Da.*"

He had no reason to trust Alexi. He fully expected the former mercenary to throw him to the wolves at the first opportunity.

But until he could figure out where Norm was being held and spring him, he had to play along.

6

Victor Malyuchenko considered himself a refined man.

He selected his wardrobe each day to reflect that refinement: suits, shirt and ties in silk, platinum cufflinks to match his platinum Patek Philippe wristwatch, a pair of six-hundred-dollar Dack's brogues on his feet, shined to an inky glow.

His gray-black hair was swept back and sprayed, his bushy mustache groomed immaculately, a slight up-curl to each tip. On this day, he favored a dark gray suit with black shirt and gray tie. He kept one hand in his left trouser pocket, a casual air as he strolled back and forth across the luxury apartment's hardwood floor.

The other hand held an aluminum baseball bat, its barrel perched on his right shoulder.

Ten feet ahead of him, a thin, balding man in grubby, loose-fitting clothing was kneeling, hands tied behind his back.

His guest looked terrified, eyes sallow and bloodshot. He trembled slightly.

That was good. Victor hated the idea that his deference to class and style might make anyone think he was weak. He was still quite willing to get his hands dirty.

Sometimes, he had decided, it was important to show the men that he was still the boss. Sometimes, when you wanted something done right...

"Ruben, Ruben, Ruben... Tell me, my friend... what am I supposed to do with you?"

Ruben looked up briefly at him, his expression one of defeat and terrible fatigue. "I... Victor... I didn't mean..."

"Shhhhh! Shhh... Be quiet, now. You know I have men scouring city for Alexi... but you fail to mention to me that he stayed at apartment above your cigar shop. You don't call Jerry; you don't try to keep him there... you don't do nothing except give him a place to stay for a few days."

He kept pacing, knowing his movement further unnerved the man, walking behind him and out of sight, then back in front, exuding the unpredictable.

"I owe him, Victor! He saved my ass..."

"I OWN YOUR ASS!" Victor snapped, his pleasant demeanor evaporating, his rage obvious. He swung the bat sideways with one hand, a Chinese vase on his desk shattering. "I protect your business! I keep beat cop from sniffing around the sales out your back door! Without me, you do not have ass to save, Ruben."

Ruben cowered backwards from his kneeling position.

Victor inhaled deeply through his nose, composing himself. "See? Now you cause me to lose my temper, Ruben. I... do not like this. I prefer for things to remain civil. If you are disrespectful, then I will have difficulty maintaining this tone... and I will cut off your testicles with rusty spoon. Then I will feed them to my dogs while you watch."

"I'm sorry, Victor. I'm real sorry, I swear..."

"Who is he meeting with? I know he has something set up, is in wind. Spill."

"He said something about Artie..."

"Artie Chee? What the fuck he want with that guy?"

"I don't know, really..."

"I'm sure you don't. Where is Alexi?"

Ruben had a frantic expression, his eyes darting from side to side as he tried to think it through, tried to parse the entirety of a friendship for a useful morsel of information.

Whatever he might have been good at in life, it was clear thinking on his feet was not on the list. "I... don't know?" he said, in precisely the wrong tone.

"Are you... asking me for correct answer?" Victor said, incredulous. "Well, Goddamn... GODDAMN YOU, YOU INSOLENT LITTLE SHIT!" He stepped into the swing, the baseball bat coming around with proficient speed, the barrel smashing into Ruben's head like a wrecking ball crushing concrete. The little storekeeper slammed sideways to the ground with equivalent ferocity, instantly unconscious.

Victor stood over him, looking down, muttering to himself, lips curled back in a half-snarl as his self-control deserted him. "You make me lose my temper again. For that, you have to pay. YOU..." A hammer blow, the body recoiling. "DIRTY..." Another. "LITTLE..." Another. "BASTARD!"

JUNE-MARIE HAD that sinking feeling she got whenever Victor was in a bad mood.

She hadn't seen him since breakfast. She'd gone to

church down the road with his head weasel, Jerry, then begged off to shop at the thrift store a few blocks from the neighborhood.

She'd ducked through the back of the store and met up with Alexi, expecting an hour of time with him, only for him to send her on his little errand.

She'd borrowed her old Dodge Shadow back from the Russian. Then, instead of calling Jerry or answering one of his dozen phone calls, she'd gone shopping for some new shoes.

She'd left the car for Alexi, outside the breakfast joint, briefly spotting him at the back table through the side window.

A hire car had taken her back to the penthouse apartment, where Jerry had grabbed her by the elbow and demanded to know where she'd been, like he was her father and she was some silly teenager. Then he'd told her to go to her room while Victor dealt with some business.

She carried the two shopping bags up the sweeping staircase to the second-floor hallway. Halfway to her room, she passed Victor's study, the door wide open.

The scene made her freeze in place momentarily, shocked.

Victor was bent over a man who was turtled in a fetal position on the floor. He was beating the prone man with a baseball bat, mercilessly pounding the man's skull over and over again in rapid succession. Even from twenty feet away, his victim was clearly now just a pile of pulped brain and bone.

She turned away quickly, her stomach turning. "Geez..."

Victor looked up and saw her in the hall. He clutched the bat in his left hand. His face and clothing were spattered with blood and brain matter. "Where have you been? Jerry Perry was worried."

June-Marie tried to focus ahead of the scene, to keep herself from retching. She averted her eyes as she held up her shopping bags. "Clearly you're not a golfer."

He squinted, puzzled. "What?"

"It's from a movie. Forget it. I went shoe shopping, is all. Look, I'm going to my room. The Uber driver was a maniac, the AC in the mall was pitiful, and my feet hurt."

She kept her eyes locked on the hall ahead of her. She didn't want to think about what she'd just seen. Thinking about that — recognizing that it was real — wasn't going to help that guy, or make Victor less intimidating.

"You spend too much money shopping. How many pairs of shoes one woman need? And don't give Jerry slip! Is dangerous..."

"Whatever."

"I got business to take care of. Dinner is at six. You're having pheasant. That's your fucking favorite, right? Fucking pheasant?"

What a psychopath. He fed me pheasant under glass once, damn near forced it down my throat. Now, he's twisted that into it being my favorite. Fuck my life.

"Perfect! You're not going to come help me eat it, I take it?" She let the question hang there, already knowing the answer, that he'd be having dinner with his family. She turned and headed down the hall as quickly as possible.

In her room, she closed the door and leaned against it for a moment, her eyes closed, the bags clutched to her chest. For a moment, she needed to shut everything out.

She took a deep breath, exhaled purposefully, and composed herself. June-Marie dropped the shopping bags on her king-sized bed. Then she flopped down next to them and stared up at the Louis Comfort Tiffany glass ceiling insert, a fake skylight, a fortune in antique art masquerading as a window to the outside world, where people were free.

"Fucking psychopath," she murmured. It wasn't the first time she'd walked in on Victor beating one of his flunkies to death. It probably wasn't going to be the last time.

But it's not going to be me.

That was all she could do, she knew: plan as best she could to get away from him. Alexi had plans; maybe they'd work; maybe they'd fail. But trying something was better than staying with Victor.

Alexi. He'd been on the run, barely able to communicate with her, jumping from place to place as he tried to find people who'd offer him shelter. If he was smart, she knew, he'd have left town, started over somewhere else. But he was proud and not very smart, which meant he wasn't going anywhere.

She steeled herself with a deep breath, then got up.

She followed the same routine each time she went back to her room: she walked around the bed, to the drawer in the bottom of the frame.

Opening it, she removed the two levels of undergarments and socks, to reveal the layer of cash underneath, each stack of hundreds neat and even.

Still there.

At last count, it was just over forty-seven thousand dollars.

She'd promised herself that until she could skim a hundred grand — enough to buy multiple plane tickets and start somewhere else with relative ease — nobody was going anywhere.

Victor was her tormentor, but she was determined that he would pay for the privilege, by being her ticket to something better.

Her "shopping trips" had led to some close relationships, girlfriends who worked at the department stores and could list her cash advances on Victor's store and credit cards as part of her purchases, for a modest tip.

It was slow and laborious, fifty dollars here, a hundred there.

Initially, she'd kept it all in a bank account. But he'd grown suspicious of her having financial independence, forcing her to close it. Instead, she kept the cash close and, in just over a year, had done well, without a hint of concern from her wealthy boyfriend.

She knew she had to speed the process up.

Can't survive another year or two of this.

June-Marie was tough. Her father had been nonexistent, her mother a whore with a crack habit and nine kids from seven different men.

She'd grown up in a group home for children from troubled families, where the homeowner hadn't minded slapping them around or copping a feel from the older girls.

She'd been out on the streets by sixteen, hustling for cash, taking whatever work she could get. She never sold herself, though. She was proud of that.

Alexi had been a ticket to easier things, even though he was almost as crazy as Victor. Initially, so had Victor. Then he'd become jealous, possessive, controlling, harder to manipulate.

The clothes back in place, she closed the drawer and sat back down on the edge of the bed.

Eventually, she was sure, Alexi would figure out something, some escape for her. Her last resort was to get a gun, buy a beater and just drive, deal with Victor's damage as it came at her.

But June-Marie was patient. She'd taken a kicking from life for twenty-four years, eight months and thirteen days.

A few more months of waiting for Victor and Alexi to kill each other weren't going to make things any worse.

7

Bob sat in the beaten-up purple Ford Focus, the windows down to accommodate the heat. He waited and watched for the café doors to spill out his new associate.

Alexi had been a merc and, judging by his whining, a security professional before that. That almost certainly made him former Red Army, which in turn meant he'd been a soldier, foremost, not a tactician. He'd have become accustomed to following orders and watching his own behind.

But he also wasn't looking ahead. Bob knew that after their meeting concluded, Alexi expected him to go about the assigned task. Instead, he waited outside the café, because saving Norm was the priority.

For that to happen, he had to know where the jackass had him stashed.

Sure enough, ten minutes after he'd left, Alexi exited the restaurant, took a quick look down the sidewalk in either direction, perhaps to avoid familiar faces, then walked twenty feet to a faded red Dodge Shadow parked at a meter.

He got in. It pulled out into traffic moments later.

Bob kept the Ford Focus five car lengths back, occasionally letting it drift a little farther forward. The key was to remain in normal traffic patterns, be unnoticeable. The car's pedigree made the job easier.

Ten minutes later, Alexi pulled the Dodge up to the curb in front of a seven-story apartment block in Cordova, a sleepy neighborhood off Trinity Park Road.

Bob parked half a block behind him. There was no percentage in following him into the building. He needed to see how careful Alexi was being, whether he had more than one stop.

Bob turned off the engine and waited, watching as the other man walked through the front door.

Ten minutes turned to twenty.

Bob kept an eye on his battered old Seiko wristwatch. He'd decided that if ninety minutes passed without an appearance, it was probably Alexi's home base. He wouldn't stay anywhere insecure for longer, not with his friend "Victor" hunting him.

He used the burner phone to search the internet for either man's name, guessing on spellings. Neither produced anything tangible.

Movement in his left peripheral vision pulled his attention from the screen. Alexi had walked around the back corner of the building and was headed back to his car.

So probably not his crash pad. Maybe he's looking for a new place to stay?

The Russian walked around to the front of the building and back to the Dodge Shadow.

A moment later, both vehicles were back in traffic.

. . .

Margie O'Hearn knew something was very wrong.

It was Sunday afternoon, and the New York Jets were playing Buffalo — not just a Jets game, but a regional rivalry with the hated Bills.

But Norm wasn't in his armchair.

It sat empty in its faded clay-red glory, sagging and covered in clumped burrs of worn material.

She'd gone to church and then to the ladies' church auxiliary meeting. Her Sundays were always like that; if a volunteer group needed help, Margie liked to be first in line, especially if they'd let her take charge.

Being in control meant less to worry about when it came to the unpredictable behavior of others. If there was one benefit to being raised by the colonel, it was that she refused to brook nonsense.

The ladies had agreed the autumn bake sale had become so popular it needed to expand: more tables, more volunteers, a bigger venue.

She'd stopped at the store and picked him up a bottle of J & B whiskey, his favorite. Getting home had taken an hour longer than expected, because Margie knew half the working-class folks in the city and stopped to see a bunch.

When she got there, he wasn't in his chair. The front door was ajar, and a newly opened bottle of Miller beer sat beside the beaten-up recliner, the game on the TV.

But Norm was nowhere to be seen.

Damn it.

He's in trouble.

Maybe... nope. Trouble. There's no way Norm ever leaves that much of an open beer untouched. And there's no way he just skips out on the Jets. Either he's in trouble, or someone else is.

Margie had always been a no-nonsense kind of gal. When they'd met, Norm had just returned from his tour in Vietnam and was still readjusting. They'd married three weeks after he'd lit her cigarette in a bar.

She'd been eighteen. Within two weeks, she'd become the breadwinner, giving up nursing school to take a factory line job, operating a commercial icing machine for a company that made cupcakes while Norm looked for work as a boxing coach.

In return, Norm had promised that her father would never hurt her again, and neither would anybody else. And he'd stuck to it for fifty years.

She knew all about the kinds of people he ran into in the trade: damaged young men from tough families and neighborhoods; mobsters and other criminals, trying to sink their claws into vulnerable young fighters; promoters who'd sell their own brothers to make a buck.

He'd always tried to make light of it, but he'd also always told her there might come a day when he didn't come home. They'd insured him up the yin-yang just in case.

But she had no intention of cashing that policy.

Instead, she pushed down her fear and anxiety, suppressing them so she could get to work on finding him.

She stood for a moment in the living room and tried to put herself in Norm's shoes. The front door was ajar; maybe he'd popped outside for a smoke? He could've seen someone he knew passing, waved at them...

But he wouldn't forget to close the front door, she knew. She'd been gone for nearly two hours, but the beer beside his chair was still sweating and a little cool, which meant he'd probably been gone for an hour at most.

Margie left the house, closing the front door behind her, and checked the street for traffic before ambling over to the little two-bedroom across the road.

Ellie Grainger was ten years younger than Margie, tall, with sandy blonde hair that she kept short. She wasn't a churchgoer, but the two women had been friendly for years, enough for Ellie to share her concerns with Margie about "porch pirates," thieves taking advantage of frequent deliveries being left on front steps.

Ellie answered on the second knock. "Margie..." The younger woman frowned. "You look like you saw a ghost or something."

"Norm's missing. Y'all see anything strange going on over here?" Margie didn't believe in beating around the bush. She'd always wanted kids, but a tubal ligation required during cancer treatment had prevented that from happening. She'd been back at work three days after the surgery. "He disappeared while I was at church, and there are signs it was sudden."

"Oh my!" Ellie looked shocked. "Well, we've got to call the police..."

Margie shook her head. "No point, not yet. They won't go looking for a missing person until they've been gone a while, not unless they have dementia or something. Norm... Lord, I wish he had an excuse like that, but he's just a pigheaded fool all of his own account. Y'all still have that doorbell camera for them porch pirate fellas you mentioned?"

"Sure do!" Ellie said.

A few minutes later they huddled around Ellie's husband, Mike, as he downloaded the video to the family PC. The grainy footage bore fruit, a clear image of a middle-aged man with receding, longish hair — maybe brown? —

leading him down the front steps, ordering him into a boxy, older sedan. Norm was clutching one side of his face, as if nursing an injury of some sort.

"They both got in on the passenger side," Ellie said, frowning. "Why'd you figure?"

Mike ran an auto-detailing shop and had zero experience in law enforcement. But he'd watched a whole lot of crime shows. "He's holding a gun on Norm. He's forcing Norm to drive. Probably hit him with it, which is why he's grabbing his face."

"Oh damn," Margie muttered.

"But if he lets Norm walk around the car, there's enough distance between them that Norm could try to run. So he keeps him close; look, honey, Margie... this might be enough for the police to..."

"You got any more footage?"

Mike shook his head. "The camera was designed for live streaming, and it cuts to two other angles. So this is the only forward-facing material from an hour ago."

"Uh-huh," Margie muttered. "Trouble is, we can't see a gun in the video. Response times for burglaries in this burg are already slower than molasses in January. They're not coming out for this, not today, probably not even tomorrow." She leaned over Mike slightly. "Fast-forward to them leaving, Mike. I want to see if you got his plate number."

He did as requested, but the angle was too sharp.

The car pulled out of frame.

"Well, dang," Ellie said.

Margie had a think. "Have y'all talked to anyone else on the street about the porch pirates? Anyone else got a camera or cameras?"

Ellie's eyes widened, and she snapped her fingers to

point at her friend. "Now you're thinking! Gary Gottlieb, at the end of the block. He's one of them paranoid sort of fellas, cameras all over his property, on the gate, on the windows. You name it."

"Achh... Damn it." *Had to be the old kraut lunatic.* "He and Norm argue constantly about sports."

Mike chuckled.

Margie frowned. "What's so funny?"

"Women. You never get men at all, but we're supposed to be the dummies."

"Spit it out, Mike," Ellie asked with weary familiarity.

"That means they like each other. That means he and Norm are friends. You rip on your friends, not the people you actually dislike. Guys Norm and Gary's age know that's counterproductive."

Margie and Ellie looked at each other, the notion occurring simultaneously. "Let's go visit Gary," Margie declared.

Victor's guards dragged Ruben's remains away, hands under each armpit. The corpse left a smear of blood that thinned as it stretched from the desk to the study door.

"And clean that shit up!" Victor barked after them. He felt his tension release, as much as it ever did.

Jerry Perry entered the office, careful to avoid the trail of blood. He was tall and reed-thin, with heavy, pockmarked features and gelled, thick hair, silver-gray above his steel-rimmed spectacles. He could've been a college professor or a diplomat. In the four years since recruiting Jerry, it had always irritated Victor how smooth he was, how he seemed to glide around rooms despite his gangly frame.

"Really?" Jerry asked. He had always been utterly fearless, almost emotionless. That also bothered his boss, although he recognized the value. "Did Ruben fuck your wife or something? Because the bodies of landmine victims on D-Day looked in better shape…"

"He was a coward who shielded Alexi from me…"

Jerry stopped walking. He kept one hand in his trouser pocket, relaxed, a slight stoop to him as he pushed up his glasses. "This vendetta of yours is not only ridiculous; it's also costing us time, which means it's costing us money. Plus, that's going to stain the hardwood…"

"*Bozhe moi*… Fuck the hardwood, Jerry Perry! As if the value of a wooden floor mattered to Stalin or Genghis Khan! Besides… is not vendetta. It is justice. Alexi steal money from me; he tried to turn allies against me. He would have taken over my business if I showed hint of mercy. So I take his girl, and I kill him."

He saw his right-hand man's look of disapproval. "Jerry Perry, why do you give me this long face? What!? Ruben was just shopkeeper…"

"That's sort of my point. This kind of shit, it makes people think you're unhinged…"

"That's good, though, yes? If they think I am mad dog…"

"They'll fear you, sure. But they won't respect you, which means eventually they'll come for you and your job. We should deflect the flak from this, find someone lowly to pin it on, send some money to support Ruben's family."

Victor nodded in short, sharp motions, clearly irritated, sucking on his tongue. "Yeah, yeah. So what you are saying is we should send big fat gift to family of dirty little bastard who stab me in back? I don't know, Jerry Perry. I always dig your crazy sensible advice, but… this goes against who I am.

In Siberia, they have saying: frost in ground guarantees shallow grave."

Jerry ambled over and put an arm around Victor's shoulder. "You want them to fear you... but also to want to be you. They have to like you at least a little, Victor. That's why you go ahead with the Robin Hood schtick. Pretty soon, any time someone like Alexi tries to stick a knife between your shoulder blades, one of your many community supporters will warn you before he gets within five feet."

Victor nodded thoughtfully. He leaned towards the taller man ever so slightly and kept his voice low. "Jerry Perry... you are within five feet now, yes?"

Jerry removed his arm and gave Victor some space. "Point taken, boss. But you know what I'm saying."

Victor rubbed his chin and considered his place as the benefactor of his people, the citizens of south-central Memphis paying tribute to him. "Yeah. Okay, Jerry Perry, I dig this plan. We go ahead."

"And June-Marie?"

"What about?" Victor walked over to the liquor cabinet and picked up a hand towel from the ice bucket. He wiped the spattered blood off his hands and face.

Jerry held up both palms in mild surrender. "Hey... I'm not saying she's a problem. Yet. But she gave us the slip again today. She's hard to control; she thinks for herself a whole lot more than is good for a man in your position. And maybe..."

Victor put the towel down. "Don't even fucking suggest what I think you're going to suggest... Because she loves me, Jerry Perry. I know she does. Sure, she may not like security detail and all of this; but she left backstabbing prick to be with me. I did not force her."

"Okay."

"Damn right, 'okay.'"

"Still… maybe it would make sense to keep someone on her without her knowing, at a distance. Just to be careful. You have enemies; if she slips away and nobody has her back…"

Victor didn't buy Jerry Perry's mock concern for a minute.

His right-hand man thought his mistress might betray him. Victor knew better. He knew she was terrified of him but also admired him, adoration tempered by the threat of the back of his hand. He had her trained like a good dog.

"I love her, you know this," he said.

"I get it, she's your girl. But—"

Victor cut him off. "I knew it was love first time I see her, first time I know I must have her. I never know love in Russia, when it was all whores, or with stupid wife. But when I see her, she is like perfect fragile figure, her big eyes soft and gentle, like they stare into my soul. I feel the blood rush, demanding I overpower her, hold her and dominate her. When I have to take her, I know right then it must be love. And for her, of course, it is more than love. It is chance to love a great man."

"It is also a chance for her to be around someone with a lot of money and power."

Whether he meant it or not, Jerry Perry had a point. "Fine. Send Oleg. He's strong and fast, able to handle himself. But he better not upset her, or he'll answer to my home-run swing. Yes?"

"Of course, Victor." Jerry Perry turned to leave, skirting past the puddle of blood on his way to the door.

. . .

Dead Drop

MARGIE'S HUNT HAD WIDENED. Gary at the end of the block had a plate number. Now she just needed to find someone who knew how to search for its owner.

First, however, they'd stopped at the corner 7-Eleven and gas bar, just to make sure a greasy middle-aged guy in a Dodge Shadow hadn't bought gas in the prior hour.

The clerk, Lyle, leaned on the counter and listened, then shrugged at Margie and Ellie's request. "Can't say I have. Can't say for sure, though, Margie. I only remember the regulars."

Margie smiled at that to keep from slapping him. Lyle seemed like a nice man, but he wasn't quick on the uptake. "It's real important, Lyle. Whoever this guy is, Normie's with him, and we need to find them."

Lyle had sighed a little at that, in the resigned manner of someone who knows he's not going to make a difference. "I'll help as best I can..." he said.

"Y'all know the other gas bar managers, right? They're all over town."

"A couple, sure."

"And they know more. So put the word out for me! This fella has to stop and get gas at some point today. Maybe he stops at one of your pumps. I can give y'all his plate number..."

She shared the information, and Gary smiled and nodded, but Margie didn't feel much commitment.

"Needle in a haystack," Ellie muttered as they walked out. Then she noticed Margie's sharp stare and added, "Sorry. But you know what I mean."

"I do. But we have to try everybody. We've both lived here for decades, El. Someone's seen that car or will see it."

Margie knew her friend meant well and was grateful for the help. She also knew her mom hadn't raised her to be a quitter. She wasn't giving up until she'd gone over Memphis by the inch.

8

By five o'clock in the afternoon, Victor was back at his mansion in Germantown, his feet up on an ottoman as he sat in his favorite wingback chair.

His sons, five and seven, were playing with Tonka trucks in front of the French doors that led to the back patio. His wife was flitting about the house, gossiping by phone with the other local socialites.

Victor couldn't stand her. She was arm candy, a prop in a five-thousand-dollar Alexander McQueen suit. She'd never been a companion of any real sort. They had nothing in common, no real attraction, very little time for each other generally. But he was rich, and she was the daughter of the Memphis Chamber of Commerce's vice president, a well-connected man who was slowly introducing Victor's investment clout to legitimate outlets.

They put up with each other while a nanny raised the boys. Once dinner was done and she was off to another society get-together, he would slip out and go visit June-Marie for sex.

It was an arrangement that worked for him. It also meant that most of the time, he could leave his business matters at the office or the condo rather than bringing them back to the mansion.

Most of the time.

His phone buzzed in his pocket. He took it out and checked the screen.

Jerry Perry.

Damn.

Calls from his right-hand man could not be ignored, generally. Jerry knew disturbing him when with family was out of the question unless it was a major issue.

"What?!" he barked on answering.

"Can you meet me out front for a minute? It's urgent."

Victor pocketed the phone and smiled at his wife as he rose and headed for the front door. "Business. Nothing serious, I am sure."

Outside the double front doors, Jerry Perry was pacing the front walk, smoking a cigarette.

"What?!" Victor barked.

"Yeah... I figured you wouldn't be happy about the timing. But we have a sighting of Alexi."

"So... you are calling me instead of grabbing him?"

"It's complicated. He's in a public place, lots of civilians around."

"They'll get out of the way once they see guns," Victor suggested.

"It's on Beale Street. It's crawling with police and so many tourists that there's nowhere to 'get out of the way' to."

Victor's head tilted back in a moment of silent prayer. "This son of a bitch... he chaps my balls, Jerry Perry. Why would he go somewhere so public? He is sure to be seen..."

Then Victor paused, eyes narrowing as realization set in. "Artie Chee."

"The smack guy? Hooked up with some San Jose outfit, right?"

"The very same. He has a garment factory a block off Beale, above one of the buildings on MLK."

Jerry Perry looked skeptical. "Alexi's only ever handled the physical stuff for you: protection, numbers, expanding territory. Why would he suddenly think he can get into that end of things? He's no dealer."

"No, but heroin gets most return per pound, and Ruben say he mention Artie's name. So maybe he figures he needs cash quick in case he needs to run. He knows I have man watching his bank, so he can't touch his safe-deposit box. Cops have already frozen his main account for warrants. He is stuck with whatever he was carrying when you tried to kill him and failed."

"I told you: he had help from someone other than Artie or Ruben. Someone tipped him that we were coming over to his place. Someone close to you, someone who hears a lot of your conversations and planning."

Victor looked at his right-hand man. They'd known each other less than three years, but Victor felt like Jerry was family. They were on the same wavelength. He'd come recommended by Chaim Popov, the Brighton Beach consigliere who'd given Victor his own break fifteen years earlier.

"You are not going to give up on this notion that June-Marie is a problem, are you?" Victor demanded. "If I did not know better, Jerry Perry, I'd think maybe you had a thing for me yourself."

Jerry flicked the ash off his Marlboro. "You're really

funny. You know it's because of her erratic behavior. I still think you should be paying more attention to how much she spends when she's..."

Victor chuckled, unable to avoid it. "Well, I am sorry, my friend, but now you are just being silly. This money... a thousand here, two thousand there... this is what the bookkeeper would call 'rounding error,' yes? Now, do me favor and drop this thinking, yes?"

"Fine." But it didn't sound fine.

"Beale Street. Where was he spotted?"

"Having a vodka and Pepsi at BB King's."

Victor's blank expression spoke volumes. "You're kidding. He goes to see a band? You know, live music?"

Jerry shrugged. "I don't know. I've never been."

The gangster frowned. "You joke with me? You live in Memphis three years and you never go to listen to the blues?"

"Victor..."

"Yeah, yeah, issue at hand. Sure. Okay, we send Lev, Oleg, Martin. Better yet, you take them down there, sweep street. Lots of bodies, so start between where it is usually closed to traffic at both ends, Second Street and BB King Boulevard. If he is gone, head towards MLK. Look around Artie Chee's but don't start nothing with his men. He has too many guns to just roll over. Not enough to cause problem, but enough to make noise, draw unwanted attention."

"And if he's sheltering Alexi?"

"Oh... If he takes sides, that is different. Then, of course, you kill everyone."

. . .

In a van parked less than a hundred meters from the mansion's back fence, FBI Special Agent David May took off his headset for a moment.

The back of the van had been converted to a functional workspace, with a horseshoe of shelving built into each wall and the rear wall of the cab. On it sat an array of listening equipment, including laptops, a tiny server stack with a cooling unit that whirred more loudly than he preferred. Next to it were black hard-shell storage cases filled with microphones and routing boxes.

May stared at the laptop ahead of him. He'd just heard Victor Malyuchenko give the all clear to have multiple people potentially murdered. And they had a digital recording, clear as day.

It didn't mean much in the scale of a massive government racketeering and organized crime investigation, but it signified that their person on the inside had completed one of their most difficult tasks: replacing the SIM card in Victor's phone with the one provided.

Under the sealed warrant that accompanied the investigation, they had full right of interception. Even so, it was the first time in eighteen months that they had words coming directly from Victor's mouth other than the office bug, and he never said anything in the office that didn't involve golf or lunch.

Business, ironically, was never discussed in the study.

It was progress.

Still, it would be a long time before anything they gathered was useful or led to arrests.

RICO investigations were time-consuming, massive beasts, spiderwebs of criminal connections in which the intent was to wrap up as many of them as possible at the same time. Victor could probably brag about murder until styles changed, but he wasn't going to jail any time soon.

As far as the bureau was concerned, he was a small fish. He would never suffice as a main course, just as bait for bigger fish in New York.

It was Sunday, which meant free meter parking. In his reduced circumstances, Alexi appreciated anything free. He sat at the bar at BB King's in a high-backed wood chair and sipped a vodka and Pepsi over ice, feeling proud of himself.

It was a ballsy move, he knew. No doubt one of Victor's little sycophants would go scurrying back to the gang boss to report seeing him. But he didn't plan to stay long, and for all of his many, many flaws, Victor was not stupid enough to shoot anyone on Beale.

He checked his phone for the time. It was four thirty; the club was getting busy.

The bartender stopped on his way to some dirty glasses. "Are you sure I can't get you a bite to eat?" he said. "The chicken and waffles are pretty darn tasty, if I do say so myself."

Alexi winked at the man and tipped his glass his way. "I do not have time to eat and must be somewhere for dinner... but you keep making offer, you might convince!"

The bartender scampered off.

The club's audio public address system kicked in with a crackle. "Check, testing, check."

Twenty feet behind him, a band was setting up for a gig on the club's raised central stage. Alexi looked over his shoulder. Three young guys were plugging in amps, another settling behind a drum kit. The line of monitors at the foot of the stage suggested it was going to get loud in short order.

Artie Chee was late.

He'd said four thirty, and that had just ticked by without sight of the man. Artie was an old friend. Alexi knew that idea would surprise the Victors of the world, with their insecure need to surround themselves with admirers. But he'd always liked Chee's ruthless ambition and his sense of humor.

They'd met over a bet to see who got to hold on to an eight-ball table at the Absinthe Room. Artie had inherited his father's conservatorship of Hong Kong Triad interests in Nashville's and Memphis's respective Chinatowns. Mostly, that meant moving heroin and illegal immigrants into the United States, wholesaling both to smaller gangs involved in street-level interests.

Alexi needed to be in a coalition, get some players with juice on his side before taking on Victor properly. He had to assume the former sniper, "Bob," would fail.

When Victor eventually caught up with him, he needed friends, and Artie wasn't making any money off Victor's crew as things stood. Victor eschewed heroin and cocaine, instead underwriting meth and marijuana producers. He thought the more expensive drugs drew too much heat.

Replacing him, Alexi wanted Artie Chee to know, would mean installing a friend, someone who wanted his business, to the tune of millions of dollars.

He downed the last of his drink and held up the glass, shaking it slightly to get the barman's attention. The other bar seats were filling up. He'd taken a seat one stool from the corner, to lower the chances of someone taking the single to his left. Most of those on the street were couples or families, out at the nightclubs for a good time, bathing in the neon and the down-home soul and blues.

He scanned the room. *Still no sign of him.* Alexi felt the bulge in the small of his back, where his pistol was stashed, under his white golf shirt.

Something felt off. Artie wasn't the type to be late for a business meeting without a damn serious reason.

Calm yourself, Alexi. This is not Iraq or Moscow. This is Memphis, and here you fear no one.

But he checked his watch again anyway.

Four thirty-one. I give him five more; then I go. Fuck, Artie. Where are you?

"Is he...? He fucking is! Jesus Christ..."

Jerry Perry craned his neck from the outdoor patio of BB King's and stared through the open front door as best he could.

Alexi was sitting at the bar, opposite the stage, about halfway across the nightclub.

The place was busy, customers moving between the small, colorfully decorated wooden tables, the walls lined with old memorabilia: old Fender and Gibson guitars, vinyl LP records, posters of movie stars from the forties like Garbo and Gable; photos of Texas and Memphis blues and jazz royalty: T-Bone Walker, Dinah Washington, Louis Jordan. It was an easy place, when busy, in which to lose someone.

But Alexi Pushkin was in full view because he was sitting on a high-backed tall stool.

Perry shook his well-coiffed head of hair. "The balls on this guy. Jesus flippin' Christ."

Next to the tall, reedy Perry, Oleg Sharmanov looked

even larger, like two refrigerators in a purple suit, arms crossed, dark eyes beady under a close-cropped haircut. He peered through the door, following Jerry Perry's line of sight.

"Balls he won't have pretty goddamn soon. So... we go take him, yes?" Oleg shuffled his feet in place, as he tended to do when bored, nervous, or a little of both.

The consigliere sighed. None of Victor's crew were going to challenge their boss for the title of most wise. Not that Victor was exactly a *Jeopardy!* contestant. "No, we don't go into one of the busiest clubs on one of the busiest nightclub strips in America and kidnap someone. Oleg, let me ask you a question..."

"Sure, boss."

"Why here?"

"Why...? He's here to meet Artie Chee."

"And why do you think he chose to meet someone here?"

Oleg shuffled nervously from one foot to the other, like a child who'd pretended he knew an answer only to be called out. "Because... he like blues music very much?"

"Because it's insanely public, and there are about a thousand people within two minutes of him. There are two police cruisers thirty feet away, parked at the curb. Knowing Alexi, the cultural and aesthetic considerations came a distant second."

"Ace-tas-tic...?" Oleg sounded puzzled.

"Yeah, exactly, Ace-tastic. I mean, my Russian is pretty shit too, so..."

"So... how you want we should handle?"

Jerry thought about it for a second or two. "Well, my enormous Muscovite friend, I guess what we need to do is use a little hunting strategy. You ever go hunting?"

Oleg's voice was flat, devoid of emotion. "When I was

boy, I would drown mink at my uncle's ranch near Zelenograd, in a steel oil barrel."

"You'd drown… Geez. Not exactly what I was thinking of, big guy. But it'll have to do. We're going to flush out some game."

"Okay." Oleg's expression suggested continued mild confusion.

"You and I are going to go in the front," Jerry explained, slowing his speech consciously so the dimwit could follow along. "Lev covers the side exit, where the customers normally come in for ticketed events. There's probably a bouncer there, so Alexi will probably head for the rear doors, through the kitchen. Martin sits in the alley behind. Whichever way he goes, we back up whoever he heads towards. Got it?"

"Sure," Oleg said, nodding, then shuffling his feet slightly from side to side, his grim expression suggesting he was just going to follow Jerry and hope for the best.

9

By the time Alexi had found a free parking space at a meter and pulled in, Bob had been following him for nearly two hours. The tiny compact was hot as hell. The pedestrian traffic kept surprising him by stepping into the roads surrounding Beale Street.

But he'd managed, barely, to keep an eye on Alexi as he'd walked into the building on the corner.

The first multistory parking garage that wasn't full, about three blocks from Beale, had seemed like a grateful reprieve. He just hoped, as he walked quickly back to the busy pedestrian-only street, that Alexi hadn't already moved on in the ten minutes that had passed.

He looked up at the massive sign. Giant, playfully tilted letters on neon were suspended vertically from a frame and read "B.B. King's Blues Club."

Bob crossed himself like a kid at mass. "The King," he murmured.

His father hadn't given a damn about music or other electronic distractions. But his mother had raised him on old blues records, none more prominent than King's 1967 "Greatest Hits" collection. He'd seen most of his blues heroes live — Gatemouth Brown, Buddy Guy, Otis Rush and Philip Walker.

But the timing had never worked to catch Mr. King.

Most of the artists he'd grown up with had since passed, including Mr. King, but they still loomed large in Bob's upbringing.

He felt a sense of calm for a moment. There had to be something in that, some sort of good karma.

He followed the sidewalk to the next corner and looked down the length of the pedestrian concourse. A handful of people dined out on the club's small front patio, enjoying the warm evening.

He felt the hair on the nape of his neck tingle.

Just past the patio, at the Beale Street entrance, two men in suits stood just wide and to the left of the door.

Bob panned his view slightly to the right, tracking back to the street. Two more men were on the sidewalk by the road, about eight feet away, waiting indolently, watching families, friends and couples stroll the boulevard. One leaned on a lamppost, under a "One Way" street sign; the other hovered at the corner of Beale and South Second Streets, as if waiting to cross, hands in trouser pockets.

Well now, what's going on here?

He looked past the post, down the street. There were two white Memphis Police cruisers parked not forty feet away.

If Alexi was still inside the club, the guys loitering outside could well have been waiting for him to make an appearance.

But they won't do anything with him on Beale. In fact, they can't even really touch him there. Any sign of a gun in public will bring down all sorts of hell.

Bob considered how he'd handle it if he were leading the crew. The place had a side entrance, visible from his corner. There appeared to be a cinderblock back wall, which suggested some sort of outdoor yard or storage area and probably another exit.

They'll cover his points of egress, then flush him out. But...

Bob frowned. He wasn't so sure Alexi was as rational and stable as to be predictable. *He probably picked the place because he knows they can't touch him there. So...*

He'll walk right out the front door.

Alexi had parked four blocks south. Could he make it there before they jammed a gun into his rib cage and forced him off somewhere nice and quiet?

Hell no.

But who knew where he'd stashed Norm. *If Alexi is picked off by this Victor fella, maybe nobody gets to him in time.*

Bob sighed deeply. He kept his left hand on the FN 5.7 in his jacket pocket.

I have to go rescue his ass.

Goddamn it.

ALEXI ACCEPTED a third vodka and Pepsi gratefully and checked his watch again.

Four forty. Ten minutes late.

That is it. I should finish this and...

He glanced sideways and caught some movement at the main doors. There was someone standing just beyond them, partially obscured by colored glass inserts, but still visible. Whoever it was, he blocked out the glass, like he was at least six five, four hundred pounds, shuffling from heel to heel like...

Oleg.

Fuck.

It had seemed brave and determined to hold the meeting in public, even though they were looking for him. *Why, Alexi? Who are you trying to prove something to? Yourself, for hiding under that truck?*

If it was Oleg, then Martin wasn't far behind. They were sent out on jobs together all the time.

How many would Victor send to fetch him?

At least four. They'll cover all the exits, give me a chance to go nicely.

He pondered his next move. Maybe his best bet was to just try to walk right by them, flash his piece if necessary, make sure they knew he didn't give a shit who was nearby or could get caught in the crossfire. There were cops parked just down the street when he'd entered. They wouldn't want a scene of any kind.

They might even just let him do it, Alexi thought.

"Don't even think about it," the voice to his right suggested.

He turned quickly and realized who it was, then redirected his attention straight ahead, as if Bob were no one in particular. "Why are you here? You are supposed to be going after Victor..."

"Kind of irrelevant to the point right now, which is that you're in deep shit."

"Irrelevant to you, maybe..." Alexi took a long swallow from his drink, then set the glass on the bar. "But... you followed me, clearly. From our meeting? Probably. Look, I do not know what you are trying to pull, but I plan on walking right by them..."

Bob lowered his voice to a subtle growl.

"If you flash a piece at those guys near the front door, the cops will see it and lock off every street exit within a mile via containment points, cruisers blocking intersections, guys in uniform flooding the area, a chopper, K-9 units. This is a major tourist destination. They don't want another Las Vegas."

Behind them, the band launched into its first song, the bass thumping, a guitarist bending strings, notes flying as he soloed into an old Big Brown song. A velvety baritone came in, promising to love his woman "Morning, Noon and Night."

Alexi turned on his stool and watched the band for a minute, a few couples already up and dancing. "You like?" he half-yelled, to be heard over the music.

"I like the song," Bob yelled back. "The band's just okay. Look, we need to get out of here..."

Alexi nodded to the back of the room. "Fine, we take kitchen."

"They'll have someone on the back door, maybe more than one guy."

"Uh-huh. So we kill that guy..."

Bob held up a hand. "No, we don't. I realize you have a complete absence of scruples, Alexi, or you wouldn't have gone back to loot a village where a girl had just been raped. But I try not to kill people if possible. And any gunplay here, even in an alley, is going to bring trouble down. And if you get killed by a stray bullet..."

"Then maybe you don't find your friend," Alexi ended

the thought. "*Da*, I get it. I understand. I just don't care. We have to go; that exit seems better than" — he jerked his head towards the front doors — "that exit. So..." He rose off the stool.

Bob pushed him back down with a hand to the shoulder. "Sit down. They don't know me, so I can get a close look at what we're dealing with. They're not going to come in here guns blazing, so let's have them sit tight where they are for a couple more minutes. Okay?"

Alexi didn't look like that was okay. But he nodded his head. "*Da, da...* sure." He lifted his vodka and Pepsi from the counter and finished the last third in one long swallow. "But get going, Mr. Bob. I have treacherous Chinese snake to deal with for standing me up. Probably tipped them, too..."

"Hang tight." Bob rose and made his way to the side entrance. It appeared to be locked. A small sign on the adjacent wall said "Ticketed Events Only."

That made things a little easier. They wouldn't have to worry about being flanked by a surprise arrival.

He made his way back through the bar, past the happy diners and drinkers, and outside via the front doors. The four men were still there, looking annoyed. One of them was smoking a cigarette clasped between long, bony fingers.

He put a hand on Bob's forearm as he passed.

"A moment, friend," he said.

Bob pulled his arm away. "Don't touch me," he warned.

The man looked unworried, a small smile playing across his face. "Not intending to offend, friend. Just wondering how you know that guy you just talked to."

Bob looked him in the eye, pretending to ignore the giant beside him. "He was in my seat. I asked the barkeep, John, to hold the last two stools for me, and the fucker gave it away. You got a problem with that?" Bob demanded, irritated. He sniffed hard and wiped his nose with the back of his hand, a pissed-off tourist who didn't like confrontation.

"No problem, friend, no problem. Do we have a problem, Oleg?" he asked the giant. It was a subtle nod to the fact that they weren't going to brook any bullshit.

"Well... good then," Bob muttered, gazing up at the giant and trying to sound like he'd just noticed how big the man was. He walked towards the corner of the street with their eyes on his back.

Around the corner, half a block down Second Street, another guy in a suit was leaning against the wall next to the side entrance. He seemed preoccupied, trying to light a cigarette with a mostly dead disposable lighter.

Bob crossed the street near him and walked past, looking for the telltale bulge at the man's waistline, spotting it as the man turned to shield his cigarette from the wind.

He walked on and crossed back at the next corner, then turned left down the alley behind the club. It was crowded, businesses using it for staff parking, storing items and refuse.

Another man was waiting by the back gate set into the cinderblock wall, his hands clasped ahead of him. He avoided focusing on Bob, staring straight ahead like a bored doorman.

Bob walked the alley to the next street. He turned right and followed it to Lt. George Lee Avenue, directly south of the club, where he turned right again. After a block, he turned right once more, heading north until he returned to the side entrance.

The guy smoking the cigarette was distracted, paunchy

around the midsection, with the kind of flitting gaze that suggested he was uncomfortable. *He'd be easy enough to take out.* But the side door was locked and would need to be forced or picked, with the club full of people.

That's not going to work.

They had to keep things quiet. That meant the back door.

He approached the side entrance guard. "Hey…"

"Fuck off," the man growled.

"You got another cigarette? Here: I've got fifty cents…" Bob reached out with the two coins.

The man looked annoyed, but reached into his pocket and took out the pack. He flicked one Bob's way, and he awkwardly caught it before it hit the sidewalk.

"Thanks!" Bob said.

The man held out his hand. "My money."

Really? Bob handed him the two coins.

The man reached into his pocket again for his lighter. "You need a—"

"Nope! I'm good, thanks!"

Bob turned and walked back to the rear alley. Once past the corner and away from the side entrance guard's point of view, he walked up to his colleague at the back gate, gripping the cigarette's filter between his lips.

The man eyed him warily but said nothing.

"You got a light?" Bob asked.

The man rolled his eyes a little at the imposition. But he reached into his pocket with his right hand. *Probably his strong hand, too.*

Bob's fist came around with lightning speed and precision, a short cross that caught the guard square on the button — the mental nerve in the chin. The man's eyes rolled back, and his legs buckled as he slumped to the ground.

He had to move quickly. Most knockout victims were down for about thirty seconds at most. He tried the rear gate, then stepped over the man. He turned and crouched, stripping the Sig Sauer P365 9mm from the man's waistband. He popped the magazine and threw it over his shoulder into the collected trash behind the club, then worked the slide to eject the round in the pipe. Then he stuck the gun back into the man's waistband and continued inside.

The kitchen was sweltering, steam rising from giant pots of gumbo on the commercial stoves. A small crew of four men were preparing meals.

"Hey!" a young employee in a white chef's coat barked at him. "You're not supposed to be back here!"

Bob ignored him and walked through to the restaurant. The heat picked up, bodies on the dance floor warming proceedings. The band was in full swing, amps pumping out "Lowdown and Dirty," an old Luther Allison tune. He was only ten feet away by the time Alexi turned and finally noticed him.

Bob nodded towards the back entrance. Alexi nodded back once and rose quickly, following him. He caught up to him at the kitchen door. "What are we facing?"

"One guy on the back is all. If we're lucky, he's still out cold."

"So we can just walk out?" Alexi said. "I am lucky man today for having blackmailed you, Bob."

"Today." Bob headed towards the back door.

SOMETHING WAS WRONG.

Jerry Perry took his eyes off Alexi for a moment to glance down Beale Street. The roadway was heavy with strolling tourists despite being Sunday night. Memphis was still the South, so the street effectively closed at midnight when the clubs stopped serving. But that was hours away.

He let his eyes wander, to the police cruisers, to the two officers strolling a beat on the opposite sidewalk, to the older couple on their mobility scooters.

The guy who spoke with me; that could've been something. I should've tracked him as he left.

He turned his attention back to the front door windows just in time to see Alexi rise from his stool and walk towards the back of the room. After a couple of seconds, he lost sight of him completely.

Jerry tapped his Apple Watch. "Lev, you copy?"

"Here, boss," Lev replied, the sound coming in through his cordless earpiece.

"Everything okay?" he asked the side entrance guard.

"Is boring," Lev replied. "Side entrance must be closed inside. No one is using it."

"Okay, keep me informed." He disconnected the call and repeated the procedure to call Martin.

It rang four times without answer.

He nodded to one side. "Oleg, go around back, make sure Martin is okay."

"You sure, boss? He could..."

"Just... do it, okay?" If they blew this, he knew Victor would be apoplectic.

Oleg nodded sternly and set off.

. . .

BOB IGNORED the complaints from the sous chef and opened the back door. The man by the gate was no longer lying down but had instead raised himself to one knee and was rubbing his jaw.

They jogged down the steps. The guard, Martin, heard them immediately, a look of shock on his face as he scrambled to his feet. His hand flashed to his belt, the nine-millimeter Sig Sauer raised to eye level in a flash.

"Stop or you're a dead man," Martin commanded.

"That gun feel a little light to you?" Bob asked, walking towards the guard at pace.

Martin looked taken aback. Then he curled his lip in a slight snarl and tried to pull the trigger.

The gun's slide drew back and forth, but there was no shot, no sound except the click on an empty chamber.

Bob hammered the man with another right cross.

The guard staggered to one side but did not go down. He reached unsteadily into his coat and pulled out a switchblade, opening the knife and crouching slightly.

Bob saw Alexi's hand come up from the corner of his eye. "NO!" he yelled, reaching over in a flash to slide his finger into the trigger guard, blocking him from firing. "Jesus Christ! There are cops everywhere, you idiot!"

The guard took advantage, reaching in, brandishing the knife in a sweeping arc. Bob and Alexi jumped back, out of range.

Behind them, they heard rapid footsteps. Bob chanced a quick glance.

Two men, both armed, side guard and giant.

He leaped forward, anticipating the stabbing motion that followed, turning slightly, the switchblade passing his side. The adrenaline zone kicked in, everything seeming to slow down as he slammed into the man's passing arm with his left elbow.

The knife clattered to the cement as his right hand flashed across their field of vision, hammering the man in the chin once more.

Before he could crumple, Bob grabbed him around the waist, turning them both toward the two oncoming attackers. The side entrance guard's gun hand rose, three shots fired in quick succession, Martin's body shielding them, bullets slamming into his torso.

He's wearing a vest. That helped. He had no idea what caliber the slugs were, but they weren't getting through the wounded back door minder.

All bets were off. Alexi's hand rose, and he fired back, the bigger man, Oleg, going down immediately. Lev trained his pistol on Alexi.

Bob let Martin's unconscious body fall away and used the moment of indecision, springing forward to close the distance between them. Lev tried to turn his aim Bob's way, but he was too late, the taller man dropping low, swinging his foot around in a leg sweep.

Lev lost his balance. He crashed to the asphalt, and the gun went off one more time, flying from his grasp and bouncing off the alley floor.

Bob tried an elbow drop from close, but Lev's hands came up in time to block it. The Russian rolled to one side and found his feet.

Bob righted himself and darted towards him. Lev flashed a front kick that Bob blocked.

Alexi stood back from the pair initially, but was done fooling around. As Lev drew back his hand for another short, hard punch, Alexi shot him twice in the torso. Lev collapsed to the ground beside his comrades, clutching at his chest.

"We go, now!" Alexi barked. He bolted for the end of the alley, Bob two feet behind him.

At Second Street, they ran south, police sirens wailing. The sidewalk was nearly empty. Alexi slowed for a brief moment and dragged Bob sideways, into a multistory parking garage, the berths crammed full of cars. "This empties into hotel... a block away," Alexi exclaimed breathlessly as they ran up the slope to the second floor.

The sirens were drawing nearer. On the second level, they ran past rows of sedans and trucks as Alexi directed them to the parking garage's back right corner. He yanked a door open, and they found themselves in a brightly lit corridor. A sign on the wall with an arrow read "Westin Hotel."

They followed it to another set of doors. Inside, they found themselves ahead of a bank of elevators.

The Russian turned abruptly, raising the gun. "No! You wait here for twenty seconds until I'm gone."

Bob raised both palms. "Will you chill out, please..."

"I will not. You follow me to the club, which means you were looking for your friend, not doing what I asked. You go now! You go and you kill Victor, or..."

"I just saved your life."

"You just saved your friend's life. Me? Me you would kill without blinking. I know. I was in Iraq, remember?" He reached behind him without taking his eyes off Bob and hit the elevator down button. A few moments later the doors pinged, and he entered the car. "Remember our deal, or old man is dead."

The doors slid closed.

Bob noticed the corner security camera in his peripheral

vision. If he was lucky, it was entirely internal and closed-circuit. Businesses hated coughing up footage to authorities and usually demanded a warrant.

He pulled down his cap and hit the elevator button again. He had no doubt by the time he got to street level, Alexi would be long gone.

10

The man behind the 7-Eleven counter stared back at Margie with dark-ringed, slightly puzzled eyes.

His green store shirt and tennis visor, with matching tag that read "Hi, I'm Corbin!", suggested he was there to meet her needs. But her request clearly had him puzzled, and he stared, slack-jawed, his lower lip disconcertingly droopy, as if he might let go a long string of drool at a moment's notice.

"Wha...?" he blathered.

"I said Gary's porch cam gave us a plate number, and he filled up with gas at Murph's gas bar about eight minutes later on Foster Ave. Xian at the 7-Eleven on Lamar said he was in there for smokes ten minutes later. Elise from the VFW caught the same Dodge Shadow on her doorbell cam five minutes after that and about eight blocks east of there on Airways. That means you're less than a block from where he was last seen. So... you seen him, or what? It's real important, sweetie. I'm looking for my husband, Norm."

Corbin held up both palms. "I can't help you, ma'am. I

can't access the security tape. Only Mr. Husain can do that, and he's not in until tonight. So…"

Margie held up the grainy black-and-white still image they'd been given by the much more helpful clerk, Xian, at the 7-Eleven on Lamar. She said she'd been about to quit anyway, so privacy could take a short dive off a long pier.

Corbin studied it. "That the guy?"

"Uh-huh."

Corbin nodded. "Yep. Came in here yesterday. I was having a smoke out back when he walked off with a bag of stuff. Headed…" He turned in place, an index finger raised as his eyes searched for the correct compass point. "That way. Down Tunstall."

Margie's eyes blazed with self-satisfaction and determination. "Corbin, sweetie, when I find Norm, I'm going to come back here and plant a big fat kiss on that mug of yours."

Corbin frowned. "I think that may be against company regulations."

Margie strode back to the Subaru. "We've got a live one," she said as she climbed into the passenger seat.

"We do?" Ellie asked from behind the wheel.

"We do. Take a right off Park, there, and then we start looking. He's somewhere around here, stole a bag of groceries yesterday."

"Okay then," Ellie said, starting the car. "Off we go!"

Margie crossed her arms, a sense of satisfaction creeping into her worry over Norm.

She'd gone from terrified to determined to confident.

. . .

It was nearly eight o'clock by the time Margie answered her phone.

"Norm's missing," she blurted before Bob had even had time to talk.

"I know. The guy who took him is blackmailing me."

"WHAT?!?" She did not sound happy. "JUST WHAT IN THE SWEET HOLY HELL IS GOING ON?! WHERE'S MY HUSBAND?"

Bob moved the phone slightly away from his face. The beaten-up old Ford Focus was on Madison Avenue, heading east.

He pulled over to the curb. "Look, I get how upsetting this is, I do, but I'm going to get him back."

"Already all over it," Margie said. "And that wasn't what I asked you. I asked you where he is. Y'all show up after not talking to him for ten years, and all of a sudden this happens? I don't buy the coincidence, mister."

Really? She's blaming me? "You didn't call the cops, did you, Margie? Because the guy in question is pretty unhinged. If he even sniffs a police car, Norm's in serious trouble."

"Well, I figured that much. I mean, he's obviously in serious trouble already. What I can't figure out is why Normie didn't tell me y'all had legal troubles or enemies, or whatnot..."

"It was out of the blue, a guy who knew me in my military days." Her agitation was making him feel the need for a drink. But that was out of the question. "I don't think he has any great urge to hurt Norm, Margie, but he's the kind of guy without scruples when it comes to decision time."

"Uh-huh. Like I figured. So this is your fault."

"It's..." He tried to think of a reason it wasn't, but nothing was coming. "Yeah, it's my fault."

His instinct had been to deny it, to blame the Russians. But Bob knew his past choices had led him there, back into Norm's orbit. *I should've thought about the risk, to anyone who knew me back then.*

"Yeah... well, no thanks to you, we tracked him," Margie said. "The guy who took him, I mean. He lives somewhere in Orange Mound; that's southeast of downtown. We just haven't figured out which house yet..."

"You... tracked him?" Bob realized as soon as he said it that "incredulous" probably wasn't the politest tone to take. "Sorry... that came out badly."

"No, I get it. It wasn't easy. But folks all over this town have cameras: on their porches, on their doorbells, on their fences, in corner stores..."

"And you..."

"Tracked the dirty so-and-so like a cat cornering a mouse, yes, sir. I aim to catch him, too, soon as we spot that car..."

"No!" Bob declared. "No, you won't."

"Now just a doggone minute, there, Mister Expert. I am sixty-eight years old, and I can darn well make my own decisions—"

Bob cut her off. "It's not about you or your abilities. It's not a judgment on age or womanhood or anything else. He's a sociopath with a history of killing people for a living."

There was a moment's pause. "Oh."

"That's why..."

"Oh Lord... and Norm's stuck with him."

Bob realized the inference. *Ah, hell. Can't I say anything right the first time? Do it now, idiot. Say the right thing.* "He won't hurt Norm. He's his bargaining chip, and this guy doesn't just kill people. He needs a reason."

"So if I get to him first..."

According to the file Alexi had provided, Victor Malyuchenko's home was still a few miles east, ten to fifteen minutes into the suburbs.

"Margie, do NOT go anywhere near this guy, okay? Just because he figures he needs Norm, that doesn't mean he'll extend the same to you. If he thinks you're a problem, he'll shoot you dead, and Norm will be gone before I can help. Do you understand?"

Another pause. Then she murmured, "Well, y'all know that don't sit right with me, really, no, sir. You got my husband into a dangerous situation; now y'all want me to just sit on my hands?"

"I know. But if you want to help, just find the house. Find it, make sure no one spots you, and get out of there. Okay?"

"What's this guy got you doing, anyhow?"

"You don't want to know that."

"I think I have a right. Is it... you know..."

"Illegal? Of course it is."

"I was going to say 'potentially fatal,' but I'm getting the sense that y'all are correct; I probably should stay out of that end of things."

"I'll call you back as soon as I know more, okay?" Bob promised. "Give me a few hours." He looked at his watch. "It's eight o'clock. I should know what I'm dealing with and be able to update you before the end of the day."

"End of... Bob, I'm not going home without Norm. Fix this, Goddamn it! Y'all fix this, and y'all make things right, and do it now!"

"This isn't getting done tonight. It's too complicated and too dangerous. But I'll be back before midnight, I promise. If you find the guy's car, note the address, and get out of there."

"But..."

"No buts! You can't help Norm if you're dead, Margie." He said it bluntly. He wanted the weight to sink in.

Eventually, she relented. "Well, fine then, I guess. I guess that's all we can do."

"Talk soon," Bob said. He ended the call.

Worries about Margie aside, it was good news. Her enterprise had provided a break. If she found the car, he might not even have to worry about killing Victor.

Then it would be time to have words with his old friend from Iraq.

VICTOR MALYUCHENKO KEPT TWO RESIDENCES, according to Alexi's file: a penthouse apartment in Richwood, south of the Bill Morris Parkway, and a massive family home in Germantown.

Bob stopped at a donut shop less than a mile from the Russian's mansion and bought a cup of green tea. He sat in a booth near the back of the restaurant and sipped it while he read through the details.

Alexi was old-school military; rather than just handing over a USB stick full of digital files, he'd printed them out at some point and cross-referenced related points with colored tabs. Doubtless, he'd originally planned to do the deed himself.

The layout of the apartment, off Long Creek Road, was included; a note said he was only there for a few hours each day. It was allegedly for work, he'd told his wife, due to late-running business commitments. In fact, it was his de facto second home that he shared with June-Marie Kepler, a place where he could indulge in whatever hedonism he wanted away from prying eyes.

But he was wise enough, most of the time, to return to his mansion. As far as the public record was concerned, he was an import-export specialist who made a solid living bringing Russian goods into America. He had a façade to maintain, membership in the Chamber of Commerce and the Better Business Bureau, a second-floor office above a strip mall where some actual, legitimate business was carried out.

Not that he was ever there. Alexi's file suggested appearances were important to the man. He was always perfectly coiffed, his suits tailored, a platinum Patek Philippe wristwatch on his left arm worth more than some people's cars. He wouldn't have been seen dead near a strip mall, for pretty much any reason.

He was chauffeured, using an extended-wheelbase Bentley Arnage or a Lincoln Limo, usually driven by one of his men. He had, typically, four guards at the house along with his right-hand man, Jerald Perry, whom the file suggested had been recommended to the role by Chaim Popov, a senior gangster in New York's Brighton Beach neighborhood.

He's connected, part of a bigger outfit, something nationwide.

That was a potential problem, Bob knew. Even if everything in Memphis worked out just fine, any aspect that hurt Malyuchenko's partners could put yet another price on his head... and none of this was his business.

Alexi's schematic of the mansion was complete, drawn on graph paper to offer proper perspective and scale. The house was ostentatiously large, over five thousand square feet across two stories. It was rectangular, the exterior designed by a famous artist, replete with cornice work, sculpted cherubs and angels, as if a Renaissance villa from Tuscany had been blown up to the size of an aircraft hangar.

There were multiple entry points possible, including ground-level windows; front, back and side doors; and a flat roof that featured skylights.

The security system was sophisticated and could be applied by zone and time; the house itself was not armed until after midnight, when the early-rising gangster and his family were asleep. But the front gate and the side doors were all active as long as locked, passable only with a code.

Alexi had provided the most recent code he knew, with the caution that it had probably changed.

When home, Victor spent most of his time in his library/study or the vast open-plan living room, which backed onto the expansive, manicured gardens and hedges. There was usually a man with him and another on the back door. Despite his outfit co-operating with other criminal organizations in Memphis to avoid turf wars, the threat was always there.

Bob studied the schematic, rotating it, comparing the distances from entry points to the house, considering the layout of the garden and patio, where he might be able to find quick and effective cover. It wouldn't be hard to reach the house unseen. From there, things would get more complicated.

But...

He pulled a black-and-white print of a panoramic photo from behind the house. The back fence to the home was a hundred and ten feet. Behind it...

Maybe...

Maybe I don't need to get into the house at all.

11

Margie was becoming frustrated as night settled in.

She sat in the passenger seat of Ellie's Subaru and watched the east side of Tunstall Street.

Most of the homeowners had left their cars on driveways rather in garages. It was the same throughout Orange Mound.

But so far, no red 1991 Dodge Shadow.

"You see anything over there?" she asked Ellie.

"A whole lot of nothing. I'm surprised how many people in this neighborhood can afford a Lexus. Other than that? Not a peep."

The tip at the corner store had seemed so solid that she'd practically expected them to spot the car around the next corner.

"How many blocks have we covered?" Margie wondered out loud. She looked at the dash clock. It was ten thirty.

"A few dozen, easy," Ellie said. "You okay?"

The tone was pure concern. "I'm just fine," Margie said. "It's Norm we should worry about."

"You don't seem fine. You seem driven and desperate, which I understand. But that also means you get to talk about it, not just carry this all on yourself. I mean, you've never been shy about bending my ear off before..."

Margie pursed her lips and tried to hold it in, but a few tears managed to squeeze their way down her cheeks anyway.

"It's because his heart is too damn big for his body," she said. "He's always had a spare room for some kid who has prospects as a fighter but nowhere to go. He always has time for some bum who should've made a good life but instead slipped off the rails. His cronies at the club are all former somebody gangsters and businessmen. There isn't a loser on this planet Norm doesn't find loveable."

"Yeah... he's pretty awesome, Margie."

"And everyone knows it. This fool shows up after ten years, and what does Normie do? He invites him to stay with us! That makes it worse, that someone has the dad-gum nerve to take advantage in the first place. I remember when people in this town were respectful and honest and..."

The notion that Memphis was ever totally on the straight and narrow struck them both as silly at the same time, and both women giggled.

"Sure, and the trees in my backyard used to grow caviar and T-bone steaks, too," Ellie said. "Now all we can get is some damn peaches."

Margie laughed again. Then she realized how much her old friend meant to her, just then and always. She reached across and hugged her. "You're a caution, Ellie Grainger. But I do not know what I would do without you."

"Whatever it was, it would be a lot less fun. Or" — she nodded to the street as they passed more homes — "you know... bearable."

Margie nodded and crossed her fingers, a surprising sense of confidence hitting her. "We'll find him. We'll get him home safe."

She didn't dare doubt it.

But the truth was they were a solid five-minute drive from the store and the clerk who'd spotted Norm's abductor.

Maybe they'd just missed it, or maybe the car was off the street to keep people like her out of this man's hair. The prospect of backtracking and spending another two hours looking didn't seem appetizing.

But if it was necessary, she knew, that's what they'd do.

"THERE!" Ellie exclaimed, tapping the brake slightly too fast, both women thrown momentarily towards the dash before their belts locked up and jerked them to a halt.

"Sorry... there, at the end of the block."

The street was devoid of traffic. The last house was a new build, one of those fancy kits with big square footage.

Probably has central AC, too, Margie thought with no small sense of jealousy. They'd worked so hard for so long, and here this crook was in a place twice the size of theirs. Didn't that just figure.

But sure enough, a fading red Dodge Shadow sat just ahead of it, in front of the garage door.

"Pull up," Margie said, undoing her seatbelt.

"Margie... you're not going up to that house on your own. Are you crazy, girl? You know what Norm's friend Bob told you about this guy..."

Margie paused, buckle still in hand. She reluctantly did her belt back up. "Bob don't run this show, I do."

Ellie shot her another worried look.

"Well... pull over anyhow. We can at least keep eyes on him."

"If we park here and he spots us, he'll move Norm," Ellie said. "We got lucky finding him, Margie. We might not be next time. We know where he is. From what Bob told you, he's got people after him, so he's not going anywhere."

"I can't just go home and do nothing!" Margie lamented. "My nerves can't take it, thinking about him all tied up and worried."

Ellie grasped her friend's hand tight. "Then you come stay with me tonight, hon. We'll be there for each other."

"I'll have to call Bob, fill him in," she said. "I wonder what he's up to now."

12

Behind the gun store counter, Arturo Ramirez rubbed his chin and pondered the question.

He had salt-and-pepper hair, a Latin complexion and deep, sallow eye sockets. He'd probably have looked contemplative while watching cartoons, Bob figured.

His name was one of several on a list provided by John Butcher in New Orleans, friendly dealers around the country who didn't ask too many questions.

"Well, sir... here's the issue: you need a .30-30, preferably a Winchester 94 or a Marlin 336. Something that you can reload quickly with lever action that also has stopping power and accuracy over two hundred feet. Problematically... I can't do the money you're talking."

"How much are we off, Mr. Ramirez?"

The gun shop owner's eyes flitted for a split second to the clock. "Geez... I mean, these are premium hunting rifles, Mr. Welling. I couldn't let the Marlin go for less than $900 and the Winchester... I mean, you can call them common as church suppers all you want; the fact is, that's a $1,200 rifle even when they're not in demand. I'd have to say $1,400 on the Winchester. The scope will run you another $1,500."

"Fifteen hundred for a scope!" Bob had trouble hiding his disgust. "Are you kidding me?"

The man shrugged. "You want my most accurate, that's the Vortex. I'm not even marking you up on that, amigo, or on the ammo, or on the… ski mask." He shook his head. "I really don't want to know. But the scope? They use the best glass available."

"I noticed you glancing at the clock," Bob said. "When it comes to retail price, the time and day shouldn't really matter."

The man shrugged. "Yeah… but they do. Because anyone who contacts me by email at ten o'clock on a Sunday and begs me to reopen the store two hours after I've shut for the night is desperate. And, if you don't mind my saying, probably not up to much that's legal, given the time of night."

Bob felt the weight of the stun gun in his pocket. If it had been fifteen years earlier, the conversation would probably have been taking place in some third-world backwater, with him in deep cover, and the man would be unconscious or dead already.

But those were the bad old days.

"I've got twelve hundred," Bob said. It was almost everything he'd liberated from criminal developer Sammy Habsi and biker boss Deacon Riggs before leaving New Orleans. "What can we do to close the gap a little?"

Ramirez rubbed his chin again. "Hang tight for a minute. I've got an idea."

He disappeared through a door behind the front counter. Bob heard metal on metal, a locker door opening. A few seconds later, Ramirez reappeared. "Here." He put the oilskin down on the counter and unwrapped the gun.

It looked ancient, rusted around the screws, although the rest of the metal on the stock had been cleared up — with steel wool, based on the abrasions. "What IS this?" Bob asked. "It's so beat up I'm surprised the barrel's still straight. It looks like it was dropped out of a plane into a lake, where it sat for a while."

Ramirez shrugged. "It's a 1998 Henry .30-30, currently loaded for 160-grain Winchester. And I believe... it was dropped in a lake, where it sat for a while."

"The scope... I don't recognize the maker. I've been... off the grid for a while."

"That's a Tract TORIC, good long-range scope. They're pretty big now in the hunting community," Ramirez said. "This one's used, so I can throw it in for $500. Say another five hundred on the beat-up Henry..."

"Five hundred? For that piece of junk!?"

"Hey, man..." Ramirez held up both palms in low-level surrender. "I've tried her myself on the range in the basement, and she'll fire a tight group still. I'm not so hot, but at twenty-five yards, I had them an inch apart."

Basement targets at limited range were one thing. A mover at nearly three times that was something else entirely. But he didn't have much option. "You can't knock even two hundred more off?"

Ramirez crossed his arms, his expression stern. "It's ten o'clock on Sunday night. Amigo, you're lucky I'm even here."

Bob felt frustrated. Money was always going to be an issue as long as he kept moving. If everything went well, however, it would be solved in another day and he could compensate the man properly. He looked around the room one more time, as if he might spot some alternative. "Wrap it all up. And thank you for..." He paused, spotting something behind the counter. "Is that a Daisy?"

Ramirez glanced at the old BB gun. "It is! I keep it around for nostalgia's sake, although I really should give it to one of the neighborhood kids, get them interested early."

"Can I take it?"

The shopkeeper shrugged. "Sure. It's been sitting in the attic for years, so you'll want to give her a test. I'll throw in some ammo."

"You're a good guy, Mr. Ramirez."

"Pleasure doing business with you," Ramirez said as he re-covered the gun in the oilskin. "As for the urgency given that it's Sunday night in Memphis... I do not want to know."

THE HENRY WASN'T PRETTY. But she'd do the job; she'd let Bob kill a man standing just shy of a football field away.

He sat in the parked Ford and kept an eye on his entry point. Ingress was going to be tricky; though he didn't technically even need to step a foot on Malyuchenko's property, the same couldn't be said of his neighbor. And whoever that was, they had money, too, and doubtless an excellent security system.

Probably better than the Russian's. *I would if I lived next door to a sociopathic gangster.*

Of course, "next door" was all relevant. The property was an acre, probably more.

He checked his battered old Seiko watch. It was a half hour to midnight. Only a few extraneous lights were left on in the house. Malyuchenko's study was on the other side of the vast, open living room from the stairs to the bedroom.

That meant he had to walk across the room... which meant he would pass before the giant folding glass back doors that opened to the garden.

It had occurred to Bob while looking at the schematic that sometimes the old ways were the best ways. Most of his overseas assignments had involved such objectives. Get in silently, hit someone from a distance, get out just as quietly. There was no reason to ever meet Victor Malyuchenko. He'd seen enough of the man's background in Alexi's well-cobbled file to know nobody would mourn his passing.

One less sociopath, and Norm could go home. There was also little reason to expect betrayal from Alexi after the fact. The deal was simple: he kills Victor, Alexi lets Norm go. The Russian wanted Victor's role, not a feud with a man who once wiped out his entire merc unit. That didn't mean he wouldn't look for it, of course.

He picked up his laptop off the passenger seat and checked the satellite image again. The property directly behind Malyuchenko's was still grand, but less ostentatious, a modern three- or four-thousand-square-foot mansion with a decent yard. But there were proximity lights along both sides of the house.

The little extra he'd picked up at the gun store would come in handy there.

Right behind the neighbor's home, in a giant old oak tree, the satellite image revealed a small, boxy formation. Bob had seen them on overhead images before.

A tree house.

Assuming modern parental paranoia was in play, there was no chance it would be occupied at midnight.

He leaned over and opened the glove box, removing the full-headed black ski mask, which he put on.

He got out of the Ford, pushing the front seat forward to retrieve his kit bag and the wrapped guns. The street was clear in both directions, just walls and gates.

Bob hiked across the road. The cameras on the gatepost were irrelevant; the house wasn't large enough for full-time security personnel, which meant it was a tape for police to look at later. But he doubted they'd put huge effort into finding Victor's killer.

The rooms on the front side of the house were dark. There was a keypad next to the barred gate. He looked up at the gatepost, a seven-foot-tall pillar. He'd probably have to climb it, he realized.

A car came down the road, headlights bright. Bob stepped in close to the pillar and hugged it, hoping the shadow was enough to hide his frame.

The car passed slowly. Bob averted his eyes; nothing he was wearing reflected too much light.

The car rolled slowly by.

Bob gave it a five count. He leaned left slightly and peeked around the pillar. The car rolled around the far corner, lights disappearing into the night.

He looked back up at the top of the pillar, eyes scanning downward until he saw a good foothold for a toe, an irregular piece of decorative stone protruding slightly, just above the ground.

After checking the street in both directions one last time, he slid the wrapped guns through the bars and let them fall onto the gravel path on the other side. He returned to the pillar and planted his left foot upon the foothold. He pushed off, grabbing the top of the pillar and pulling himself up to its concrete cap. He dropped over the other side, his feet finding the grass and soft soil silently.

He retrieved the guns. A pair of large manicured ornamental trees sat eight feet apart on either side of the front lawn. Bob crouched low and moved behind them, using them for cover as he approached the house. At the second topiary, he unwrapped the oilskin and took out the Daisy BB gun.

Classic is right. This thing must be from 1960.

It wasn't the slingshot he'd used in Tripoli when knocking out a spotlight; that had given him a clear shot to eliminate an international terrorist. But it would serve the same purpose, thanks to the pump-action lever that allowed maximum air pressure in the chamber. A BB wasn't enough to do much more than prick a person's skin painfully... but it was effective against light bulbs and made just a slight popping noise, far quieter than any suppressor could manage.

Bob worked the pump until it would barely snap shut. It was an old-fashioned ball sight with a V reticule. He lined up the light bulb with the ball, then placed the ball in the groove of the V. He was less than thirty feet away, and the muzzle velocity was likely well into the hundreds of feet per second, so worrying about drop or wind was pointless. He breathed in and held it, then squeezed the trigger smoothly, the BB gun kicking forcefully from the sudden expenditure of air pressure, the *pop* louder than he remembered it.

The proximity light bulb shattered.

Bob wrapped the gun up again and waited. He had to be sure neither the shot nor shattering bulb had been heard before proceeding. If a light went out just as someone stepped outside, or while they were staring out a window, his cover was blown, and the homeowner would doubtless call the police.

He waited a few more moments for any sign of disturbance.

Go time.

He grabbed both guns and crouched before scurrying down the left side of the house. The windows were set well above the ground, and he remained out of sight. Halfway along, he stopped, unwrapped the BB gun again and took out the second light, pausing in place again to judge any betrayal of his position.

He followed the fence line into the darkened backyard, to the rear corner.

A small wooden ladder led up to a tree house about eight feet off the ground, just above the height of the rear fence. It was big, the kind ambitious dads built so that their sons could impress their buddies with a clubhouse.

He rested his foot on the bottom step and pushed up, to make sure it would be able to take his weight. The hand-built ladder creaked slightly but held.

Bob kept the guns under his right arm as he used his left hand to haul himself up a few steps. He reached up through the open trapdoor and deposited the guns into the tree house, along with his kit bag.

A moment later, he followed them.

The beaten-up Ford Focus had looked out of place immediately in one of the city's wealthiest neighborhoods.

The only people driving that car in that neck of the woods were pizza deliverers, FBI Agent David May figured.

The listening gear had an effective range well beyond their immediate radius, at least five hundred feet of play.

That meant he could go mobile if necessary. *Time to see what this guy's up to*, he decided.

He waited until the Focus passed the van and took the next corner, heading north on Wentworth Lane. He moved to the driver's seat and started the van, put it into drive and executed a U-turn. A few seconds later, he was at the corner, watching the lights of the Focus as they went down Blair Lane, a block north.

He followed, then pulled the van over; its day running lights had been disabled for surveillance purposes, and he left the headlights off throughout. There was no point attracting attention.

May returned to the operations area and rummaged in the bin under one of the counters, coming away with a spyglass. He got out of the truck, closing the door quietly, then followed the road to the corner.

A car was approaching. He ducked back into cover long enough to see it turn left and drive away.

May looked back down German Place. The Ford Focus was parked about halfway up, a house away from Malyuchenko's rear neighbor.

The driver had disappeared, he thought. But a split second later, a shadowy figure separated from the wide gatepost ahead of the house for long enough to jump up and grab it, using the post cap to vault over the fence.

Now what the heck is going on here, exactly? He tapped the mic button on his belt, the bone-conduction earpiece scratching to life. "Hey. Yeah, I know, I'm sorry it's so late. But we've got a problem."

. . .

In his office, with the lights low, Victor Malyuchenko picked up the receiver on his landline and dialed a New York number.

He hadn't been looking forward to the conversation. But when Andrei or Artur called, he was expected to answer and provide answers. They were underbosses, go-betweens to the organization's top men.

The phone rang three times. They always answered, eventually. That it was not immediate filled him with dread. Victor understood speaking with Brighton Beach meant a level of tact he otherwise eschewed.

The leaders of the outfit were strong, indivisible and ruthless. They commanded respect, manpower, and many, many guns. Like a single shark among a pod of killer whales, the one could never hope to overcome the many.

"Victor." Andrei didn't elaborate.

"You asked for me to call... My man Jerry did not mention it until just a half hour ago. My apologies."

The other man had little interest in fawning. "Why are you making such a show of dealing with Alexi Pushkin? He is an underling, unworthy of so much public noise. He stole from you, yes?"

"He is more dangerous than that," Victor said. "As I told you in the summer, we have a mole in the organization. There are details, agreements between us and other groups, that have come to light. Given his direct involvement with one of these groups, it has to be him. If he still has any information he is holding back, or access to more of our business..."

The line was quiet momentarily. "The gentlemen would like you to act more tactfully, if you must. Consider this a warning, Victor Ivanovich."

The line went dead. Victor hung up the phone and checked his watch. It was late, time to try to get some sleep, put the pressures of the day behind him.

BOB KNELT by the tree house window. He unwrapped the guns and took off the ski mask. He drew a sterile wipe from his kit bag and wiped down the BB gun, tossing it aside. Then he checked the load on the Henry before taking the scope out of the small leather pouch and sliding it into place with a click on the rail mounting bracket.

He used the window ledge to rest the barrel, like an improvised tripod. He adjusted the scope's focal depth and focus. Then he drew his eye away and checked the nearer trees, trying to get a sense of wind speed from the branch and leaf movement.

Maybe ten klicks south-southeast, nothing significant. The muzzle velocity of the Henry was sufficient that even at two hundred feet the bullet would take a tenth of a second to travel to its target.

And unlike the FN, which suited close-quarters accuracy at the expense of power, that same muzzle velocity guaranteed a headshot would take down the Russian.

He looked back through the scope. There was no situational need for an active left eye, so he shut it tight, allowing optimal focus on the target. He slowly turned the barrel on its fulcrum point until it was pointed at the study doors. There were occasional shadow movements over the doorjamb, confirming Malyuchenko was still inside.

In the moment, he suddenly realized, he'd gone into work mode, operational performance focused on essential tasks and issues.

Bob felt a sudden rush of discomfort, a flush of heat bordering on nausea.

It was everything he'd given up, everything he'd tried to get away from. And Alexi had pulled him back into the mire. Malyuchenko was undoubtedly scum of the first order, but Bob had done his time and turned his back on the business of death in the public interest.

But dwelling on it wasn't helping Norm. He swung the scope back onto target.

Walking normally, Malyuchenko would move less than three inches forward in a bullet's travel time.

Bob would line up the crosshairs with the man's left eye, which experience suggested that, assuming no sudden wind interference, would punch his ticket via the left temple — although the hard-point .30-30 ammo wouldn't require such accuracy, just a hit.

A lamp light went out in the study. Through the room's glass block inserts, he saw shifting shapes, shadows drifting.

Target is moving. Bob trained the crosshairs on a spot about six feet ahead of the door and six feet off the ground.

A few seconds passed before Malyuchenko walked out of the room, stopping immediately to turn and close the office door. Bob remained still, waiting patiently.

Malyuchenko turned to continue... then stooped unexpectedly, crouching down as if kneeling to tie a shoe. Bob adjusted as required, keeping the crosshairs on the man's left eye. The crouch lowered the Russian's target profile, so that a low or high miss might not do as much damage, or even hit him.

Wait him out. He still has to walk across the...

Bob lowered the rifle. Even without the scope, he could

see the second figure who had entered the picture, the little person running up to hug his daddy.

Oh, goddamn it.

They were both crouched, as if Malyuchenko was telling the boy something important, a life lesson of some sort. The fact that he seemed to love his kid was disturbing enough. *I'm not switching him off in front of a kid. That shit would haunt him forever.*

The boy looked to be nodding about something. Malyuchenko rubbed the kid's head, tousling his hair, then gestured behind him. The boy scurried off, towards the stairs on the other side of the wide room.

The Russian rose to full stretch again. Bob retrained the scope just ahead of his left eye.

On first stride...

He took a deep breath.

Malyuchenko took a half step. Bob's finger curled around the trigger.

He heard a rustle behind him.

The rifle was released and his hand had drawn the FN before he'd finished turning towards the ladder.

"I'm unarmed; don't shoot," a male voice declared.

The head that popped through the trapdoor was familiar, salt-and-pepper hair sprayed in place or gelled.

It was the man he'd seen outside the club.

It was Victor Malyuchenko's number two, Jerald Perry.

"Tell me why I shouldn't drop you where you stand," Bob asked. "You get one answer."

"Because if you shoot me, you'll be killing a federal agent... and you're in enough trouble already."

13

Bob weighed the news.

On the one hand, the dude could've come in guns blazing.

On the other, it seemed insane that the second-most powerful gangster in Memphis was a fed.

THAT bore further examination.

He hated to admit it to himself, but it was intriguing.

And he'd met more than a few bureau guys all full of bravado when they were Stateside. He wanted to see how the man held his ice.

"If you're thinking I might miss you, don't. I once tagged a Somali warlord who'd run for their Olympic team as a two-hundred-meter guy when he was younger. Got him on a dead sprint from a rooftop a half klick east, into the sun. Course, that was a BAR .50..."

Perry stood on the ladder, his top half in the tree house, hands raised. "You're missing your shot any second now..."

Bob resisted the temptation to look away. Instead, he set

the gun down on its butt, propped against the wall. "Okay, I'll bite. We'll play this your way."

The other man wagged his head back towards the road. "Not here. If we wake up the homeowners, who knows what shakes loose. I have a cover to maintain. We've got a van…"

"Not going to happen," Bob advised. "Somewhere public, where I can keep an eye out for your help and any scene you make might blow your cover. That way I can be sure you'll behave and you won't bring any friends. An operation this deep can't possibly be something you're working alone. I passed a van on Malyuchenko's street. Was that you guys?"

"It was."

"Fine. Give me your phone."

Perry did as demanded. "You want to lower the FN a little bit?"

Bob ignored him. He checked the number, then handed the phone back. He used his free hand to withdraw his burner from his coat pocket and save it. "Go. I'll move in five and call you tomorrow with a place. If I see anyone who doesn't fit — and I will spot them, no matter how civilian they look — I disappear and you've got a whole new problem to worry about."

Perry began to climb down the ladder. He paused momentarily, as if about to ask a question.

"Yeah?"

"You a fed?" Perry asked. "I figure some hitter or vigilante, he's not playing it this cool, agreeing to protect my cover. But by the same token, that rifle is a piece of shit… and this kind of domestic black ops shit died in the sixties."

Bob shooed him ahead with the FN. "Go!"

Bob gave him a 180-second count before following. By

the time he reached the street, there was no sign of the undercover agent.

He had little concern that Perry would move against him immediately. Undercover operations of the kind of magnitude required to place a man in the Russian mob were ponderous, massive ventures. Protecting that cover would mean avoiding any contact with local FBI or police, which would almost certainly filter back to Malyuchenko.

The operation had been a wash, but at least he'd learned something important.

He could only hope Margie O'Hearn had better luck.

It was nearly one in the morning by the time Bob got back to the O'Hearn house. He parked the Ford in the driveway and gathered up his gear.

Clearly, Alexi knew he was staying there, which meant others could find out. He'd have to move on, after first making some plans with Margie. Her amateur snooping had been impressive, and he was beginning to think her help could prove pivotal to freeing Norm.

"Bob! Over here!" The shout was muted, Margie trying to avoid waking the neighbors. He turned around. She was calling to him from the opposite home's porch.

Bob crossed the road, his bag over one shoulder, the oilskin-covered rifle under his other. A tall woman with pale skin and straw-blonde hair was hovering to Margie's right. "Bob, this is Ellie. Ellie, this is Bob, the guy who's making my husband's life hell right now."

"Come on," Ellie suggested, gesturing towards the house. "I'll make us all some tea, and we can figure out just what the heck is going on."

In the living room, Margie slumped onto the low-slung, plump white couch. "This has been a very, very long day."

It had. Bob had been trying to exercise regularly, but he had to admit that, post forty, it wasn't like the old days. He'd been going all day, and he felt a palpable fatigue; not the aching in the bones and muscles after hiking miles through difficult terrain, or the sting of lactic acid buildup from lifting too many weights; this was just bone tiredness, like he hadn't slept.

Margie read the look on his face. "Fun getting old, isn't it? I'd like to think I'm going to keep doing it with Norm. Makes it bearable."

He decided not to bring up the ten years he'd probably taken off his life by living on the street. "I'm sorry for all of this, Margie." He couldn't stand the idea of this strong, proud woman losing her man because of him. That couldn't happen.

"It's not the first time one of Norm's guests has brought trouble to our door, Bob. It's crazier and scarier, that's for damn sure. I know my husband's got a big heart and... heck, y'all are probably trying, or whatever. Whatever it is you have to get over, or deal with. Whatever your problem is. But... now it's our problem, and I don't think I'm going to sleep tonight, wondering if Norm's okay."

Ellie re-entered the room carrying a tray. It bore a brown ceramic teapot and three small cups, each adorned with faded Chinese art in red ink and script. She poured them each a cup. "So... what's next?" she asked as her guests sipped the green tea.

"I have a rather profound complication at my end of things," Bob said. "I was tasked with taking care of a problem for the guy who took Norm..."

"And that's your way of describing something worse, I'm guessing," said Margie.

"Yeah... anyway, it became impossible. So now I have to look for another way to deal with him."

"Or... I could go get Norm's shotgun out of the basement, and we could go down to that house Ellie and me found in Orange Mound, settle his hash the old-fashioned way."

Her face was a mask of determination, but Bob could read the anger simmering just below the surface. "Margie... it didn't take long into knowing you to realize you're a pretty capable, direct person. But you're also a smart woman; please don't do anything dumb like trying to get him back without me."

"Because you've helped so much up to this point?"

"Point taken. But I was in the business of dealing with bad men for a long time. I guarantee you, where Norm's being held — and it's probably not in that house you found, for a variety of tactical reasons involving constant resident traffic — wherever it is, we'll find him and get him back. He'll want his wife in one piece, I'm guessing."

She scowled slightly but nodded. "Fine. Dang it..."

"The key to this is leverage," Bob said. "Right now, Alexi — the guy who grabbed him — has all of it."

"So?"

"So he has someone important to us. First, I'm going to get some sleep."

"And then?" asked Ellie.

"Then I'm going to take someone important to him."

14

The Monday morning sun was warm and invigorating, and Andrew Kennedy jogged up the concrete steps towards the Lincoln Memorial, thin blue dress tie flapping in the breeze. He hadn't felt so vigorous in some time. He was not a small man, and the crown of white hair gave away his seventy-four years.

But he felt like a young bureaucrat again.

After months of waiting — which, in turn, had followed a nearly calamitous year of bad history revisited — they'd learned just an hour earlier that the agency's budget expropriation committee had approved, with the director's sign-off, a substantial increase for covert operations.

That meant more money for Team Seven. More than that, it meant the director once again had confidence, in the wake of the Gerald Dahlen scandal, that he could handle things just fine without outside interference.

That was the point of Team Seven, after all, to operate outside the boundaries of accountability. Without that freedom, the exercise was pointless. And without the team,

Kennedy's power and influence on Capitol Hill would be reduced to that of a middling civil servant.

It was only by the grace of a special exemption from the director that he was allowed to continue past mandatory retirement age to begin with.

Now, he had to placate a senior bureau man over something Team Seven related. But he could hardly have worried less. Anything short of Bob Singleton getting involved in a public gang war wasn't going to alter his mood.

It did not bode particularly well, however, that the man wanted to meet somewhere public but anonymous.

The sun cast long shadows as it crept higher in the sky, the giant statue of the seated emancipator cast in a half-pall of darkness despite the bright day just a few feet past the tall, fluted Doric pillars that surrounded it. A few tourists flitted about.

His associate was on the other side of the Greek revival-style building.

Alan Manseth was the bureau's deputy operations director. He was shorter, stocky, always in need of a shave no matter how much he tried to keep up. He'd gone gray at the temples, but was otherwise youthful despite nearing retirement.

"Al," Kennedy said, slowing to a casual walk as he approached, reining in his elation.

The two men had known each other for nearly thirty years. Manseth did not look happy. He had his hand shoved into his pockets and turned slightly to acknowledge his colleague.

"Andy... what the fuck is going on in Memphis? And why am I finding out about it from a deep-cover agent, on the verge of having that cover blown by one of your guys?"

Kennedy looked at his watch. "It's... eleven fourteen in the morning on a Monday, Al. And while I am chock-full of goodwill right now due to our funding being renewed..."

"Congratulations."

"Thank you... and while I'm chock-full of said goodwill, I'd really appreciate you reining in the aggressive tack because I have no idea what you're talking about."

Manseth frowned. He seemed genuinely puzzled, Kennedy thought.

"You're kidding, right?"

"I... am not. But you've got me wondering what I missed in the time it took me to get here from the committee hearing... what, twenty minutes ago? What's going on that has you looking like you're on a third week of constipation?"

"As you may be aware, we have a deep-cover operation going in Memphis involving Russian organized crime. You should be aware, at any rate, because our ultimate targets, the New York-based leaders of the gang, have strong political ties back home... which is why it's been updated in our cooperative initiatives briefing package."

Kennedy nodded thoughtfully, letting him continue rather than venturing the truth, which was that he got at least sixty such briefs monthly from other intelligence agencies and departments, and he read very few of them.

He'd relied on Eddie Stone's judgment over their involvement level for years.

"Last night, he got a tip that his mark, a local boss named Victor Malyuchenko, was about to be assassinated by an unsub. We got an image of him from our street-level surveillance team. It took until about an hour ago to get a hit, via our liaison at the NSA..."

Kennedy felt a sinking sensation in his gut.

"... and it appears he's a former Marine named Robert Singleton, who at last mention had been seconded to your folks at Covert Ops. He disappeared from there... but that record was in 2002, twenty years ago. The bureau has him declared dead in 2012. Andrew..."

"Yes, Al?"

"What the fuck is going on? And I mean that as nicely as I can put it. According to our guy, your guy — I'm assuming he's involved in that spookfest you have going in that Arlington basement — your guy was perched in a tree house behind Malyuchenko's back fence with what looked like a .30-30 and a long scope, like Carlos Hathcock decided to go on a suburban hunt."

Kennedy sighed. "He's need-to-know, Al, and I can just say..."

"Oh bullshit, Andy!" Manseth huffed. "We go back too far for you to pull that oblique shit on a domestic operation that, in case things haven't changed since yesterday, is completely outside your mandate! Now I don't care how much faith your director has in you budget-wise. I'm pretty damn sure he hasn't signed off on a mob hit in Memphis. In case you don't recall, the US government doesn't have the best damn track record with regard to snipers in that neck of the woods."

"He's... off the reservation," Kennedy offered. "We're on it, okay? Just... don't worry. As long as he knows he's treading on your feet... well, let's just say he's developed a rather ponderous and annoying level of conscience in recent years."

Manseth squinted and peered at him, incredulous. "So... this is some sort of vigilante thing one of your boys has decided to take on himself? Is that what you want me to believe?"

Kennedy shrugged. "It's the truth, Al, I swear it."

Manseth took a deep breath and looked around, his eyes sweeping the ceiling of the monument aimlessly, as if an answer might crash down from Lincoln himself. When it didn't, he said, "Okay… let's say I give you some leash on this without reporting it… what do I tell my director if this floats up to him?"

"You… tell him I asked him to call me. Leave it with me. I promise, Alan… we've been friends and colleagues too long for this to bounce back on you."

Manseth stared sternly. Then he nodded once, his expression screaming that he was unconvinced. "Don't lose my number," he said. He turned and headed off, past the tourists and back out into the sunlight.

Kennedy watched him amble away.

Burning Alan Manseth wasn't any kind of ideal. They needed to sweep Singleton up as quickly as possible. That hadn't proven easy on earlier attempts. But they had a jump on him again.

He took out his phone and speed-dialed. "John, bring the car around to the Memorial, south side. Good man." He needed to meet with Eddie, discuss tactics.

Perhaps the best approach was something more surgical than the last attempt, something Singleton wouldn't see coming until it was too late.

15

June-Marie hated Mondays at the penthouse.

When she'd had free rein to come and go as she pleased, she'd used it to shop for clothes or get caught up on what was going on back home in Nashville. Once, she'd driven all the way to Dollywood and back, getting home late, and no one had noticed.

But it was rare that a day went by without a request for sex from Victor or, worse, a shoulder to cry on. As much as she loathed his short-lived thrusting, listening to him mewl about how hard his life was had to be even worse.

He was unappreciated. He was an unrecognized genius. His father didn't love him. It was generally pathetic, a man who'd been born with silk sheets but complained like he slept in a barn.

Then, after smoking a cigarette, he would get up, shower and leave, without saying another ten words to her.

Today was a rare pleasure: he had meetings all day and had to have lunch with his wife's parents, who insisted on occasionally seeing their grandsons.

She'd prepared her own meal, dismissing the cook until lunch to make an omelet on the giant gas range. She'd blasted the apartment-wide stereo system, both music and a handful of her favorite influencers. She'd eaten chocolates and drunk three glasses of champagne by noon.

For just a few hours, her usual dread at the start of another week had given way to a giddy, slightly drunken sense of freedom, as if neither man existed, as if she had the freedom of her adult self but the responsibilities of a kid.

By one o'clock that afternoon, she had retired to her room to lie on her bed and read Hollywood gossip. It was as close to blissful relaxation as she'd had in months.

There was a knock on the door. "Got a minute, there, June-Marie?"

She felt a swell of anxiety. If anyone could ruin the party, it was Jerry Perry.

"Go away!" she yelled back. "I'm taking a day off!"

"You get every day off."

"You know what I mean: from Victor, from you, from doing whatever anyone else tells me."

He opened the door a crack and peeked in. "Look, I have better things to do with my time, too. Believe me, if I didn't think it was an issue, I'd be honest about it and save myself the bother."

"Didn't think what was an issue?"

"We have a security threat, some guy who might be working with your former boyfriend."

She hoped she hadn't shown any reaction. June-Marie had been wondering when that guy might make an appearance. "So? What does that have to do with me?"

"Come on, kid; you know Alexi's still crazy about you. Maybe this guy's job is to grab you, put Victor in a position where he has to negotiate while he 'reunites' you with Alexi. Either way, I need you to stay in tonight."

"You have no right to treat me like a little girl, Jerry," she spat. "You're such a jerk!"

"Now... be reasonable..."

"I hate you, Jerry, I really do! Can't you just... I mean, I was having one day, one day to myself where I could do whatever I wanted, be whoever I wanted! And you had to step in and fuck that up."

"Nice mouth, with the swearing..."

"I'm not a child!"

"Just... keep a lid on things today, okay? I have to meet someone. I'll be back in an hour. Jesus Christ..." he muttered as he closed the door.

She could hear his dress shoes clopping down the hall.

She wasn't sure why, but there had been something ominous in his tone. June-Marie felt a chill run through her, that sensation she'd only felt a few times in life, a premonition, a warning to move on.

She sat up on the bed and threw her legs over the side. *Don't ignore it. Be smart. Be smarter than the nutjobs around you.*

She got up and approached the walk-in closet. From inside, she retrieved a small soft-sided suitcase and a carry-on-sized satchel. She spent ten minutes meticulously figuring out how to fit as many changes of clothing into the case as possible and still look human. She went to the bathroom and retrieved her makeup bag, toothbrush and nail kit, depositing them in the case on the bed.

Crouching beside the bed, she opened the drawer underneath and emptied out the money, placing the bound piles in the satchel. She grabbed a few more items from her bedstand and then zipped up both cases.

Then she sat back down on the bed. Something was brewing; she could feel it. One way or another the apartment door was going to open at some point in the day, and she vowed she was going through it.

"I JUST DON'T UNDERSTAND why you have to go right now."

Margie didn't want him going anywhere until she had her husband back. They sat on Ellie's porch, a cup of her green tea in front of each.

"It's not just your safety," Bob suggested. "I need somewhere to hold on to a person for a few days until this is all worked out. But I have to be smarter about it than Alexi, namely somewhere anonymous and just out of town, probably a motel. Most have parking away from the road."

Margie seemed to take that in stride. "Okay, I guess. But if something changes quickly…"

"The burner I've… the disposable cell phone I've given you is programmed so you just have to hit the first number in the call list, and it'll ring me."

"A disposable phone? Why can't I just use mine?"

"When this is done, you toss it, and there's no record you knew me, which… just believe me, that's a good thing."

"Okay. If I'm being honest with y'all, that's not a hard sell right now."

"I promise I won't be far away. And once this is taken care of, we can figure out how best to spring Norm."

He rose and picked up his kit bag, slinging it over his shoulder. Then he stooped and picked up the rifle. "Thank you for the car. I can't promise how quickly I'll be done."

"Just try not to let her get too beat up, okay?" Margie said, crossing her arms nervously. "And call me as soon as we're on the move again. I don't like the idea of knowing where Norm might be and just ignoring it."

The place he'd picked to stash June-Marie was far enough out of town to no longer qualify as Memphis, just off South Parkway west and Kentucky Street, near the I55 Expressway.

He'd puzzled Margie by asking to borrow one of Norm's suits. The man was at least six inches shorter than him, for one. But Bob had explained it was purely for show; Motels see one visitor more commonly than any other: salesmen, guys who spend all their time on the road. And they had one thing in common: they always had a separate suit on a rack hanging inside the car. Looking sharp was their bread and butter.

"If I check in carrying a suit draped in dry-cleaner plastic," he'd explained, "the guy doesn't even register my existence. Then, if Alexi or Victor has an information network, he has nothing to tell them."

He felt mild satisfaction when the ruse worked perfectly, the motel counter clerk barely looking up from his phone as Bob paid $129 cash for two nights.

"Receipt," Bob had muttered. The clerk had ripped one right off the register tape, handing it over with an irritated look that said he hated getting the same request over and over. Then he'd sat back down on his stool behind the counter and gone back to his phone.

In the room, Bob texted his tech contact, Nick Velasco, in Washington.

> Want to earn some more favor credit? Need intel, ASAP.

The phone rang three minutes later.

"Nicky, how are you?"

"Alpha, you know, you're ahead of schedule. It's been less than a month. I figured you'd take at least a week longer before calling for my help again. You already owe me at least one solid favor."

"I'm sure you're not going to complain about me owing you more than one."

"True enough. What do you need?"

Bob gave him the request. Nicky had back-door access to numerous intelligence databases, and what he couldn't find domestically, he'd locate overseas or on the Dark Web.

"Give me a couple of hours," he said. "As usual, I assume I'd rather be anyone on Earth than these people."

"Not yet. But the way things have gone so far, eventually."

"Talk soon." Nick ended the call.

Once he had a schematic on the apartment, he'd work on access to the building. Alexi had Norm; but that wouldn't mean much, Bob figured, once he had June-Marie.

16

Jerry Perry had his poker face on. He was leaning an elbow on the diner booth's faux-wood table, his chin propped atop his hand as he studied the patrons coming and going.

His other hand held a fork, a plate of fried eggs and toast ahead of him.

"Okay, I promised you I'd meet and listen," Bob said as he approached.

The place was nearly empty, just an older patron, hunched like a regular at the counter, another man reading a paper at a two-person wall table, an emptied plate ahead of him. The tables had mini-jukeboxes on them, the posters on the walls of old western stars. It looked like it hadn't changed since the fifties, but it was all a sheen; it was all new, all designed to evoke an era, a feeling.

He took the seat opposite.

"You seem relaxed for a guy pursuing a suicide mission," Perry said. He forked another mouthful of egg and wiped some off his plate before transferring it to his mouth.

"Hmm... I thought maybe... excuse me..." He swallowed. "I thought maybe you wouldn't show. Figured you'd expect me to send a couple of agents instead..."

"You didn't strike me as a stupid man," Bob said. "Maybe return the favor. You know, like, maybe put the fork down and get on with it because I have limited time."

The undercover man sniffed slightly as he swallowed, dropping the fork with a clank. "Fine." He picked up a white linen napkin and wiped his mouth, then tossed it down beside the plate. "So here's the deal: Malyuchenko's father, Ivan, is a bigwig in the Kremlin inner circle, an unofficial advisor and retired former KGB. He's leadership tight. If we can pin down Victor legally, we can not only take his bosses in New York down, we can offer him as leverage to our boys at State and Langley, maybe put the squeeze on the old man."

He said it matter-of-factly, Bob noted. The side players — Norm, Margie, local residents and police — didn't even enter the conversation. "That it?"

"It? It's a multimillion-dollar investigation with massive political and intelligence ramifications. How much more do you need to realize this isn't the place to be?"

"We share different priorities."

"So you'll... back off?"

Bob peered at him quizzically. "What part of different priorities didn't you understand, 'Jerry'?"

"If you interfere with the investigation, they'll send someone to deal with you. You know that. You can't take on the entire government."

Bob shrugged. "For now, I don't have to. I just have to deal with Victor. And whoever gets in my way. Am I being totally clear on how this is going to go next time?"

Perry looked resigned to it. "It is what it is, I guess."

Bob rose. "Take a piece of advice from someone who's been doing this as long as you but in a far nastier world: go back to DC, Jerry. Take whatever wins you have until now, play it safe. This is just career shit for you, not real life. But the people I'm representing? For them, this all really matters. And that means... you don't. I won't warn you again."

Bob left the way he'd come, satisfied the undercover agent had looked duly uncomfortable.

At the side table by the wall, the man reading the paper put it down. Agent David May strolled over to Perry's table.

"Did you catch all of that?" the fake consigliere asked, nodding towards the phone on the table.

"I did." May took off his earpiece headset. "You're right about him refusing to budge. But I kind of wonder if he doesn't have a point."

Perry's squinted as he studied the younger man. "How do you figure?"

"This has been ongoing for two years, and we have so much evidence already. The risk to people in Malyuchenko's orbit who aren't really culpable of anything — his family, some of his staff, locals... it could be argued that at this point it's no longer necessary."

He had a point, Perry knew. But he also knew that pinning Alexi Pushkin's murder on Victor would put him in their pocket forever, trials be damned. He'd do anything to avoid a possible death penalty charge or life in prison.

That was worth any risk.

The man pretending to be Jerry Perry knew it meant more than that. It meant resuscitating his career; it could get him out of undercover work and tracked towards an executive role, as a director or senior advisor. Something fat, slow and easy, with lots of time for travel and golf. He'd had enough of being the bearer of bad news and consequences that were even worse. It was time for him to be on the winning end.

"There's more at play, more information that he has on the bigger organization than we've even come close to securing," Perry said. "Leave that end of things to me. Just remember, Agent May, that if you stick with me on this, you can go places. The bureau likes winners. And there is no victory without risk and collateral damage. You feel me?"

"I feel like we should be calling in backup, immediately, to take this dude out of the equation."

"But you also know Victor has enough local law enforcement on the payroll to at least get word back that it happened. Then he's going to wonder why the FBI was protecting him at all. It's not going to take him long to figure out we have bigger plans, at which point..."

"Your cover is blown. Or tenuous, at best."

"Exactly. Just... play it cool, Agent May. We'll deal with this in due course."

May nodded, his look uncertain. Perry made a mental note to ask that the young man be reassigned as soon as possible, maybe to somewhere in Alaska.

THE TIMING SEEMED TOO good to be true.

Bob sat at the curb and watched as Victor Malyuchenko and his men paraded out of the luxury condo building in Richwood. The Russian gangster led his men to his limo and a pair of black Mercedes.

A few moments later they were gone.

He'd counted eight men in all.

Jerald Perry wasn't among them.

He'd stayed parked outside the diner for another twenty minutes before Perry had emerged with the man who'd been sitting along the far wall. Bob had made the undercover agent's associate as soon as he'd walked in, the paper held a little high, as if he was subconsciously trying to hide behind it.

They'd walked in separate directions, Perry to his car, a few spots ahead of Bob's, the other man towards the van he'd seen near Malyuchenko's house.

He'd followed Perry. The Mercedes had led him right to the apartment block in Alexi's file on Victor.

What to do with Jerry Perry? The undercover FBI man was a serious wrinkle, a complication that so far left him unsure of how to proceed.

Nicky had managed to snag a copy of the man's personnel file. His real name was Simon Cross. His present assignment wasn't even mentioned in it, likely in case of prying eyes, just his pseudonym. And technically, Jerry Perry was assigned to the Buffalo, New York, field office.

His file said he was from Trenton, New Jersey, and had been at the bureau for twenty-three years, all out of the public eye.

Bob looked up at the building again. Malyuchenko's condo was on the eighth floor. A private elevator led all the way up there. But safety regulations meant there had to be a back door.

In this case, that meant a second stairwell, with the lower door only opening from the stair side, meaning it was designed to be used as a private exit only.

He could probably pry the door open, he realized. From Alexi's description, it was just a normal door with the latch removed on the street side.

But that would sound the alarm. If Perry was smart enough to have someone stay with him, it could be a problematic extraction, Bob knew. If the consigliere was there alone with June-Marie?

He's had his warning. He knows my objective, or thinks he does.

He wouldn't be expecting an outside party to grab June-Marie. Given her comments about Victor Malyuchenko, Bob did not expect much of a fight from the girl.

Perry was another matter. His guard would be down, with the Russian away from home. But taking the girl would infuriate his boss, escalate pressures in the city, possibly upset his plans.

Bob drew the FN 5.7 and checked the load. Sometimes, operational pressures were to be expected, collateral unavoidable.

Bob walked around the building to its rear parking lot and waited near the back door, just around the corner. It took twenty minutes before someone used the door to leave. He heard the click of the latch handle and walked around the corner as if he'd just gotten there, allowing the departing resident to hold the door for him.

"Cheers," he said pleasantly as he passed the woman.

According to the schematic, the emergency exit was at the end of the rear lower hall. He followed a concrete corridor under tube lighting. Sure enough, the latch on the door had been removed.

Bob reached into his jacket's inner lining pocket to remove the half-sized pry bar.

Inevitably, things are going to get noisy.

He placed the fine edge of the bar against the tiny crack in the doorjamb. He was about to force it further when a thought occurred. He looked up at the ceiling.

A line of tiny shower heads was embedded into it as part of the emergency fire control system.

If there's a fire, they shut down the elevator.

He reached back into his pocket and found the small packet of Kleenex tissues he kept at hand.

But they'll make great kindling.

He held the packet under the nearest smoke detector and lit it with his disposable. In seconds, the tissues were engulfed in orange flame, a wispy trail of black smoke rising up and into the detector. He stretched upwards so that the heat source was as close to the detector as possible, the tissues scalding his hand.

The alarm sounded frantically, a bell at the other end of the hall clanging a dire warning. The sprinklers activated, three jets suddenly opening up, their shower-style nozzles unleashing a torrent of indoor rain.

After a few seconds he began to hear deep *thunk* sounds from the stairwell, heavy doors opening and closing on the various floors. Seconds after that, the first resident pushed open the lower stairwell door.

Bob held it open for them. "I've got it," he said. "Let's go, let's go; this looks legit."

He repeated it as residents streamed past. The volume from the stairwell suggested it was busy, a surprising number of people home for a Monday afternoon.

"What's going on?" an older woman asked him.

"No idea," said Bob. "Something on an upper floor."

He leaned against the wall, keeping his face behind the edge of the door, watching people as they passed. Soon, the steady trickle had been reduced to a few late departures, then no one.

But there was no sign of either Jerald Perry or June-Marie.

He chanced a glance through the door, up at the stairwell.

"... don't understand why we couldn't just go right away," a familiar female voice said from two or three flights up.

"We don't know what it is yet, that's why." If Perry was nervous, he didn't sound it. "Just... stay behind Constantin, okay?"

So two men, one likely a bodyguard. Perry would be armed as well.

He spotted a familiar red canister on the wall nearby. *Advantageous*, he thought as he retrieved it. He secured himself behind the door again.

Twenty seconds later, Jerald Perry walked past him, followed by another football linebacker-sized hunk of muscle. He didn't wait to see June-Marie, swinging the fire extinguisher with baseball bat speed, catching the guard square in the face.

The man's eyes drifted lazily around, the concussion setting in even as he collapsed, face-first, to the hard concrete.

Perry reacted like a professional, without delay, hand flashing to his belt line to draw his pistol. He wheeled around, his arm met by Bob's palm punch to the sensitive wrist bones, tendons splaying, grip lost. The pistol clattered to the ground even as Perry lashed out with a short front kick.

Bob spotted it late but leaned in slightly, his midsection withdrawn, the brunt of the blow muted.

He jumped back two paces. Perry sensed an advantage, rushing in with hammer blows to Bob's head, trying to catch him on the mental nerve, to end the fight quickly.

Bob's own instincts kicked in; he dropped the extinguisher and raised his forearms to guard his head. He kicked out his right foot, hooking it slightly so that it would catch Perry's ankle. The undercover agent tripped, falling sideways even as Bob spun in place on his left foot, his right foot coming around again in a whipping roundhouse kick. His heel met Perry's chin halfway to the ground, the blow dazing the bureau man, who slumped down on all fours.

Perry was shaken, having trouble rising. "Why...?" he muttered.

"Leverage." Bob grabbed June-Marie by the upper arm. She had a small soft-sided suitcase in her other hand.

"You know what'll happen..." Perry struggled to his feet.

"They're already looking for me. I don't think this changes much," Bob said. He spun on his left heel, his right foot whipping around from the knee, catching Perry across the jaw again.

The bureau man crashed into unconsciousness.

A few feet away, the bodyguard began to rouse. Bob kicked him, hard, in the chin. The man went down again.

"You're coming with me," he told June-Marie.

"Oh, sweet Jesus, thank God!" she exclaimed.

"I'm not here to rescue you," Bob said as he marched them toward the back door. "You're just leverage for your boyfriend. He's holding a friend of mine."

"Fine!" she said, shaking her head slightly as if irritated at any other notion. "Y'all need to kill them both, or I'm dead anyway."

Bob stopped just shy of the door. "What?!"

"You need to kill them both, Victor and Alexi. They're the same person, both crazy, both infatuated with me. Do that, and y'all can take me anywhere you want."

Bob pushed the door open. He let it close behind him.

He wasn't sure what to make of it. He hadn't expected a grateful hostage. "Move! Head for the rusting Ford."

They pushed past the other residents. "Did you kill Jerry Perry?" she asked.

"He'll be okay."

"Too bad. He's as mean as they are," she said as they reached the car. "Where are we going?"

"Just... get in. I'll explain on the way."

17

Artie Chee paused and held the phone away from his ear for a moment, then pushed his glasses back up his nose with his index finger.

He'd had glasses since his teens. But in the twenty years since, he'd never found a pair that fit quite right, even with adjustments.

Then again, he realized, the sweat wasn't helping. The heat in the back of his limousine was stifling, the car's air conditioning having crapped out that morning. He couldn't roll down his windows for safety's sake, and he needed the partition up for privacy.

It was way too hot. He pushed back his thick, shoulder-length black hair, clearing droplets of perspiration from his brow.

His glasses slipped down again. *Damn it. You keep meaning to get these fixed, but you don't get around to it, and now it's sweaty, and...*

Focus, Artie. The man just made a hell of a request.

"Hello?" a faint voice asked through the phone's tiny speaker. "Are you still there?"

He put the phone back to his ear. "Yeah. Yeah, I'm still here. I just have to think about it, is all."

"It's the safest option, believe me, Artie. If you stay out in the open and Victor Malyuchenko really wants you dead, he's going to find a way to reach you."

For a policeman, Detective Michael Grandini was hardly sweetness and light. The Organized Crime Unit officer had approached Chee in the past, hearing rumors he didn't enjoy the trade his father had left him and wanted out.

But this time, Chee was the one who had reached out. He had to place some faith in the man, even though the notion of talking to law enforcement curdled his stomach. He needed allies, and he needed them quickly.

"Then what do you suggest?" Chee asked. "If I go back to the warehouse, eventually he will send a crew. Even if we survive that, he has resources, cops on the take, people backing him with hitters on retainer, available at a moment's notice to take care of 'problems.' I'll never be able to step out in public again."

"I'm going to give you an address, just off Virginia Avenue, by the old rail bridge. It's just off Riverside."

"You want me to come to your office!?" Chee asked. "That seems insane."

"It's the only way. We can take your initial statement here, then work with the feds to set up a proper safe house and protection. But first, you have to show us you have something of value."

Value? There wasn't much of that left in Memphis, not for him. He was a volume heroin wholesaler, and soon, with Victor putting the squeeze on them, no one would want his product. He had one more shipment to move, one more large sale. Once the money was moved offshore, with the bulk of the family finances, he could get out of the city, go to Hong Kong or Macau, at least until things cooled off in the States.

It was all so depressing. All he'd done was agree to meet with Alexi Pushkin, see what he had to say.

There was no heroin deal, no agreement to help Alexi deal with his myriad personal problems. And when Victor's right-hand man Jerry Perry had let the word get around that his boss was angry, he'd agreed not to go.

But the word on the street was that Victor wanted him dead for even agreeing to meet with Alexi in the first place. He wanted a message sent to anyone else who might offer the outcast Russian gangster assistance.

"I know lots, believe me," he said. "Just... make sure nobody knows about me except you, at least until the feds get involved. I don't know your guys, and Victor likes to splash the cash."

"Not a problem. We'll keep you in my office until they've provided a protection detail. Where are you... never mind, don't tell me. When can I expect you?"

Chee chewed on his lower lip and pushed his glasses up again. Discussing any specifics over the phone was stupid. Really, the whole move probably was. "Soon."

He ended the call. Chee leaned forward, across the back of the front seats. "Derrick, take me to 223 Channel 3 Drive, and don't spare the lights."

Derrick had been with the family firm for two decades, a Hong Kong expat with a neck as thick as a child's waistline. The driver grunted and nodded once.

The drive took less than ten minutes. Chee ignored what was going on outside the limo; he had enough to worry about already. Once he'd talked to the feds and been assigned protection, he figured he'd have plenty of time to determine his best exit.

Via Mexico seemed likely. Victor would have people watching the airport and bus terminal, so he'd have to take the limo to Nashville.

The car followed the sweeping bend that took them off Riverside Drive and onto Channel 3 Drive; the television station was just up the road.

It began to slow down.

"What's going on?" Chee asked his driver.

"I have to pull over," Derrick said.

Chee felt a flutter in his stomach. "Why?"

The driver did not reply, instead pulling the limo over to the side of the road. "What are you doing?" Chee demanded.

The driver did not respond.

"Hey! Answer me, damn it! What are you..."

The driver got out of the car and shut the door behind him. Chee leaned forward and stared between the seats, through the windshield to the road ahead.

A pair of cars were blocking the limo's passage. The police building was immediately to their right. Surely Victor wouldn't try something in full view...

Two men got out of the cars, each carrying machine pistols.

Chee reacted instinctively, his hand finding the door handle as he bailed out of the limo and began to run. He sprinted east, up an embankment, and found himself on the railway tracks that snaked over the old iron suspension bridge, crossing the Mississippi River to Arkansas.

He looked around quickly, then heard the pop-pop of the

machine pistols. A bullet whistled slightly as it pinged off a rock near his feet.

Chee ran for it, following the tracks. He looked left. The road bridge thirty yards away was backed up, traffic slowed by something ahead. If he could get across the rail bridge, he reasoned, it would take men in cars too long to find a route across, making it difficult to catch sight of him again.

He was not in good shape; he hadn't had to do any sort of manual or physical labor at any point in his life. His father had been a wealthy criminal back to the old days with the Triads in Hong Kong and had left him everything. The soles of his shoes pounded the loose gravel and stones between the tracks with a constant rattle, the surface just uneven enough to feel like it was slipping out from under him with each stride.

The heat was brutal. He was unaccustomed to running, and by the time he reached the bridge proper, he was already panting.

A bullet pinged off the bridge's towering metal superstructure, the iron and rivets stained dark with age, beams curved like a rollercoaster in partial collapse. A split second later he heard the gunshots. Chee slowed his pace, unable to continue at full sprint, his chest heaving.

He turned slightly to see where they were.

His pursuers were less than fifty feet behind him, apparently willing to continue the chase into Arkansas.

He turned to the rails ahead, praying he wouldn't see the top of a locomotive skirt the horizon. His toe caught a rock that was partially embedded. Chee sprawled, tripping, falling to the ground knee-first.

His glasses flew off his face and bounced off one of the old wooden railroad ties.

"Oh God, no!" he whimpered. He was essentially blind without them, the world instantly converted into a mass of blurred images. He rose to his knees and felt around himself on the ground, gravel and iron cold under his fingertips. They had to be there. *Come on, come on, please...*

The footfalls closed on his position. He could see the men as distinct blurs now. There was no time to find his glasses, no time to...

He rose to flee again, not seeing the outline of the rail amidst the blurry ground. His toe caught metal as he tried to run, and he slammed chest-first to the ground, the track bruising his shin.

He was halfway to his feet when he felt the hand clamp onto his upper arm.

18

The Bentley limousine pulled up to the front of the lot at Mud Island Marina, parking horizontally across four spaces, parallel to the Mississippi.

"I keep telling you... he's not on the boat." Artie Chee looked sullen sitting on the jump seat, Oleg the giant on the seat adjacent, holding him at pistol point.

Chee had black eyes and a broken nose, twin rivulets of blood tracing down to his top lip from each nostril. He clutched one hand around his ribs, which were also broken.

Victor Malyuchenko sat on the bench seat opposite and puffed on his cigar, holding it between the first two fingers of his right hand, his eyes narrow as he peered through the blue-gray smoke at his unwilling passenger.

"You know problem I always have with you, Artie? You are weasel. Most crooks, I expect them to try to cheat me, to lie, to steal. It's their way. But they do not try to hide behind cover of..." He waved a hand up and down at the beaten man. "This... bullshit. This front-company of a man. You act like you are big businessman in this town, but you know without heroin, your company is shit. Without your old man's money, Artie, you are just pool hustler with bad attitude."

Artie motioned as if to say something, then held back, fearful.

"Yeah... I did not think so," Victor said. "You are also coward. Yet you are one who, in moment of panic, suggest Alexi is not hiding on your boat. I asked you about warehouse, your home. But I did not bring up boat. Truth is, I did not even know you own one. So, question is... why you don't want us coming here, no?"

He nodded to Oleg. "Take him. We go to the boat now, see what Artie Chee has been up to."

They got out of the limo, Tommy the driver staying behind, Mattie Chicago joining them from the front seat. Oleg and Chicago grabbed Artie under each armpit and marched him down to the slips. At the last row, a sixty-foot Galeon 640 FLY cabin cruiser was waiting, floating placidly in the harbor shallows. *Spirit of Memphis* was emblazoned across one side of the boat in flowing text.

"Your crew is on board?" Victor asked.

"My skipper and two assistants," Artie said.

"They are armed, yes?"

"They are."

Victor stopped walking, the boat still thirty feet away. "You call them off now, tell them to stand down. When we go aboard, I give them chance to stay alive but... under new management."

Chee took out his phone. "Yeah, it's me. I'm coming aboard. I've got some guests. Make sure any weapons are stashed, please. Thank you, Max." He ended the call. "Okay."

Tommy climbed the gangplank to the aft deck, a flat area fronted by a short flight of steps up to the main galley.

They led Artie up the steps slowly. His three crew members were waiting in the aft dining area, standing astride next to the table and curved banquette benching. Their eyes widened when the men led him in.

"Keep cool, everybody, and we will all be happy," Victor advised. "I am Victor. I am your new employer. Mr. Chee has decided to get out of the import-export business and take a long vacation to Hong Kong."

They looked frightened, Victor noted, which was the desired effect. "You understand? Good. You go back to your cabins now, yes? Anyone call anyone, all of you take much longer vacation. You get what Victor tells you?"

The men hesitated. Chee nodded, wincing from pain, towards the bow of the boat. "Do it," he said. "Don't worry. It'll be okay."

The men departed through a separate set of steps at the other end of the room.

"Now," the gang boss said, throwing an arm around Chee's shoulder in conspiratorial fashion, "you tell me where he is hiding, or I send Oleg after them, and he hurt each man severely before he snaps their necks. Okay?"

"He's not here, I swear..." Chee said.

"Artie..."

"It's true!" His head dipped. "You're going to search the boat anyway, aren't you?"

"Of course. So... what is issue?"

The Asian-American businessman sighed. "My product for next month... it's in the hold."

Victor couldn't help but scoff a little, his chuckle throaty and deep. Then he caught himself laughing and took a deep breath to halt it. "Ahhh... that is funny! Apologies, Artie Chee. I loathe you, but no one in your situation deserves to be mocked. We already know you are stupid, stupid man, and you are going to die today. But we do not need to make it worse than that. How much?"

"About eighteen kilos."

"Eighteen kilos? Of skag?"

"Yeah."

Victor grinned. "You store $10 million in heroin on a sixty-foot cabin cruiser in middle of Memphis? Artie... my goodness! You are pig-shit stupid, yes?" He turned to Mattie Chicago. "This is pretty good day so far. We have new boat, we make $10 million profit in dope, and if Artie does not tell me where his friend Alexi is, I will kill him. Is good day, yes?"

"I swear..." Artie began to say.

Victor stepped in quickly and punched him hard in his fractured right rib cage. The drug lord winced hard, blanched, then turned to his left and vomited.

Victor winced in disgust. "Jesus. Clean that shit up now!" he ordered his lackey. He reached down and hauled Artie to his feet using his shirt collar. "Where is he, Artie? I don't want to kill you on this nice new boat of mine..."

"I can't. If I tell you, he'll kill me. He'll just make it last longer," Artie said. "You know him, Victor. Alexi is crazy."

"You think?" Victor said, scowling. He turned to Chicago. "Call Salukhin. Tell him to set up at the warehouse. Apparently, stupid fuck-ball want demonstration of how long I can make his pain last before he dies."

THEY'D BEEN BACK at the motel for five minutes when Bob's phone rang.

"So?" Margie asked.

"Smooth as silk," Bob said.

He looked over to the second bed, where June-Marie had perched herself, next to her soft-sided case. He lowered his voice slightly. "Our leverage is secured."

"Now what?"

"Now I get back in touch with Alexi and arrange a trade. You, in the meantime, need to head back to Tunstall Street with Ellie and keep an eye on the house. If he decides to be difficult, or doesn't agree to trade, we need to know if he's moving and where he goes. Okay?"

"Okay. But, Bob…"

"Yeah?"

"If he won't agree and we know where he is, we're going to get Norm back. I mean, I figure if we call the cops — even if they don't cite the fact that it's only been a day since he vanished — this guy will kill him and disappear."

"If we have to take the risky step, then that's what we do," Bob said. "But in that case, I'll handle it solo. You two will just slow me down."

There was a pause. "Well… that's not a very nice way to say we're old…" Margie groused.

"You're not old, you're civilians. Alexi may come across as a deranged criminal, but he used to be a mercenary. He'll know how to fight and to shoot and to protect his home from invasion. Plus, he'll see three of us coming. One person has a better chance of getting in before he knows what's happening."

She didn't sound convinced. "Fine, but…"

"No buts," Bob ordered. She needed to understand that once they were active, one person had to be in charge. "No buts, no creativity, no deviating from the plan. You guys are there for surveillance only. Are we clear?"

"Fine." It didn't sound fine.

"I'll call you when I know more. For now, get in position; let me know if he goes anywhere."

He ended the call.

Across the room, June-Marie sat on the edge of the bed, eyeing him suspiciously. "Tunstall? That's where Alexi is staying. Leverage?" she asked. "So... you're just going to hand me back to him?"

"I don't have a choice," Bob said. He walked over to her. At the last moment, he kneeled beside her, drawing the wrist restraint from his pocket. He grabbed her ankle and, before she could pull away, attached it to the bed frame.

"HEY!" she yelped.

"I can't take the chance you'll wander away."

"And what? Escape? I'm grateful, can't you understand that! I don't want to be around either of them. And I don't even have my car."

"It'll be fine where it is."

"It'll be towed by the end of the day. Have you ever dealt with the Memphis Parking Authority?"

"I'll retrieve it, okay?"

"No! Hell no! I didn't agree to any of this!" She yanked at the restraint with her leg, shaking the bed frame violently, then reached down and tugged at it. "Asshole! ASSHOLE! HEY! SOMEONE HELP ME!"

"No one can hear you. There's no one in the room on either side, and we're on the back of the property." Bob frowned. She was going to be difficult. He gestured past her. "What's in the bag?"

"My clothes."

For a fire alarm? "You were anticipating a trip?" He stared at the girl, her expression plaintive and slightly anguished. She didn't want him looking at her stuff. "You were planning on running."

As he approached her, she reached over and pulled the suitcase closer. "Don't touch my shit!" she barked.

He pushed her away and snatched the bag from her grasp. "Let's just take a look and see..."

He carried the bag over to the luggage storage shelf and set it down. He flipped open the lid.

Clothes, in bundles. He reached under them and felt paper. He moved the clothing away.

"That's a lot of cash."

"That's mine!" she squealed. "Don't you touch that!"

He closed the lid. "Let me guess: you skimmed this off Victor. This is your escape plan."

She hung her head. "Please. Please don't take my money. It's my meal ticket. My future..."

"I'm not going to take your money. I am, however, going to put it away for safekeeping." He carried the bag into the washroom. There was space behind the sink pedestal, and he wedged the bag in as well as he could.

He rejoined her in the room. "Anyone coming here isn't going to be looking for it, so you shouldn't worry. If you're being straight with me about everything, and you're not just going to run back to one of these guys, it'll all be there when you get it back. But I can't leave it out in the open."

June-Marie held up the restraint. "I told you I won't run. In fact..." She lowered her chin slightly and looked up at him with saucer eyes, batting her lash extensions. "I can show you just how grateful..."

"Yeah... I'm not Alexi. My brain isn't in my pants, and

that shit won't work on me; just... preserve your dignity a little and stow it, okay?"

She yanked at the restraint forcefully. "You can't keep me here; this is kidnapping!"

"A minute ago, you were eternally grateful," Bob said dryly. "Maybe move on past 'pissed off' to 'resigned to your fate.' I need to make some arrangements, and you need to keep your head down. So... just live with it for now."

He dialed Alexi's burner. It rang twice before he answered.

"Go for Alexi... No, I kid! I know it's you, big man. You are only one with number."

"I have your girlfriend," Bob said.

"What!?"

"June-Marie. She's sitting with me. She's healthy, for now."

"MOTHERFUCKER!" Alexi squealed. "Mother— wait a minute: you're joking with Alexi, yes?"

"Of course not. Do I seem like the type?"

"No. So... you take her to trade for your friend, I assume. Is good. Is clever move. I like this. But..."

"But?"

"But girl is no good to me if Victor is still alive, because if Victor is alive, I am dead."

"You could leave town with her. She's got some money socked away, a fair chunk of cash. Start over somewhere with no Victors, no Jerry Perrys."

There was a pause, then a deep breath. "I consider this, it's true. But... here, I have contacts, associates, ways to make income. If I go, all of that goes with me. I must make new allies, find new boss, work against new boss from inside to take his job. Is... massive hassle."

"If you don't trade..."

"What? You'll kill her? Maybe... but I don't think so. You forget, American, that I know who you really are. You are stone killer, sure... but you take side of the underdog, as they say. You fight for her like you fight for the poor Iraqi villagers. That is not man who will just murder helpless stripper."

"So you're not going to trade..." Bob was trying to cycle through his options. Alexi had made a show of how crazy he was about June-Marie, but apparently it had either been just that — a show — or he was colder than Lake Michigan in December.

"I will trade, sure... but only after you kill Victor. You kill Victor, I meet you, and we trade. Nothing changes except... now you have June-Marie for company. Ah! You touch her, I kill you, Mr. Bob... Okay? Okay, bye-bye."

He hung up.

Bob shook his head in disbelief and stared at the phone.

"Let me guess: your clever plan just went up in smoke," June-Marie said. "That's Alexi; he's completely nuts. I mean, he's better to me than Victor, but he doesn't give a damn about anyone but himself."

Bob glared at her. "Anyone ever tell you that you have truly horrible taste in men?"

"It's been suggested. Hey, I just flirted with you, didn't I? And so far, you're pretty horrible."

Bob exhaled deeply and pocketed the phone.

What the hell am I doing in Memphis, dealing with these lunatics? He still hadn't emptied the safe-deposit box, and Monday had almost passed. Before he did anything else, he'd promised to retrieve her crappy Dodge Shadow for her.

"He wants me to kill Victor. He wants you back, too. But mostly... he just wants me to kill Victor."

She shrugged. "At least he picked someone who's easy to find."

"How so?"

"Victor only goes to three places: the apartment to try to crawl all over me, usually while drunk; his mansion in Germantown; and his main warehouse, in Oakhaven."

ALEXI GOT off the phone and looked down at his captive. "Your friend, he is not so concerned about you as I think, eh?"

Norm was tied to a chair, the only furniture in the near-empty basement. He had a welt under his eye from being clubbed by a pistol a day earlier, and a sour look that would have been there either way.

"I'm betting he cares a little more than you do," he retorted.

"He is a little bit crazy, yes? He kidnap my girl, try to make trade..."

"Let me guess: she's not as important to you as you are."

Alexi's eyes narrowed, his smirk disappearing instantly, replaced by a thin, cruel line. "Don't think that because you are old, I will take your insults, Norm O'Hearn. You want another smack to the head, eh?"

"You're going to do what you want regardless of what I want."

The Russian inhaled heavily through both nostrils, letting his anger subside. He did not want the old man seeing weakness, and reacting angrily was weakness.

"If we have prepared correctly, it is quite possible your

friend and my enemy will both be dead this afternoon. Then all of this becomes unnecessary, and... I let you go."

Norm looked up at the man, trying to gauge his expression for the slightest sign of sincerity. "Yeah, sure you will."

"I will. I say I will, so I will."

"Alive?"

Alexi smirked slightly. "We see."

"I don't know Bob real well, but I think I got a little measure of the man a decade ago, when he helped out a few guys at the club. If he wants to, he'll find you. And I don't like your chances of making the bell for the second round."

"Maybe." Alexi took his left hand out of his jacket pocket. It was holding a small canister with a curved handle on top. "This is MK3A2 concussion grenade. Enough explosive in confined space to turn Bob into bloody pile of dead. All I have to do is pull this pin" — he pulled the pin but kept its trigger depressed — "and friend Bob is corpse. He get as close to you as I am now, maybe I let go, and take all three of us to hell together."

Norm just stared at him implacably. "You forget to put that pin back in because you're busy showing off, we won't have to wait for him."

Alexi slid the restrictor pin back into place. He felt a surge of annoyance. The old man was either not afraid of death or a very good actor.

But it would not matter. Soon, they would find the address of the house rented the day prior and come for a visit. Whether it was Bob or Victor or both, he intended to be ready.

19

The wood framing was complex, an entire side of a house laid out and connected while lying on the grass. Now, the team of twenty men stood behind it, a trail of ropes leading over it and back to them.

A foreman held up his hand. "Ready? On three, gentlemen: one, two... three!" The men all heaved on the ropes together and walked backwards, the massive frame lifting off the ground, pulled upright until it sat precariously balanced against the rest of the would-be home's bare bones.

Another team moved in quickly and began to fasten it in place.

Earl Monroe let go of his end of the rope and brushed his work gloves against one another, dust and fiber particles flying. He wiped the sweat from his brow with a beefy forearm, the T-shirt under his overalls drenched through.

"Good work today, Earl, good work," the foreman said. "That's going to be one grateful family when this is all done."

The home was the third the volunteer crew had put up in a week. In an earlier life, Monroe had worked in construction, and it felt satisfying, warm, to have contributed so much effort to something, to see hard work go towards someone who deserved it.

"Good working with you, Larry," he told the foreman.

His phone rang, and he retrieved it from his overalls. The number was unlisted.

"Yeah?"

"I've sent you something." The call ended.

He put the phone back in his pocket and began to walk back to the parking lot. The volunteer agency liked everyone to report their comings and goings, but his stint with them was over.

He was going back to work.

"Earl? You're good for this afternoon, right?" he heard the foreman say. "Earl?"

He ignored the man. Once operational, everything else was secondary. That was how it had been in the SEALs, and that was how he conducted business now that he operated alone.

At his truck, he pulled a metal strongbox out from under the front bench and opened it, using a five-number combination tumbler.

He withdrew the phone from within. It was encrypted; any texts or messages sent by it purged from memory within a second of delivery.

He hit the green dial button, and it automatically speed-dialed a phone in Arlington, Virginia.

"Monroe."

"Mr. Monroe, it's been a while."

"Stone, what's up?"

"We have a situation in Memphis. The target we were

tracking — the subject of the open contract we sent out last month — has resurfaced."

"And?"

"He's mixed up with some sort of gang business. I don't know the hows or whys. But he was spotted last night. He's driving a purple Ford Focus, rust on the doors and wheel wells. You have a pen or something to tap a note? Here's the plate number." Stone read it out. "We have some help on the surveillance side. And we know he's working some sort of case involving a Russian gangster named Victor Malyuchenko. Stick near the Russian and Bob is bound to make an appearance."

"Okay," Monroe said. "You know my fee has gone up, correct?"

"Two hundred thousand wired to your preferred account."

"Stay tuned." He ended the call.

MEMPHIS, Tennessee

VICTOR SLOUCHED in the oversized armchair, a beaten-up leather recliner rescued from the warehouse office.

The building was owned by a holding company, which was in turn owned by his import-export firm. Surrounded by tall shelves and crates, he'd gathered his men and their captive in the polished concrete loading area near the front of the building.

Ahead of him, Artie Chee sat on a wooden chair, pants around his ankles. A large hole had been cut in the seat, as if allowing access to a toilet bowl. Instead, a pair of wires and alligator clips had been strung through the hole. The clips were attached to the loose skin at the top of his scrotum.

Underneath the chair was a car battery.

Chee was unconscious; the first blast of electricity to his testicles had been enough to make him pass out.

"Wake him up," Victor ordered.

One of his men tossed a bucket of cold water into the gangster's face. Chee was shocked back to consciousness. He shook his head vociferously and spluttered.

"Did you enjoy that, Artie? Did you enjoy the sting? Now you know how I feel when I find out you're fucking me in the ass."

"Please..." Chee begged.

"Please? You have balls to ask favor? Not for long." Victor nodded to the man at the wooden table by the door. The man reached down and turned up the dial on a potentiometer, allowing more current through the line.

Chee spasmed, his muscles contracting, locking up in a series of cramps instantly, his nerves shot through with pain. His teeth were gritted, just the tip of his tongue showing. His eyes rolled back in his head.

Victor waved for his man to stop.

The current subsided.

Chee's head slumped forward on his chest, but he was moving, just barely.

"Artie, do you know why you are still alive?"

Chee could barely moan acknowledgment.

"Because I give you chance to help, one last time. You are going to die today. But you can die quick and painless, or you can die slowly, so slowly in horrible agony. You think Alexi would be worse somehow? You must ask yourself, my friend, what you want your last moments, your last feelings of life to be."

"Please..." Chee begged again. He'd begun to sob, tears rolling down both cheeks.

"Is too late for this. You knew like everyone else in city what I decide about Alexi Pushkin. But you agree to meet with him anyway. Then you arrange to work with him, to buy product for him. Now, you pay the price so others can learn from your mistake."

Chee heaved spit and phlegm out, most of it running down his chin and shirt. His hair was matted down by sweat. He could barely see through the tears in both eyes, his wrists tied to the chair, hands unavailable to wipe them clear.

He only had one thing of value to Victor besides the modest chunk of criminal business run by his company. And he'd always vowed that if he went out early, if life seemed like it was about to abandon him, he would be a bigger man than his father; he would not be a snitch.

At least... not again, anyhow. The cops had been a necessity, he told himself, the only way to stay out of Victor's grasp.

And look how well that had gone.

"I..." he panted, trying to get the words out. "I... do not snitch...?"

"Do not insult both of our intelligences, please. I want Alexi. Hit him again."

The torturer turned up the current. Artie's jaw seized, locking with the rest of his muscles, his teeth clamping down hard on the end of his tongue, the tip flying off, blood spurting out of it, running down his shirt. After about five seconds, the man released the switch.

Artie slumped back into the seat, barely conscious.

"It will go on like this for hours if necessary. I do not enjoy watching you suffer, but neither does it bother me. So we could be here for a very long time. Eventually, you will talk to me. Do you know why, Artie Chee? Because eventually, everyone gives me what I want. My father, Ivan Malyuchenko, is great man. He would tell me this is one thing we learned in former Soviet Union: when opportunity comes, the man who is willing to do whatever it takes to seize it, that man is king. For average man, man like you? You have no destiny, no greatness worth protecting. You are... how do you say... you are commodity. You are piece to be moved around chessboard, taken out of play whenever I feel it. Such is the fate of lesser men."

The pain was bad enough. Listening to Victor praise himself was apparently too much. "Why... don't you... go fuck yourself," Artie muttered in a moment of uncharacteristic bravery. "You're... just a... douchebag with... lots... of guns."

"HIT HIM AGAIN!" Victor bellowed.

The man at the table turned up the juice, and Chee began to spasm again, shaking in place so hard that the chair began to rattle. Victor slumped down in his seat slightly, chin resting on the palm of his right hand, elbow on the armrest. He watched the man convulse and this time said nothing even as five seconds became ten.

"Boss, he's going to have a heart attack before he tells us..."

The Russian raised his hand again. "Stop," he muttered, sounding disappointed.

"He's unconscious again," the man by the table said.

"So wake him up again!"

A few moments passed before the man on the bucket

returned with it refilled. He tossed the cold contents into Chee's face, and he woke again, though his head bobbed as if delirious.

"So much pain, Artie Chee. So unnecessary." He wasn't sure if the man was still conscious or absorbing what he was saying, so Victor raised his voice. "YOU WANT QUICK, DIGNIFIED END, YES? YOU WANT PAIN TO END, YES? THEN JUST... GIVE ME ADDRESS, ARTIE, NOW!"

Chee's eyes rolled around in their sockets, his ability to focus obviously gone. He was barely conscious, and he stammered as he said, "Twelve-thirty Tunstall Street."

Victor rose from his seat and smiled. "Thank you, Artie. Now you are done." He nodded towards Chee and looked at the man to his right. "Take him out the back door and kill him."

His men untied Artie and picked him up under each armpit.

"No... NO! Please... I have a family."

Even after being tortured, he had the resilience to beg, Victor noted. That seemed impressive.

"Two in the back, pop, pop, make it quick, no suffering," he called out after his men as they dragged the kicking and screaming gangster towards the back door.

20

The warehouse was away from other buildings, near the end of Old Getwell Road, in an industrial park. From the street, Bob figured, it didn't look like much. The exterior grounds were overgrown; the chain-link fence sagged in a few places.

A pair of black Mercedes and a limo were parked out front. A guard in a black suit and white dress shirt stood by the front double doors.

He drove the Ford past the front of the building without slowing down, just another piece of random traffic passing by. Two corners past, he turned south, then west, then north again, until he was across the road from the warehouse's back corner.

The rear of the building looked equally uninviting, a cracked and broken parking lot, empty save for one guard on the back door and more collapsing fence. He got out of the car so that he could move closer on foot; he pushed the seat forward and retrieved the rifle from the back seat, now ensconced in a borrowed soft-sided case from Ellie's husband's collection.

He slung the rifle across his back. He used the sidewalk to walk around the building until he spotted what he'd been looking for.

There. On the west side of the warehouse were two fire escapes, black wrought-iron staircases leading up to the third floor.

Nothing about Victor Malyuchenko suggested operational caution. The likelihood of a sophisticated surveillance system or internal security network seemed doubtful at best. That suggested the guards were his only real threat during access.

He checked the street both ways for watchful eyes, but it was empty. At a point where the fence sagged extra low, he used the top of the chain link as a vault, swinging both legs over and onto the property.

He jogged to the fire escape and pulled down the lower ladder, wincing slightly at the creak. He turned and kept an eye on the corner of the building for fifteen seconds, his hand on the grip of the FN 5.7. When he was sure the rear guard hadn't heard the ladder, he clambered up it.

He kept his steps low and his footfalls light as he made his way to the third-floor landing, outside a double window. It had been boarded over, but carelessly, long nails jutting out slightly, bent over from shoddy hammering.

Bob pried the boards off, taking his time in case someone was on the upper level. He took off the gun case and passed it through the broken window, following it a moment later.

The room was dusty, musty, unused for some time. Empty desks and unplugged lamps sat in a row. On the other side of the room was a wooden door with a glass insert, long since broken.

Bob picked up the rifle. He kept his pace measured and quiet as he crossed to the door and peeked out into the corridor.

It seemed deserted. But he'd gone ten feet when he heard the faint sounds of conversation.

The hall led him past two offices, to a landing surrounded by three-foot walls. It overlooked the warehouse proper, facing toward the back of the building, thirty feet away. A set of stairs on its far side led to the first floor.

"... you are commodity. You are piece to be moved around chessboard, taken out of play whenever I feel it. Such is the fate of lesser men."

For a split second, a man paced past the overhang of the upper level. Bob caught a bare glimpse.

Victor.

He was giving someone a speech, which probably meant a captive of some kind.

Not your problem. Just hit the guy and get out.

Exfiltration would be a problem, he knew. The two exterior guards would be alerted. One might run in to help, but both? If they were on a mic system, they'd be communicating by earpiece, which meant the risk of coordinated opposition.

"HIT HIM AGAIN!" Malyuchenko bellowed from below. Bob thought he heard the sizzle and crackle of electricity.

He looked around the upper level for a better view, but the landing's low-lying wall cut off sight of the man. He could see the guard by the back door, and he knew there had to be at least one more man helping the Russian.

Victor had strayed out from under the landing once. But

even if there was a repeat, aiming and firing directly downwards with the rifle from just twenty-five feet or so was awkward due to its powerful kick and the difficulty of bracing the gun properly on a vertical. It would also leave him a sitting duck for the guard at the door.

He laid the rifle down next to the rail and drew the FN 5.7. Though some criticized its stopping power and .28-caliber center-fire cartridges, Bob preferred it for its exceptional accuracy. Used within acceptable range, the entry penetration and scope of wounding were enough to control most situations. Short of a double tap to the head from close range, most pistols were a mixed proposition at best when it came to actually killing a man.

He leaned over the rail and tried to gauge roughly where Victor had popped into view the last two times. He only had a second, perhaps less, to take the shot.

He heard something else, unsure of what at first. Bob craned his ear over the rail to listen.

"... I have a family."

Whoever it was, he was mewling, crying and begging for his life.

"YOU WANT QUICK, DIGNIFIED END, YES? YOU WANT PAIN TO END, YES? THEN JUST... GIVE ME ADDRESS, ARTIE, NOW!"

Artie? That was a new name.

Not your business. Just be patient... take the shot.

I have a family.

The man's plea was eating at him. For all Bob knew, it was just someone sleeping in the warehouse they'd discovered, or some other civilian.

Jesus H. Christ, he muttered internally, *why now?*

Before meeting Dawn Ellis, he'd have just done the task,

swallowed any self-doubt until he had the luxury of considering it.

Scratch that. Before Nurse Dawn, you'd have just gone back to the street and ignored it all.

He was probably just another gangster, like Alexi. In a moment, he knew, Victor would reappear for just long enough for him to squeeze the trigger…

The sound of scraping and squeaks registered first, two men dragging a third, coming into sight a moment later. They were headed for the back door.

Damn it.
Don't get involved.
You don't know this man.
You're not a cop.
You're not here for this.

Instinct was telling him to be patient, wait for Victor to make another appearance.

And if he doesn't? You have to try to hit him elsewhere, and this dude dies.

Goddamn it, Nurse Dawn, get out of my head.

Training suggested there was no option to debate. The third party was collateral, an unfortunate in the wrong place at the wrong time. It was just his time. *Accept it. Talk the emotion out of it, or things will go from bad to worse.*

But you're not that guy anymore.

He crept back to the office window and headed back down the fire escape. At the back corner of the building he chanced a quick glance.

The two men had their captive kneeling. He had his hands behind his head but was dipping and jerking around slightly, afraid to look back, terrified to wait for the sting of the bullet. "Please... I'll give you anything..." he said. "I didn't know he was off-limits, I swear..."

So, a gangster of some sort.

Just let him die, Bob. He's not your problem.

But something was preventing that from happening. At some point, he knew, his conscience had expanded beyond letting people be executed in public, behind some dive warehouse.

He ran from cover, waiting until the men started to turn to drop into a kneeling crouch, gun hand braced, the dot sight finding the man with the raised pistol first. A smooth squeeze of the trigger and the gun retorted, the volume knocking out his hearing in his left ear slightly. There was almost no recoil, the gun's design minimizing kick.

The gunman went down immediately, his body jerking slightly, the headshot incapacitating him. His partner turned and tried to draw a piece from his waistband. Bob shot him twice in the chest, the man collapsing before he could finish the move.

Thirty yards away, the back door guard was sprinting, gun raised, yanking the trigger wildly as he ran, his movement virtually guaranteeing he couldn't hit his target. Bob closed the distance between them, running past the prone, terrified victim. He dropped to one knee again as the man got to within twenty feet, firing twice in quick succession. The guard collapsed to the ground.

He swung his pistol over, training the sight on the back door. He popped the magazine and replaced it with one from his jacket pocket. The noise would have alerted the others, which meant imminent company.

At least he had the lot to his back. *Don't have to worry about my six.*

The blow felt like being hit by a hammer. He'd been pistol-whipped before and knew a second into the spiraling dizziness that he was losing consciousness, that he'd fallen over, that the cold sensation was asphalt against his cheek.

He was awake just long enough to hear the warehouse back door open.

"See?" Artie exclaimed from just behind him, breathless. "I'm... no snitch... see?"

A gun fired twice. A body thudded to the ground a few feet away.

Bob's world faded to black.

21

The dreams were confusing, nonsensical. Bob careened from one person to another, hurt souls, accusations, a chase, a shooting. Jon Rice's disappointed, youthful expression as he lay on one side in a Tehran street, life eking out of him like a dripping tap, the puddle of blood growing.

The cold water hit him like a blast of ice, the dream gone instantly, reality coming back into momentarily hazy view, his head feeling mildly concussed.

He tried to move, but his arms and legs were restrained, tied to a chair.

"Good, you are awake and back with us in the land of the living. For now."

Bob shook his head to clear the cobwebs. He could feel water trickling down his neck.

He blinked and looked around. The lights were high above and dim, but an open front door to the warehouse helped visibility.

He was in the same chair they'd used just moments

earlier to interrogate "Artie"... who he presumed was the same person who had thanked him for the save by pistol-whipping him into unconsciousness.

"You make bad choice, my friend." Malyuchenko strolled over to him. He had his hands in his trouser pockets, like someone who was casually people watching. "You decide to save man who was not worth saving. Am I to presume you are same man who interfered with Alexi Pushkin on Beale Street?"

The time and place were different, but Bob had been in similar circumstances before. If Malyuchenko didn't need intel, he'd already be dead, he knew. That meant holding out for as long as possible, until he could figure out how to get loose.

And if you can't figure out your way out of this?

Well... you're supposed to be dead already. You've had a hell of a run.

He thought about his late fiancée, Maggie, for a split second, then pushed her out of his mind. Now wasn't the time.

"You kill two of my men, leave third dying. He may not make it." The Russian sounded more tired than annoyed. "What do I call you, anyway?"

"Bob works just fine. And I'm real broken up about your boys."

"In case you were here to help Artie, you should know: he goes to sleep with fishes now in Mississippi River. I have his two-engine boat with cabin... is pleasure boat more than luxury cabin cruiser, if I am honest. But I am simple man with simple needs."

The Patek Phillipe wristwatch and thousand-dollar-plus

Bill Blass suit suggested otherwise to Bob, but he kept it to himself.

"This is what will also happen with you. Same men who are currently driving his body to boat will come back... after we have finished with you." He paused and stopped pacing, as if waiting to hear what Bob had to say about the matter. "Cat got your tongue? No matter. We will torture you, introduce great pain into your world..."

"You're going to play disco?"

Victor smiled at that and sucked on his tongue, as if caught between irritation and amusement. "Very funny. You are funny man, Bob. Give me some Tchaikovsky any time! Still... I must know. I must know why you would help sewer rat like Alexi Pushkin, let alone Artie Chee, heroin dealer with — as far as we can be sure — no friends in world."

"Everybody has someone," Bob said dryly.

"Sure, sure. While you were asleep for a minute or two, my friend Jerry Perry call me. He say you show up at apartment and take June-Marie away from me."

"You don't say."

"So... you do this for weapon to use against me, yes?"

Not really. But if the mood fit... "The term is 'leverage,'" Bob said. "How long have you been here, anyway? You sound like you served borscht at the Moscow McDonald's yesterday morning."

That amused him less.

"I speak four languages, American. How many you speak?"

Six. But there was no point sharing that with him. Speaking Russian near fluently was liable to come in handy around Malyuchenko's ilk.

"I speak American," Bob said, because it was the kind of goofy line that would irritate him.

"Boss, you want me to hit him?" a thug asked in his mother tongue.

"Sure, sure," Victor replied. "*Slomat rebro.*" *Break a rib.*

Oleg stepped in and hammered Bob in the ribs with a meaty fist. He felt the sharp sting of a minor fracture quickly radiate into warmth, then ache. Breathing was going to be a little painful for a few days, a familiar sensation once again.

"He would be very happy if I let him do this for the rest of the day," Victor enthused. "He is like... like baby boy with new toy, yes?"

"He hits like one, too," Bob said, a deliberately bored edge to his voice.

The man stepped in menacingly, but Victor blocked him, one arm aloft. "No, not yet. You can beat him later if Salukhin allows." He turned back to Bob. "In moment, I must leave to track down and kill that fool Alexi. Then I am expected for dinner at my home with parents of my wife. I have spectacular mansion in Germantown. They are ignorant bumpkin hillbillies from Greenville but very rich, with political connections. While I am gone, my friend Salukhin will introduce you to pain you never knew existed."

He nodded towards a table ten feet away. A short, slight man with Asian features and a buzz cut was perched, leaning over instruments on the tabletop. He wore a butcher's leather apron over a T-shirt and had a maniacal grin on his face.

"Salukhin," Malyuchenko promised, "will hurt you in ways you cannot imagine."

Bob felt some of his energy returning. His headache was down to a dull throb. "He's also going to play disco?"

The Russian leaned so that his face was inches from Bob's, then lowered his voice. "Laugh now. It is a good idea, while you still can. He was interrogation specialist with the FSB in my country, the intelligence service."

"If you say so."

"I do. Salukhin can do things with a needle or scalpel that would have made Nazis cringe. You will talk eventually, Mr. Bob. Only question is how quickly… and whether it is enough to satisfy his urges. After you have told him what you know, I have ordered men to give you quick death. But… if you take too long, Salukhin has a specialty…"

"What, like crochet?"

"Hmm. No, he has toxin he prefers. It is what he calls 'paralytic.' Very strong. Paralyze everything in your body, from the outside in, very slowly. Skin first, then tissue, then small muscle groups, then lungs. Heart continues to beat as you slowly suffocate while conscious and unable to move, like drowning in slow motion. It is, without doubt, most horrible death possible. Agonizing, slow…"

"He sounds like a second date personified."

The Russian smiled matter-of-factly again. "Eh, is excessive, is true. I would just put two bullets in your head, save time, or cut head off with machete. But Salukhin is sort of 'artist' of pain and suffering. Again… not my style. I would kill you quick."

"You're too kind."

"I am, is true," Malyuchenko said. "Where is girl?"

"The girl?" There was still leverage there, Bob was sure of it. They were both too infatuated for anything otherwise. "The girl is coocoo over you, isn't she? Victor this and Victor that. 'My boyfriend is the most powerful man in the city,' blah, blah, blah."

Malyuchenko stopped pacing again and turned back his way. He was scowling, a dark, angry countenance, the face of someone about to snap. It was the first time the Russian had shown his true colors. "You ARE ALREADY DEAD MAN! Question remains, how much you wish to suffer before it ends."

"Kill me and you'll never find her," Bob said. "I promise you, she'll die in agony, choking for breath. And it won't take a special toxin to do it... just a hole in the ground with the air running out."

Given that June-Marie had been watching *The Price is Right* on the motel TV when he'd returned with the Dodge, it seemed unlikely. Again, Victor didn't need to know that.

The Russian smiled again. "You will not die, not until you tell us where she is and why you are working with Alexi. But... that will make Salukhin very happy indeed, yes?"

He turned on his heels and began to walk towards the door. "Whoever you are, Mr. Bob, you are... how you say... small potatoes. You do not belong in my world. We shall not meet again."

He headed out the front doors, two of the men accompanying him.

Bob craned his neck each way. There were two guards left, both with pistols, one drawn and on the man's lap as he sat in a chair nearby.

Salukhin stood over the table, fiddling with items. After a few seconds, he seized upon an idea. He reached down and grabbed an object, then turned back to Bob.

The scalpel caught the dim overhead lights.

At least it looks sterile, Bob thought absently.

"How long is this going to take?" the bored-looking guard by the door asked.

Salukhin glared at him. "It takes what it takes. Boss just left. You want me to call him, ask him how long it should take on your behalf?"

"Hmmph." The other guard headed towards the door. "I'm going to get a coffee."

"Don't you fucking dare!" the pistol-bearing gangster seated nearby said. Clearly, Jerry Perry wasn't Malyuchenko's only non-Russian employee. "We lose this guy, we'd better both have passports ready."

"The dude is tied tightly to a chair with baling wire. He's not going anywhere. And if he even looks like he might get loose, you can shoot the fucker."

"Okay, Tommy. And if that happens before we have the information Mr. Malyuchenko wants, do you want me to tell him it's because you decided to go for a fucking coffee?"

"I don't give a shit what you tell him. I'm going for a fucking coffee. You want one or not?"

His colleague looked irritated. He nodded his head and took a deep breath, like a parent holding their temper with a naughty child. They might as well have been two store employees arguing over who could take a break. "Fuck. Fine, one sugar, two creams."

Bob looked over at the torturer as the guard left. *Look for leverage, Bobby.* "I notice they don't even offer to get you one. You're Mongolian, right? Must be nice working with bigots."

Salukhin stared at him for a moment. Then he smiled broadly and giggled. "I am Hmong, from Laos. The name is... just a nickname. An affectation. It is funny that you think you can 'divide and conquer.' I feel nothing for you. Nothing at all. Not good, not bad. You are just object that makes noises and breathes air. Love, hate, fear, happy. All means nothing to me. I enjoy pain. Any pain. Yours, mine, theirs... but especially yours."

He approached with the scalpel. "Did you know that there is a nerve in your foot that is so sensitive, the right amount of pressure will cause unbearable agony? You immediately void your bowels, among other charming details. Men have died of heart failure from the pain if it is overstimulated. I will stop you... just short of that."

Salukhin kneeled and took off Bob's right sneaker.

"My apologies," Bob said. "I haven't changed my socks in a few days."

The diminutive torturer stared at him, puzzled, as if trying to understand his intent. "Why?"

"Eh? Why what?" Bob asked.

"Why would you be polite to someone threatening you with intense pain? This makes little sense."

Damn, Malyuchenko sure can pick 'em. "It's a joke," Bob explained. "An absurdism kind of thing."

The man frowned again. "Your accent. I do not recognize it, but it is definitely American. But not from here, not from the South."

From his chair twenty feet away, the remaining guard chimed in. "He's from Michigan, the UP."

"Ring out Ahoya with an M-U rah, rah!" Bob sang back. "Get out of here! There's someone present who isn't a complete moron."

The guard sniffed. "First off, the dude with the scalpel is the smartest guy in the city, probably. The shit he knows is frightening, and I do not use that word lightly."

"Chicago?" Bob asked.

"Gary."

"Tough town."

"Yeah... although that prick Malyuchenko has been calling me 'Chicago' for two years." He shook his head absently. "That fucking guy. Before you get your panties all excited, it's not going to get you dick, all right? My ma's got back surgery in three months, and that shit is going to run, like, six bills. Even then she may never walk again. If you think I'm turning my back on that sort of moolah, my friend... well, I ain't interested. You can take a long walk up a short gangway, okay, fella?"

"I'd rather not kill you with that scalpel," Bob said. "I'd rather you just follow your friend out the door, pretend to go for a walk or something while I deal with the little psycho, here. But that sorta seems to be where this whole dealie is headed."

The guard leaned forward, elbows on knees. "Look, Bob... whatever the fuck your last name is, Victor is unbelievably fucking rich, serious clout. He still has at least eight guns at easy reach and contacts to get more in quickly. He's protected, he's completely fucking bat-shit insane, and he's ruthless. Why the fuck are you even fighting him? For that piece of shit Alexi Pushkin? He's worse than Victor!"

Salukhin was becoming irritated, feeling excluded from the conversation. "Why do you talk to him so much? He is just an objective, a receptacle for my gift."

"He's talking to me," Bob said, "because he has a Marine tattoo on his left wrist for the 2nd Infantry, and he recognizes something in me..."

"The FN," the guard said. "Only a pro would use a gun that 'brosephs' think is for pussies. You serve?"

"In Iraq, in Afghanistan for a period as a sniper. A few other missions."

Salukhin frowned. "He is federal agent."

"Maybe," the guard said. "If he is, he's the dumbest fucking federal agent in history. I know what those guys are paid." He nodded Bob's way. "You realize Malyuchenko would just pay you off to turn in Alexi and give him back his girlfriend, right? I mean... I'm talking serious money to just fuck off."

Bob shook his head gently. "I don't care. I'm going to have to kill them both. That's how this shit always breaks down. Doesn't matter the place, doesn't matter the time. They can't help but pull evil shit, and inevitably a guy like me shows up or is sent to kill them. You two both look younger than me; I'm guessing you're... what... twenty-seven, twenty-eight, there, Chicago?"

"Twenty-eight. Pretty good guess."

"And you're... Man, I'm not so good with Asian features and age. My bad. Thirty-five?"

"Close enough," Salukhin said.

"So... I've been killing dudes like Victor and Alexi and surviving situations just like this one for literally half your lives and then some. That's how I knew about the scalpel... and that I'd have to kill Chicago here with it."

The kneeling Laotian peered up at him, studying his expression. "Even if you believe it true, it changes nothing. I still have to get answers out of you. It will still hurt greatly... and I will still enjoy it." He grinned at the notion. Then he began to giggle, a high-pitched titter, like an old Englishwoman on helium.

"Unless..." Bob said.

"Unless?" Chicago asked.

"Unless you consider the fact that baling wire, while tight and strong, will hold a pair of socks in place nicely. But a pair of socks, well... they'll give; they allow a gap between your flesh and the restraining wire that, given enough time, can be worked against, wriggled out of. And you two morons, well... you seem to love passing the time talking. You also left my socks on."

His bare foot came up before Salukhin could react, the ankle bloodied from stripped flesh, the top catching the torturer in the groin. He fell over sideways, clutching his testicles.

Bob heard Chicago scrambling to his feet even as he rocked forward with all his strength, the chair still tied to his arms, its legs coming out from under him and off the ground.

He threw himself backwards, pushing off the soles of his feet like a diver doing a reverse, his full weight coming down on the wooden chair.

It shattered just as Chicago's gun hand came clear, the guard yanking the pistol's trigger three times in quick succession. Bob rolled sideways, a moving target, all three shots stray.

He threw an elbow to his right, breaking the prone Laotian torturer's windpipe, the scalpel tumbling from his hand.

Bob grabbed it with his left as Chicago closed, hurling it backhand, snapping his wrist to balance its rotation centrally.

The scalpel buried itself in the man's throat.

The guard grasped at it wildly, flailing and tripping over, his pistol thrown from his grip, clattering to the floor, Chicago crashing down next to it. His hand found the scalpel, and he managed to pull it out, blood pouring out of the tiny puncture wound left behind.

He righted himself and staggered to his feet just as Bob

reached his gun. Chicago raised one hand to his throat to block the stream of blood, the other in protest.

Bob shot him through the forehead.

The shocked guard stood there for several seconds, blood pouring from the tiny wound to his throat and the massive hole in his head, a confused expression on his face.

He stumbled sideways, tripping again, falling to the ground. He lay on his right thigh, the other leg extended as he tried to stand, unable to reconcile that it was the end.

Bob walked over and shot him once more through the temple.

The former Team Seven Alpha had killed a lot of men at close range. He'd tried to never feel one way or another about it.

But in the moment he experienced a profound sadness. In another life, Chicago might've been someone he knew, someone he liked. Maybe his mom would walk again; maybe she wouldn't.

But either way, he was going to miss it.

He heard a gurgle and turned. Salukhin had managed to rise to his feet, clutching his damaged windpipe. He was headed for the table.

Bob glanced ahead of him. A pistol sat on the front right corner. He ran over, reaching the diminutive torturer just as his hand reached out to pick it up.

Bob pistol-whipped the Laotian across the back of the skull. He collapsed, his face slamming off the edge of the table, teeth breaking and expelled.

The table held an array of scalpels and twisted blades, spread out, along with the pistol and a vial containing a clear liquid. He picked up the vial and pocketed it.

Salukhin stirred, trying to rise, spitting blood out onto the concrete.

Bob shot the Laotian through the top of the head, then leaned over his body and shot him once more in the head and once in the chest, to make sure.

Whatever else he'd accomplish in Memphis, he'd decided, getting rid of Salukhin was doing the world a favor.

Hearing damaged by the gunfire, he could make out just the faintest *clunk* of a car door closing.

The other guard. He's back.

He walked quickly over to the door, crouching briefly by Chicago to collect his FN from the man's jacket pocket.

He kept the three spare mags. Helpful.

He moved over to the door and stood behind it. It swung open.

"I got us some donuts, too…" the guard managed before Bob hit him over the back of the head with the butt of his gun.

He went down hard, stunned. "You're going to want to stay there," Bob suggested. "Your friends are both dead. You can join them… or you can deliver a message for me. Choose."

"Unnhh… message," Tommy muttered. "The message, of course."

"Throw your keys on the ground, and your phone, your wallet and any piece you're carrying."

He pushed himself to a kneeling position, then did as asked without hesitation. "Okay, now what?"

Bob collected the gun and sprang the magazine, pocketing it. He tossed the piece to one side. He picked up the man's wallet.

It was stuffed. "Thank you very much," he said. "There's nearly a grand in here."

The gangster pouted but said nothing.

Bob retrieved his sneaker. He kept the gun trained on his captive as he put it back on. Then he stepped on the phone and crushed it under his heel.

"When you get back to wherever you came from, I want you to pass on a message to Jerry Perry. I know his brand; if it becomes a problem for me, certain folks in Brighton Beach are going to find out all sorts of things about him. Like where his parents and siblings live. Am I clear?"

Tommy looked puzzled. "No. I don't know what the fuck any of that means."

"Good. As long as you can repeat it verbatim. Do it."

The guard complied.

"Perfect." Bob walked around the kneeling man. "Nighty night." He brought the pistol butt down once more, Tommy knocked cold.

Bob headed for the door. He knew where Victor was going to be, and he knew that when his message got back to Jerry Perry, he'd have at least one less gun to face.

Then it was Alexi's turn to pay the piper.

22

Bob didn't spare the horses, stepping on the gas and holding it down as the tiny Ford zoomed across the city.

The call rang through on hands-free, his phone on the passenger seat. "Hello?"

"Margie! Where are you?"

"We're still watching the house. What's wrong?"

"Can you look out and tell me again, from where you are, what the address of the place is?"

"Yeah, it's 1230 Tunstall."

It was the same address Artie Chee had given up.

"You need to get out of there, now," Bob ordered.

Maybe it was the demanding tone, but Margie didn't like it. "I'm not going anywhere without Norm. If he's in that house..."

"There are two carloads of Russian gangsters on their way there right now. They won't be far off. They're coming for Alexi. Please get out of there."

The line went silent. After a moment, Margie said, "I

don't know quite what to do. If Norm's in there, he could be caught in some kind of crossfire situation... I can't sit by and let that happen."

"You don't have to," Bob said. "Just... get clear. Park a few blocks away if you're insisting. I'm on my way. Don't get out of the car; don't engage; don't let anyone see you. Okay? Are we clear?"

Another pause. "Fine," she said. Bob sensed the resigned tone. But he had to trust that she wouldn't do anything stupid.

"I'll be there soon." He ended the call and turned his attention back to the road, the Focus zigzagging nimbly through the afternoon traffic.

Homes were difficult to defend, making speed essential. If they showed up loaded for bear, Alexi would have a tough time protecting multiple entry points, finding a secure position once they breached.

If he was lucky, both men would be preoccupied with each other's death, giving him a chance to take out both relatively unimpeded.

The rifle would've helped. He cursed losing it at the warehouse... although in a pinch, Chicago's fat wallet-load of cash would help resolve the matter.

Margie hung up the call.

"That was Bob, I take it," Ellie said from behind the steering wheel.

"Uh-huh. He wants us to move a few blocks away. We might have some company of the none-too-pleasant kind."

Ellie looked nervous. "Are we..."

"In danger?" Margie leaned forward and opened the

glove box, taking out Norm's old service pistol from Vietnam, a Colt 1911 in .45 caliber. He'd taken her to the range a few times, and he kept it in good shape, stripping it and oiling it regularly. The first time she'd fired it, it had felt like she'd jumped backwards, such was the recoil. "Nah, we're not in danger, sweetie, not as long as I've got something to say about it."

"But... we should move the car."

"Yes. He wants us to stay put. But if I see Norm, I'm going to get him back. Are y'all okay with that?"

"Sure. I mean... not really, no. It's completely insane, but... I get it."

"We could get shot at. Still okay with that?"

Ellie took a deep breath and really thought about it. "This is not our world at all, Margie O'Hearn. I love you like a sister, you know that. But we shouldn't be here. I'm not going anywhere or nothing, because I love Norm too and you're real worried. But I don't want you to shoot anyone, Margie, and I sure as shit don't want to see you get shot. So... no, not really, I guess. But..."

"But you know if he appears, I'm going to go get him anyway."

"Exactly."

Margie looked down at the pistol as it rested against her leg, her finger outside the trigger guard, the way Norm had taught her. She lifted it up, opened the glove box and returned it to its place. "Okay. We'll do it your way. No getting involved unless there's no other choice."

"You don't look too happy about it."

She wasn't. Margie had the urge to charge the place, kick in the door, make whoever took Normie pay. Hand out a can of whoop ass. But Ellie was sensitive and... not wrong. Norm would freak if he knew she'd gone hunting for him.

Jerry Perry didn't worry about speed limits as he headed for Germantown.

He'd gotten off the phone with Tommy moments earlier to learn that not only was Bob Singleton captive and no longer a problem but that they now had an address on Alexi Pushkin.

Victor was headed over there to kill him.

Maintaining his cover meant Perry playing the gangster role even when there were other gangster lives at stake. He wasn't to break the law himself, but he wasn't to interfere, either. He would watch as they killed Pushkin.

The end game was simple: eventually, like any man, he would express ambition. To move up in the organization, to have more responsibility than being Malyuchenko's right-hand man. Just as they'd used leverage to get him a recommendation from a Brighton Beach senior hand, they would use Victor to get him to New York, a few more rungs up the ladder.

None of it sat well with Perry. He'd been an agent for two decades and had always played it straight, his undercover roles about observation, gathering evidence. Playing a mobster had taken it a rung further; he had to watch them go about their business daily and do nothing.

Bob Singleton had threatened to undermine all of that. Whatever his motivation, the damage to the investigation — and the prospect of senior organization arrests — would ruin everything Perry had worked so hard to build. His efforts would go for nothing, and his career would stall.

If Malyuchenko killed Singleton, as expected? *So be it. He's off the reservation anyway. He's not even active.*

The Mercedes's tires squealed, the centrifugal force pulling him sideways as he took the corner to Tunstall Street at speed. A few blocks ahead, he could see a limousine pulling over at the curb. Just ahead of it, four of Victor's men got out of a sedan.

His phone rang. He used the wheel controls. "What?!"

"Sorry... Boss, it's me again. Boss... he got loose. He killed Salukhin and Mattie C." He paused. "He asked me to send you a message."

Bob Singleton. Fuck you, man. Fuck you for wading into this insane mess. "So tell me."

"He said if you get in his way again, he's going to..." He paused and sighed, as if squirming at the prospect.

"Out with it!"

"It's just... it didn't make any sense anyway..."

Perry pulled the car over to the side of the road, two blocks ahead of Victor's limo. Three men were climbing out, joining the others on the sidewalk opposite the house. There was no sign of Victor himself or his driver.

"Just fucking tell me, Tom..."

"He said he'll tell your friends in Brighton Beach that he knows your brand, and they'd be interested in where your family lives."

Perry's mouth dropped open involuntarily.

The dirty sonuvabitch.

He was making the none-too-subtle point that he could not only expose the FBI agent, but have his family wiped out as a consequence. Whoever Bob Singleton really was within the murky world of CIA politics, he was nothing if not determined.

"Clean up there, then head back to the mansion," Perry ordered. "I'll deal with you later."

He ended the call and looked through the windshield. The men hadn't moved yet, instead discussing something. Two of them broke away from the group and began to walk towards the next corner.

He's surrounding the house, planning a raid.

His phone rang again, the display reading unknown. "Go for Jerry."

"Where are you?" It was Victor.

"I'm in West Memphis, taking care of some legal business, the dock leases for Mud Island," he lied. "Why?"

"Head back here, now. I'm at Orange Mound. We have Alexi's house surrounded, on Tunstall."

"Okay. Anything else?"

"Just get here. Twelve hundred block." Victor hung up.

Perry turned off the motor and sat, watching. He had no intention of getting involved; he didn't know Singleton from a hole in the ground. The chances of a CIA dog going so far off his leash as to blackmail a federal officer would have struck him as ridiculous that morning.

But that was happening.

If he could do something that unpredictable, Perry thought, he might also follow through.

No investigation, no job or promotion was worth his family's safety.

Margie and Ellie watched the two men walk past them on Tunstall Street, then back across the road and towards the back of the house. Its siding was stark white. It had a short white picket fence surrounding both gardens.

"They're going to go in there and start shooting. I can feel it," Margie said. It terrified her, the notion of losing Norm, of going on without him. She'd always displayed strength outwardly, a product of her dangerous home life as a child. But they'd been together for nearly fifty years. He was everything to Margie.

"We don't know what they're going to do," Ellie said. "But your friend Bob is right; we're not supposed to be mixed up in any of this. Margie... I don't feel safe right now. We should be farther away. We should move a few blocks back."

"Quit worrying so much, hon... We haven't even gotten out of the car yet."

She kept her eye on the street ahead, but Ellie was close enough that Margie could see her friend's eyes widen at the comment.

"Margie... we are NOT getting out of the car. I'm not. And if you do, you're taking a risk Norm would never agree to. We don't even know if he's in there."

"We're close to him. I can feel it," Margie insisted.

"Now you're just being silly."

Margie reached across her and opened the glove box. She took the Colt 1911 out again and held it in her right hand, feeling the heft of it.

"Is that thing cocked and ready?" Ellie said. "It looks cocked."

"Yeah, but that's because it uses a hammer-lock for the safety." She flicked out the safety, then flicked it back into the butt again. "See? Bar in, hammer can't fire. Boy howdy... I'll tell you what, El... it sure does make you feel like you could take on the world..."

Ellie put both hands on top of the gun and gently forced it down, onto her friend's lap. "Margie... you know I love you like the sister I never had. And you know I'll do whatever I can to help you. But you are sixty-eight years old, and you've never shot anyone in your life." She gestured back towards the street. "Look at those men surrounding that house."

Margie did as requested. "Uh-huh. So?"

"So... there are seven of them! Do you even know how to load that thing? Lordie! It's a miracle you haven't shot one of us already! A dude breaks into your house, Margie, by all means, grab Norm's gun and start blasting. But this isn't a robber at four in the morning. Those are professional killers! Land sakes..."

"Ellie May Grainger, y'all fret more than a pig in barbecue sauce. Did I get out of the car yet? No. Did I shoot anyone yet? No."

"It's the 'yet' part what's got me worried. Hey... something's going on."

They watched as the two at the back of the house clambered over the short fence and crept toward the back door.

One of the men drew a pistol from under his jacket.

"Ah geez." Margie flexed her free hand subconsciously, like someone squeezing a wrist exerciser. "Ahhh... Geez. They're drawing guns now. And Norm's in there. Ahhh geez..." She fidgeted in place, the draw to get out of the car and rush over there almost overwhelming.

Ellie placed a hand on her friend's again, giving it a reassuring squeeze. "Just... stay cool, hon. We can't be doing anything stupid."

"I know. I know, I know, I know," Margie said, rocking slightly, her last nerve about used up.

. . .

Bob felt the Ford begin to speed wobble as it slid around the last corner, as if the wheel bearings on the subcompact had finally given up all hope.

The situation didn't make sense.

Alexi seemed more than a little unbalanced, but he clearly wasn't stupid. Giving the address to someone like Artie Chee, a man who would betray his own rescuer without a second thought, was like splashing gasoline on a problem, then giving Victor some matches.

Now wasn't the time to wonder why, however.

He peered through the sun glare on the windshield. The house was five blocks away, but the street was straight and level, the scene unfolding visible from a distance. He slowed the car slightly and pulled it over, cruising next to the curb in idle.

A couple of blocks past the limo and the small group of men, Ellie's Subaru was parked on the other side of the road.

Damn it. They're too close. They could be spotted easily from there. If not for the sunshine, they probably would've been, he figured.

Another car sat two homes farther back, yet another Mercedes sedan. He couldn't make out the driver.

Bob drew the FN 5.7 and checked its load. The twenty-shot pistol was ideal for an outdoor, close-range engagement, the muzzle velocity and center-fire cartridges lowering the risk of bullet drop, the pistol's light frame nearly bereft of recoil.

He was struck by the automatic nature of his preparedness, how he just went back into old routines, training. It was like it was grafted into his bones, a trait as much as a decision. An animal instinct.

Just like the old man wanted.

Oh, but this isn't you, remember? You're not a killer anymore. You're not a bad guy. You're on the side of the angels.

Who are you kidding? Has anything really changed? Isn't this shit why you dropped out? Wasn't it better just being on your own, with a bottle and a quiet place?

He smiled wryly, and his eyes drifted involuntarily to the Heavens as he gently shook his head. "Knew you'd be back eventually. Haven't given up yet, have you?"

He'd begun talking to the alcoholic part of his brain like it was an adversary after New Orleans. Somehow, making it separate, like it wasn't really him, helped remind him the voice wasn't on his side, even as it tried to reason him back into a bottle.

You know you love me, Bob. You know you want me. I make all this shit go away.

For a split second, bourbon flitted across his taste buds, triggering the memory of its sweet burn in his throat.

Imagine how good it would be...

He snapped out of it, breathing hard through his nose, shaking his head gently. "You almost killed Dawn and Marcus in DC. No. That's not happening again."

Up the street, three of the men had crossed the road and opened the front gate to the property. They strode up the front walk, drawing pistols.

Things are going down.

They wouldn't barge straight in, too much risk of being shot. They'd door-knock him first, try to get him to come outside, flank him from the back of the house while he's talking or occupied.

From the corner of his eye, he saw movement up ahead. He turned his attention back to the limo. A head poked out of the rear passenger window for just a moment and said something, then poked back inside.

Victor.

In sending all of his men over to the house, he was leaving himself unguarded. He was only a block away, unaware.

Bob knew he wasn't going to get a better chance.

He pocketed the FN. He opened the car door and got out, pushing it closed slowly and quietly. He rounded the back of the car to the sidewalk, to ensure his approach was on the opposite side from Malyuchenko.

Getting spotted at the last second would destroy his advantage, and for all his reliance on goons, he was sure Malyuchenko was carrying.

He crouched low and moved slowly and steadily up the sidewalk.

Margie had resigned herself to waiting and was trying to be patient. Maybe, as Ellie had suggested, Norm wasn't even there. Maybe it was all a dangerous waste of time.

Then she saw a car pull up, three blocks down the road.

Then she saw Bob climb out of it.

"He's going in," she muttered to Ellie. "He's going to take all those guys on by himself. Then he'll get shot, and Norm will get hurt anyhow. Y'all can't expect me to just sit here and do nothing. Ellie May, I'm just fixing to burst right about now!"

"What did he tell you, Margie? What did the man say to you just ten minutes ago?"

"He told me to stay put. But he's not helping nobody.

Heck, he's why Norm's in trouble in the first place! I can't just sit here."

"Margie..."

"I'm going," she said, yanking the door handle and climbing out, pistol in hand, before Ellie could utter another protest.

Her friend opened the driver's side door and leaned out from behind it. "Margie! Come back here and stop being so damned foolish!"

Margie ignored her and kept walking, unlatching the safety in stride. "Y'all stay in the damned car. I'm going to get Norm."

Ellie got out and closed the car door. "Margie... dang, girlfriend... you're hotter than a chili pepper in a volcano."

"You don't know the half of it." Margie headed towards the house on the corner, mad as hell.

BOB REACHED the back end of the limo. He crouched low behind its trunk, out of sight of the wing mirrors, while he decided the best approach.

Normally taking the shot through an open window, if available, would make sense. A relatively soft target like a politician or revolutionary was unlikely to have a gun in hand or within reach. Taking the open window meant less chance of bullet deflection if the glass was reinforced.

But that would not be the case this time. The moment he spotted movement, Malyuchenko would reach for a piece, probably something unnecessarily powerful and large, to go with the chunky jewelry.

The FN's muzzle velocity and the high-velocity NATO-rated bullet would pass through safety glass like butter. At that point, glass protected him... but not the Russian.

Of course, with just six to eight feet between them, it probably wasn't going to matter much. It would take a special kind of glass to withstand a two-way barrage at that range.

The window it is. Pop out and around in one motion, scope out the target's shape, open up. He pushed off with both feet, rising to stand even as he turned to step into position.

Ahead, half a block away, he saw Margie O'Hearn jogging down the street, pistol in hand. Her friend Ellie was ten feet behind her, yelling at her.

Jesus flippin' Christ. Not now.

The explosion was forty feet away, but its concussive blast of heat blew Bob backwards, off his feet, his hearing gone instantly, replaced by a high-pitched whine, debris from the former two-story home raining down on the sidewalk beside him, as well as all over the road, pieces of siding, chunks of flooring, flaming vinyl.

He pushed up onto his backside. The ground around him was littered with tiny chunks of safety glass, the Mercedes's windows blown out. Five feet away, the taillights of the limo suddenly illuminated. A split second later, it peeled away from the curb and flew down the street.

Damn it.

Smoke was drifting across the road, people beginning to come out of their homes to find out what happened. The house next door to the shattered remains of Alexi's alleged crash pad had caught fire, the homeowner running out, rushing to get a hose. Car alarms were sounding from garages nearby.

Bob shook his head to try to get some of the fog out. He

rose unsteadily, feeling a pain in his left arm. He turned it inward so that he could see his triceps. A triangular piece of safety glass, its ragged edge surprisingly smooth and thick, was embedded a quarter inch in.

He pulled out the shard. He took off his jacket and shirt, tearing a strip off the bottom. He used the torn shirt to bind the wound. He peered past the smoke, down the street.

Margie was kneeling over her friend Ellie, who lay on her back.

Bob began to run.

23

Margie was frozen in place, overwhelmed by choices and fear.

"Oh God, oh God, oh God…" she mumbled, her hand over the seeping wound in Ellie's lower abdomen. "Please no… Please…"

Bob firmly moved her aside. Ellie's eyes were closed. He checked her pulse. "She's alive, but she's losing blood quickly. Ellie, can you hear me?" he asked loudly. He put gentle pressure on her shoulder.

Her eyes flitted open. Her voice was weak. "Bob?"

"Stay still; you've got a shrapnel wound," Bob said. "We're going to get you to a hospital."

Margie took out her phone and fumbled with it.

"There isn't time," Bob said. "Ambulance will take too long. Go get the car; pull it up beside us. GO! NOW!"

She snapped out of her initial shock and confusion and ran towards the car.

Bob realized he had his torn shirt in his left hand. He examined the wound, trying to gauge through the slick, fresh blood how deep it was. A piece of metal was sticking out, jagged and twisted. "I know it hurts," he said loudly. "But we're going to get you help. Just hang in there; keep listening to my voice."

The car squealed to a halt beside him. Margie got out and quickly rejoined him.

Down the street, a block past Margie's car, the other Mercedes pulled a three-point turn before speeding away.

Bob slid his arms under Ellie's back and under her knees. "When I lift, you have to lift with me, under her butt, to keep it level with her legs. We don't want her to dip in the middle because we don't want any pressure on the wound. Okay? On three."

They lifted her into the back seat. Margie pushed the front passenger seat ahead and climbed in back with her, crouching next to her friend. "You're going to be okay, sweetie, I promise," she said. "Make her okay, Lord. Please..."

He knew Margie was getting a crash course in dangerous consequences. She'd punched the darkness square in the face, and it had punched back even harder. If Ellie paid the price, she'd never forgive herself.

He picked up the pistol she'd left lying on the asphalt. Bob shut the door behind her, then rounded to the driver's side, pulling his light jacket back over his bare torso. He tossed the Colt onto the passenger seat.

The nearest hospital was St. Francis, a five-minute drive. He floored the pedal, zipping in and out of traffic as they hit the main thoroughfare. "Dial the hospital emergency for me, then hand me your phone," Bob commanded.

Margie passed it to him.

"St. Francis Hospital Emergency..."

"We have a bleeding explosion victim inbound in a

private vehicle, a maroon Subaru wagon. Victim is..." He held the receiver to his shoulder. "How old is she, and any medical issues?"

"Fifty-nine. I don't think... wait... she's allergic to bee stings, carries an EpiPen."

"Victim is a fifty-nine-year-old woman with no known drug interactions. She is allergic to bee venom. She has a deep open puncture wound to the right side of her lower torso from a jagged piece of metal that remains embedded."

"Where are you now, sir?"

"We're about five minutes out, on Park Avenue."

"Is the patient conscious and breathing?"

"She is, yes, but barely. She's lost some blood."

"Keep her as still as possible, and if someone can talk to her, keep her lucid, it may help if she can communicate with the doctors. We'll alert the police to not stop you if possible. Please bring her directly up the ramp to the doors, and then we'll ask you to stand well clear while the paramedics work, okay?"

"Okay."

"Okay, sir, we'll be ready, don't you worry."

He hung up the call. "Keep talking to her, Margie; let her know everything's going to be fine."

Of course, Bob had no idea if that would be the case.

"Please hang on, sweetie," Margie intoned. "I promise I won't let anything happen to you." She looked up at Bob over the seat divider. "Y'all want to step on it, please? Oh God..."

Bob stole a quick glance. There was blood all over the floor of the back seat, Margie kneeling in it. The older woman had her hand over her mouth and was trying to retain her composure.

"This isn't on you, and she'll be okay," he said. "Just concentrate on what we have to do right now. She needs us calm and focused."

"I never should have got out of the car," Margie sobbed. "She told me I was putting us in danger, and I didn't listen."

"You didn't blow up a house; you didn't kidnap Norm. It was shrapnel from about a hundred feet away. That wasn't predictable or anyone's fault. NOW SNAP OUT OF IT! We don't have time for self-pity right now."

The tonal change shocked her, and her eyes widened. Then she nodded her head quickly.

The hospital came into view. Bob used the station wagon to barge the car ahead into the center lane, horns sounding as he turned in to the hospital entrance, then up the curved ramp to the doors.

Four paramedics and a nurse were waiting.

They opened the back door immediately, one man running around the car to the other side. Margie got out and stood to one side as he supported Ellie's neck and back. They transferred her to the lowered gurney, raising it with a button, then rolling it towards the emergency double doors.

Bob took off his seatbelt. He retrieved Margie's Colt 1911 from the passenger seat and got out of the car. Margie was watching her friend go through the double doors.

"Go; be with her," Bob said. "I have to get out of here before police arrive and ask questions. As far as they'll know, you two were uninvolved, innocent bystanders."

Margie was crying gently, a single tear tracking its way down her right cheek. "Bob... what if Norm was in that house!?"

He closed the distance between them and lifted her chin

with one hand, looking her square in the eyes. "He wasn't. I'm sure of it."

"Norm has never let me down. Never. He's my hero." She looked up at him, resolute, but also angry. "You got him into this mess in the first place. So you'd damn well better save him... goddamn you, Bob... goddamn you if anything happens to him."

"The man who set that trap up knew they were looking for him; he knew from his experience with me that people would follow him. And he leaked the address to an associate, knowing that man had already betrayed him once. But it didn't kill the man he wanted to kill. For that, he believes he needs help. And he needs Norm. If Norm were dead, he knows there would be nothing to protect him."

"Protect him? From what?"

Bob headed towards the street on foot. "From me."

24

The front doors were ajar and unguarded at the mansion, the clopping of shoes on polished floors audible as Jerry Perry ran up the steps.

He threw the doors open and jogged inside.

The man who was usually at the front door was helping Mrs. Malyuchenko with four large, overstuffed suitcases. The boys were running up the stairs, laughing and screaming.

At the top landing, Victor appeared, mopping his brow with a handkerchief. He grabbed the rail and headed downstairs at double time, dodging past the boys as they nearly knocked him over.

He looked up and saw Perry. "Where the hell were you?"

"I told you, I had to go out to Mud Island. I saw what happened there, though. I mean... what the fuck was that!? It looked like you bombed the place!"

"BOMBED!?" Victor spat, his face red. "Bombed the place!? He blew up the fucking house!"

"He... wait... who?"

"Alexi. He set us up and trapped it to blow when my men broke in. He must have known what a treacherous worm Artie really was. He kill seven: Taylor, Oleg, Dmitri, Eddie Renfro... in three days, he kill all my men except Artur, Evgeny, Tommy and Piotr. And you..."

Perry held up both hands. "If you'd taken my advice and let this stupid vendetta go..."

Victor held up a single index finger. "Ah! Not another fucking word of argument. Right or wrong, I do not care right now, Jerry Perry. Contradict me again, I promise you, I shoot you in face, cut off your balls and shove them down your throat."

"We need to get you out of here," Perry said. He glanced over at Mrs. Malyuchenko's luggage. "What's going on here, anyway?"

"I am sending wife and kids to in-laws' for safety."

"You're not staying here," Perry said. "Like you said, Alexi already killed most of your men, and this guy 'Bob' is still trying to take you out. This place has too many points of ingress for a handful of guns to defend. It's also spread out, giving him a chance to isolate people."

"Jerry Perry... I JUST warn you about ball-cutting-off thing, and immediately you begin to tell me what to do..."

"HEY!" Perry raised an index finger of his own. "I'm in this job because of the largesse of Chaim Popov, in Brighton Beach. Remember him? They gave me two jobs: to give you the best options and to keep you alive. Remember that?"

He knew how much weight the old man held with Victor, who saw himself as the son Chaim should've had.

The gang boss breathed in deeply through flaring

nostrils, trying to compose himself. "You... push my buttons, Jerry Perry. But also I know Chaim never steer me wrong. So... What? What is your plan?"

"The guy trying to kill you has to be the priority now, Victor. He's come close twice. We go, now, to the slip on Mud Island. Your wife and sons go to the in-laws'. We take a few days out of town on Chee's boat, where we've got thousands of miles of Mississippi River to disappear into until we can round up new recruits and borrow some men from Nashville. In the meantime, I find out where this 'Bob' guy is hiding, who he is. Then we kill him on our terms when he's least ready for an attack. Okay?"

Victor pretended to give it deep contemplation. He nodded. "Okay. But if you fuck this up, there will be consequences. *Da?* And not Chaim nor nobody is going to prevent that. Understand?"

Perry nodded. He checked his watch. "It's... seven twenty-six. For now, go. Get the other men and head for the boat. There are weapons and food on board already. I'll collect some work material and join you, and we'll aim to cast off in about an hour."

Victor nodded twice, studying the other man. Then he clapped him on the shoulder. "I always can count on you, my friend. This business, it is nothing without trust. And I am glad to have such a capable comrade to trust."

Perry bowed his head. "Go on, get out of here before you make me all sentimental."

Bob retrieved Margie's Ford from the quieter block of Tunstall Street. He stopped at Ramirez's gun store and picked up a few more items, then at a corner store for a few more.

He took his purchases back to the motel and parked next to June-Marie's faded red Dodge Shadow.

When he got to the room, she'd switched positions, from the floor to sitting up on the bed, the TV remote next to her, her right arm still draped across the bed and tethered to its frame. The TV had built-in apps, and she was streaming a movie.

"You've been gone for hours," she said. "I'm starving."

He set his bags down on the low-slung chest of drawers. He reached into a brown paper bag and took out a ham-and-cheese sub from the corner store. "Bon appetit," he said, tossing it to her. He took Margie's Colt 1911 out of his coat pocket and deposited it in the empty bottom drawer.

June-Marie pulled at the plastic wrap on the sub. "This is the best you could do?"

"Everyone good requires reservations," Bob said. "So, tell me, June-Marie... am I really supposed to believe you're not in love with Alexi? Or that you didn't know that house on Tunstall Street was going to blow up in our faces?"

She sighed, her shoulders stooped from fatigue. "A house blew up?"

"I believe you knew that already. It killed seven of Victor's men and hurt a friend of mine."

"I don't really care what y'all believe at this point. I just want to get out of Memphis."

He worked quickly while she watched her movie, transferring items to his kit bag. "After tonight, you can do whatever you want. You've got your money. Alexi's boss will be dead. The world's your incredibly shitty oyster."

She was quiet for a moment. When she spoke again, her

voice was low, the defiance gone. "You think you know me well enough to judge me. But you don't. All I ever did was agree to go out with a guy. Now they've got me in a corner, and... you're... what, helping me see how untrustworthy you find me? Judging me as bad as Alexi and Victor? Maybe the person you need to be judging is you, not me. Maybe you're a lot more like either of them than YOU realize."

Bob sat down on the edge of the chest of drawers. He studied the forlorn woman's face for a moment, her bleak expression, eyes staring off into an invisible distance. She was probably only twenty or twenty-one, but looked at least a decade older.

"The problem, June-Marie, is that after a few decades of dealing with bad people, a guy learns to play it safe. You might be the poor, set-upon young woman you portray yourself to be, sure... I mean, you've been a dancer for years, and those can be rough circles. So... I have a hard time buying that, no matter how good the performance. Or you could just be a player, playing the same game as the rest of us, pretending to be something you're not when it's convenient. I might hope for the former... but I'll plan for the latter."

"Meaning?"

"Meaning that if I keep you tied up here and assume that, should you get loose, you'll run right back to Alexi, I keep one more threat off my back, one more person removed from the equation who could stick a knife between my shoulder blades or shoot me in the back of the head."

"And if you're wrong..."

"And if I'm wrong... eventually you're going to be free and clear anyway. All that happens is you're inconvenienced for a few days. But if I'm right, and you're as sneaky as you are pretty, letting you loose is just another problem I have to solve."

She watched him as he got up and slung the bag over his shoulder. "You're not going to find him," she said. "Alexi comes off as crazy, but he's clever, and he knows Memphis. You don't. Let me go, and I can lead you to him."

Bob walked to the door. "And right there, that's another worrisome sign: operators, scammers, players... they've always got another proposal, another idea, another way into someone's good graces. They're always trying to scam the guy with clout. The smart ones know when to shut up and play it cool. But there aren't many of them, which is why they get caught or killed eventually."

He opened the door.

"Just do what Alexi wants!" she pleaded. "Just kill Victor. Alexi will give back your friend, and everybody can go back to their lives."

"I'll be back in a few hours," Bob said, ignoring the plea as he closed the motel room door behind him.

PERRY WAITED until the small convoy had departed the mansion before heading for Victor's study.

He had no doubt Singleton would come calling soon enough. He also suspected he wouldn't kill a federal agent, no matter how big his beef with the Russian.

That gave him a few minutes to do some snooping.

Victor often left his computer on or unprotected. Perry had made a practice of cloning the man's storage drives regularly, forwarding it all to DC for the bureau's perusal.

He sat behind Victor's desk and waited as the USB drive filled.

Heads were going to roll over the former agency man's sudden involvement, he was sure of it. They'd spent millions to get enough leverage over Chaim Popov, enough to bury him and plant someone deep within the Russian Mob. But if Malyuchenko were taken out, Brighton Beach might blame him. At the very least they would be wary, checking into anyone connected to Malyuchenko, shutting down potential leaks before they led anywhere.

"You know, I'm really tempted to shoot you in the head."

He looked up. Singleton was standing in the doorway. He had a pistol in his right hand.

"That was quick. I assumed you'd be at the hospital."

"So that *was* you I saw parked up the street. Thanks for helping with her... Oh, that's right, I forgot. You're playing bad guy. Or maybe you just are one. Which is it again?"

"I couldn't blow my cover without knowing if any of Victor's men survived."

"You're kidding, right? Parts of that house are still coming down in Georgia."

Perry could feel the weight of his pistol speed holster clipped to the left side of his belt. He was acutely nervous, aware that Singleton had already decided all bets were off when it came to Malyuchenko. The agency's assassins — their "dogs" — had long leashes by reputation. Not that it ever admitted they existed.

"So... what now?" Perry said. "I've asked you politely to stay out of this operation. You know my next step is to call in outside assistance."

"It's probably already en route, whether you asked for it or not. There are bigger issues, bigger forces at play than you, probably bigger than your precious case."

"Straight up need-to-know agency shit, huh?" Perry said.

Singleton walked up to the desk.

Perry eyeballed the pistol. "Nice piece. Not familiar..."

"It's an FN 5.7."

"NATO gun. Huh... I have a friend who has the Ruger take on the same. He digs the accuracy. I take it you've got the mil-spec rounds in that, right? In case I'm wearing body armor?"

"That would be illegal."

"Oh, ha ha. Very droll. Are... you planning on killing me, Singleton? Yeah... I know who you are."

"Not planning on it, no. I might kill you accidentally if you don't give me the information I need. But I would hope not. By the time we reached that point, your agony would be considerable."

Perry tilted his head and studied the man. Would he really go that far? "So... you're thinking... what, pull a few fingernails out by the roots, maybe strap a car battery to my nuts?"

"Not really my style. That's more the purview of sadists, Jerry. Although... pain can be much more of a motivator, if carefully applied, than people think. There are nerves between the muscle groups of the hands and feet, for example, that are every bit as agonizing as what you described, just quicker and more controllable. Your little friend Salukhin liked to go on about them."

"So... you don't really expect to accidentally kill me; this is just supposed to make me nervous?"

"That's not up to me, if I have to torture you," Bob said, sitting on the edge of the desk. "That's up to the strength of your heart. Enough shock to the system and even the biggest man will crack. I don't want you to die, so of course I'll then have to give you CPR... which means kissing you, Jerry. I'd almost rather shoot you now."

Perry studied the man's eyes. They were clear, full of intent, not cold and dismissive but utterly unyielding nonetheless. "You'd really do that, wouldn't you? You'd commit the premeditated murder of a federal agent."

"There's a sweetheart of a woman with no place in our world of violence and death, and she's clinging to life in St. Francis Hospital while her husband cries and worries if she'll make it. She did nothing but help her neighbors and live her life, and now she might lose it, all over some stupid local feud between thugs."

"Singleton..."

"No, shut up for a minute. You asked, so I'm going to tell you. In the middle of this ridiculous lowlife fiasco, I find you, a federal agent, so intent on making his career arrest and taking down the big, bad Russian mob that you're ignoring the carnage your 'source' is bestowing upon all he despises. You're a public servant, sure, but you're not here serving the public. Because you don't give half a shit about any of them. So... yeah, Jerry Perry, I'll hurt you. I'll make you wish to God you'd never been born to feel anything in the first place, by the time I'm done. And I won't lose a second of sleep over it. Where is he?"

Perry considered trying to draw and fire on the man, but it seemed foolhardy. Agency dogs were trained to kill a dozen different ways, and he knew he'd take a bullet between the eyes before his gun even cleared its holster. There was no point prolonging it. He was either going to find Victor and kill him or be killed by the Russian and his men.

Perry knew he no longer had a say, not if he wanted to live.

"A boat at Mud Island Marina, off Riverside. It's a twin-engine cabin cruiser called the *Spirit of Memphis*. He'll be almost there by now. Unless you can fly, you won't get there before they leave. And that's a big river, my friend."

"I'm not your friend, Jerry. My friends don't have to worry about what'll happen to them if they ever see me again."

The former agent turned on his heel and walked out.

On the monitor ahead, Perry's files continued to copy over, a green bar reading thirty-eight percent.

25

"Target acquired, a black Bentley, moving west on Riverside Drive at Union Avenue, containing three men. Rear glass is tinted, so no word on whether it's Malyuchenko. One car ahead, a black Mercedes, containing four men. No chase vehicle."

Earl Monroe leaned over the back rail of the rented pickup's trailer. He balanced the spyglass on the rail and focused on the mansion's windows.

His support handler was a former military colleague. His help didn't come cheaply. But freelancers had tried to take out Kennedy's target, "Bob Singleton," once before in New Orleans. A slipshod approach had, predictably, failed.

The handler had contacts, a friend in the Memphis Traffic Department who could flag vehicles. They'd picked up Malyuchenko's limo on a traffic cam before he'd even reached the mansion. His assumption was that they'd left the mansion out of caution, assuming Bob Singleton was en route.

He paused at the second window to the right on the second floor, spotting movement. He waited. After a few more seconds, the figure came into view. He tapped the shutter button atop the spyglass and took a still image of the man. He held down the button underneath it, a satellite uplink sending a copy of the high-definition image to his handler, in a downtown hotel room.

"Who am I looking at, Home?"

"Stand by." The handler would be accessing public databases, using his traffic department source to check saved images against drivers' licenses.

Monroe swiveled the spyglass on the rail, aiming back towards the parking lot. It was empty save for a single Mercedes, registered to Malyuchenko's holding company.

Given reports from the two prior days, Home said analysts expected Singleton to confront the Russian at his mansion.

Malyuchenko was clearly on the move. Either Singleton was en route or had already come and gone. If he'd already visited, he'd convinced the agent to give up his boss's route, final destination or both. If he hadn't, the man probably wouldn't still be able to stand and look out a window.

If Singleton hadn't visited yet...

I'm better inside than out.

He placed the spyglass in its pouch and vaulted over the side of the truck bed.

"Your image is of Jerald Perry. The contract specifies he's not to be touched," his earpiece announced.

What's that about? A source inside Malyuchenko's camp, maybe?

Monroe looked the part of the tourist, a Memphis Showboats ball cap and tie dye T-shirt over olive green cargo pants. In the field, he favored a quick-release leg holster for his Ruger 8649, the second strap keeping it immobile. But working in the US meant tact was paramount, and he'd clipped a speed holster to the back of his belt instead, carrying a Glock 19. He had a knife sheath strapped to his right ankle, a butterfly knife in his left pocket, two extra magazines in his right.

He headed for the front gate. Vaulting the fence would trigger a response if there was anyone else inside, monitoring.

At the security panel by the wrought-iron gate, he tapped his earpiece. "Home, I'm looking at a Honeywell GSP280 Premium security panel. Can we bypass?"

"Stand by..."

He waited for a few seconds. Monroe was no Dark Web expert, but he knew it contained a trove of illicit information, including private corporate data, internal specifications from manufacturers, back doors and resets that the public wasn't supposed to know. It would not take his colleague long to determine if the system was compromised.

He used the time to check the street both ways. It was quiet.

"Asset, the manufacturer has an emergency override that resets it to its original status and turns off any potential triggers. Use code 1-A-0-0-0-0-1-R."

Monroe entered the code. The digital panel read, "System Override?" with a "y/n" prompt.

He approved the change. The red light on the left of the panel turned green, and a split second later, the gate lock whirred, a motor disabling it. He opened the gate and walked in.

The front doors were ajar. He pushed them wider open while staying in cover, to the left. He checked the atrium cautiously, then entered the house.

A double-wide opening led into a massive open-plan living room to his right. Ahead, at the end of the hall, a spiral staircase led up to the second floor. He followed it, moving cautiously, checking each doorway as he passed to ensure no one could step in behind him, into his blind spot.

A door at the end of the upper hall was also ajar. He pushed it open, peeking around the corner as it swung wide.

The man behind the desk was in a suit. He was middle aged, with salt-and-pepper hair that had been moussed or gelled stiff.

"You're Jerald Perry, right?"

"You know me, but..."

Monroe cut him off. "Where is he?"

"Who? Malyuchenko or Singleton?"

"Maybe both."

Perry took off his glasses and polished them. "Are you going to kill me?"

"I'm being paid not to, so no. But if you cause me problems, that could change. Where are they?"

"The former is on his way to Mud Island Marina. The latter is going after him, intent on killing him. Something about doing a favor for someone else... or fulfilling an obligation."

"The boat..."

"The *Spirit of Memphis*. A sixty-foot twin-engine cabin cruiser."

"He's running?"

"Of a sort. There are only so many places to run to when

you're on a river. He's getting out of Singleton's way. Or, he thinks he is."

"Singleton's already been here."

Perry nodded. "You were late. He left about fifteen minutes ago."

Monroe betrayed no hint of frustration, no sign of any emotion. His stoicism usually worked to his advantage. "Can they be tracked easily in any manner?"

"You're asking for my help?"

"Demanding would be a better description. If there's some way to track him, you'll know. If you say you don't, I'll know you're lying, and I'll reconsider whether I need to kill you."

Perry nodded. "The boat has a satellite radio with an emergency broadcast beacon in it. If you can figure out the maker, I'm guessing you could use it to lock onto a location signal."

"Okay. I'm going. Any questions before I leave?"

Perry shook his head.

"Smart," Monroe said as he turned to head back down the hall.

In truth he had no interest in Perry or his issues.

His assignment was specific and simple: eliminate Bob Singleton on sight, regardless of circumstance. He was a "must kill" target, an "XPD."

That was new, too. In his fifteen years of military and mercenary service across war zones, dictatorships and failing nation states, Monroe had never encountered an XPD — an "expedient demise" order. The fact that it was an American meant that Bob Singleton must have been very, very bad indeed, and equally dangerous.

But the details were need-to-know.

He walked out into the sunshine and headed for the gate and his truck beyond, a Dodge Ram with a Hemi engine.

His target was on the move, and Monroe needed to make haste.

26

Arturo Ramirez stood under the dome light, suspended from the tin ceiling of his gun store, twenty feet above them, the light reflecting off his balding head and the glass of the front counter.

"You cannot be serious. Another favor?"

"At least you were still open this time. And it's not like I'm asking for the world, Mr. Ramirez, just a loaner or three. I paid you what I already owed, so..."

"Hmph." Ramirez looked at the paper list on the counter. He turned back to his old-fashioned cash register and began punching in numbers. It took about twenty seconds. He looked up at Bob over the top of his glasses as he entered each price. He did not look amused.

"So... let's see: another fifty rounds of mil-spec FN 5.7 ammo, two smoke grenades, a flash-bang..." He looked up, his skepticism over Bob's ability to pay looming large.

"Hey, a guy never knows when he's going to need one of those," Bob said with a shrug. "I mean... I'd keep one in the dash if they were as cheap as Mickey Ds..."

"... another rifle, preferably in .30-30, preferably with another long-range scope..."

"The other one is in a warehouse in Oakville, I think."

"... body armor, preferably something light and meshed rather than plated and cumbersome, but good enough to stop armor-piercing rounds..."

"Because there are probably, like, eight guys with guns where I'm going, and I don't know what kind..."

"... a Skydio autonomous drone... Amigo, you are NOT getting a fucking Skydio on credit. My lord... Bob... Can I call you Bob?"

"Sure."

"Bob, John Butcher and I go back to before our time in the service. We used to go to cadet camp together when we were teenagers. Like I said before, if he vouches for you, I'll supply you what you need. But... with all due respect, you're crazy! I've got small profit margins! I can't front you thousands of dollars' worth of gear..."

"I get that, really, I do..."

"Particularly if as John says you're into, and I quote, 'some kind of black ops spook shit with dark connotations.' I mean, he added, 'but he's a good guy.' However..."

"Okay..." Bob bit his tongue and hid his disappointment. The man was one of the good ones, the kind of person worth having around. "What can you do for me?"

"The black-tip ammo for the FN and one smoker. That's it, man. That's what I can afford to risk. The Skydio drone is out, as is another .30-30. The flash-bangs, the scope and extra rifle ammo are out."

It wouldn't be enough, Bob knew. If he ended up battling people aboard a boat, he'd either do it from close range, and risk being overwhelmed by manpower, or from shore or another vessel... and be overwhelmed by firepower.

But he had to do something. The idea of Ellie clinging to life in that hospital — that once again his best intentions had contributed to someone innocent being hurt — was unbearable. Adding Norm to the list of casualties by failing at his task wasn't acceptable.

"Isn't there anything else you've got, something with some heft that could even up numbers quickly? An old grenade from WW2? Anything?"

Ramirez looked dismayed. "Man, there's nothing remotely..." He closed one eye in a squint. "Ehhh...?"

"What?"

"There is one thing. But I don't know how much use it's going to be." He lifted the counter divider and headed for the basement door. "I can tell you this though: it makes that old Henry repeater look like a titanium android by quality comparison. I mean... we're talking a genuine rusting piece of shit. But... it's free. Okay?"

What choice did he have? "Okay," Bob said.

"I'll be right back."

MARGIE SAT in the intensive care unit waiting room and tried to steady herself, to empty her mind of fear and anxiety.

She clenched the tiny crucifix key ring Ellie had given her a decade earlier, as if squeezing it tight might somehow transmit down the hall, to her friend, as she suffered through her third hour of emergency surgery.

God... You and me, we don't talk a whole lot because... well, I'm sort of mad at you about how the world is and such. But if y'all would see fit to help Ellie out... She's a good woman, Lord.

She believes in you, and in people... and she's always believed in me. Please... I'm begging you, God, don't let her die.

If Ellie died, she told herself, she was done with God forever. She would be over the notion that any positive force was out there looking out for anyone. There was nothing good in Ellie being hurt, nothing positive anyone would gain from her death.

A figure sat down in the chair next to her. "Margie, hon?"

She looked over. It was Mike, Ellie's husband. "Mike! Did you hear anything? Is she..."

"They don't know yet," he said. "They said she had an infection near the wound, but that they caught it, they think, before it spread to any of the surrounding area or organs. The metal... it lodged in the wall of her small intestine but somehow didn't breach it, which they said was a miracle."

Hear that? He still believes in you, Margie prayed silently. "Did they say when they might know...?"

"By tomorrow, if nothing else goes wrong... possibly."

She felt her heart sinking. She'd hoped when he returned, it would be with an all clear, something definitive. "Ellie tried to talk me out of it, tried to get me to go to the police..."

Mike took the older woman's hand in his. "Margie... Ellie wouldn't have been there if she didn't think it was important. She knows the police won't go looking for someone who's only been gone for a few hours. She knows they wouldn't get involved."

"But when we saw men with guns going into the house that blew up, she said I should stay away..."

"She was probably right," Mike counseled. "But you thought Norm was in there. If I thought Ellie was in harm's way, I'd have gone charging in, too. She'd react that way for me. Margie, you loving Norm isn't to blame for Ellie being hurt. That's on the lunatic who blew up that house."

She nodded and wiped away a tear with her sleeve. "And Bob. If he doesn't show up at our door, none of this happens. Are you okay?"

"I'm holding it together," he said. "That's about it for now. I can't imagine..." He lowered his head. "I can't imagine life without her."

The television on the other side of the waiting room was showing a preview of the late news, images of the burning house, a neighboring home also engulfed in flames, the wind causing havoc.

All that damage. All that pain. And they still had no idea where Norm was. They'd pulled seven bodies from the scene, badly burned. There had been seven men trying to get in. Was the math just convenient... or had the house been empty?

It had to be the latter. Whoever Bob's blackmailer was, he seemed smart enough to trap this man Victor's gang members in the explosion. That suggested he was smart enough not to be there when it happened. No Norm, no more leverage over Bob. So...

He's still alive. I can feel it. Down to her bones, she knew Norm was still out there.

27

Bob whipped the wheel of the Ford subcompact to the left, the frame of the car tipping slightly as it slid into the other lane of Riverside Drive, between two cars, the back end fishtailing.

He was changing lanes rapidly, using any space advantage to beat traffic. Ahead, the exit to the Hernando De Soto bridge was backed up. He slowed the car, the traffic jam forcing a long line of brake lights to flash on.

It was after seven, dusk setting in as the sun neared the horizon. The cars ahead of him slowed to a crawl at idle speed.

Damn it. He couldn't risk Malyuchenko getting too far upstream. There were tributaries, harbors, places where the boat could disappear, or at best be difficult to find.

He pulled the car over in traffic, throwing it into park and grabbing his kit bag from the back seat.

Bob got out and threw the bag's big strap over his shoulder. He began to run, keeping his pace quick but even, heading towards Adams Avenue. He'd checked the map carefully before leaving, making sure he knew an alternate route. There was a monorail station there with an exit onto the pedestrian footbridge across the river.

The sun beat down, a healthy sweat building as he ran the three long blocks. Behind him, the long traffic jam to the exit began to honk, angered by the immobile Ford.

At the station, which doubled as a parking garage for the nearby civic center, a couple were just coming out of the side exit from the stairs. He pushed past them and sprinted toward the second level.

MONROE DROVE NIMBLY, the big truck pushed to the limit, the former soldier moving it from lane to lane, spotting opportunities well before they arrived.

His earpiece mic/receiver crackled to life. "Asset, be advised we have eyes on subject. Traffic cam has a lone male of similar description running from a purple 2005 Ford Focus along Riverside Drive."

"Talk to me, Home," Monroe said, keeping his eyes on traffic. "Where's he going? I'm not local."

"He must have stopped somewhere after the mansion, because he was heading east on Riverside, which is the opposite direction from your current heading. But he's on foot now. He's probably heading for the pedestrian walkway to Mud Island Park. It's a big shortcut."

"They must have a security detail for the walkway and the parking areas. Tip them to a guy with a gun. It might buy me enough time to get ahead of him."

"Roger, will do."

He ended the call and stood on the gas. If he was lucky, he'd be waiting for Singleton when he exited the footbridge.

. . .

BOB TOOK the stairs to the second level two at a time. He threw the door open to the parking level and scanned for the exit to...

There. The pedestrian concourse that crossed over the twin roadway below was just twenty yards or so away. He jogged towards it.

"HALT! Do not move!"

Bob glanced to his right. The security guard was undersized for his uniform. He had a pistol on his hip, but it was holstered. He had a stun gun in his right hand. "This device contains enough electricity to render you immobile. I am effecting a citizen's arrest," the man said. "Take the bag off your shoulder slowly and put it on the ground! DO IT! NOW!"

Bob did as commanded, tossing the bag halfway through the motion directly at the man. The guard instinctively raised his other forearm to block it. Bob was already moving, running after it, leaping into a side kick that slammed into the guard's chest. The smaller man flew backwards into a parked car, bouncing off it forcefully.

He picked up his bag, the guard down and groaning. To his left, he heard another voice. "We've got a man down at the monorail, second floor," a guard was intoning into his shoulder mic. The man unclipped his weapon and drew it, even as Bob sprinted towards him.

The gun came level, and Bob cut left, then right again, zigzagging quickly and unpredictably, making himself difficult to hit. Within ten feet he drew the car keys from his pocket and tossed them, side arm, the guard ducking and throwing up an arm in fear, firing off a wild shot that ricocheted off the concrete ceiling.

Bob hurled himself forward, balling up into a forward roll, ignoring the force of the concrete on his joints, his profile tiny as the guard squeezed off two more shots. He came out of the roll but stayed low, his foot shooting out and in a semicircle, catching the man's legs and unbalancing him, the guard crashing to the ground, the pistol clattering as it skidded away.

Both men scrambled for it, the guard kicking out at Bob as he attempted to climb over the older man. The guard reached back, jamming a thumb into Bob's eye socket. He closed his eye instinctively, just in time, turning his head just enough to bite the guard's thumb, hard.

The man screamed and let go, rolling away. Bob leaped to his feet and kicked out, catching the guard in the face and dazing him.

Across the level, his colleague was staggering to his feet.

Bob picked up the pistol and ejected the mag as he ran across the covered walkway bridge, tossing it out and down to the street below.

He heard the cock of the gun's slide behind him. The second guard had reached the walkway, shots ringing out, a bullet pinging off the concrete floor.

He ignored it and kept running. The man had to be at least thirty feet behind him, the bridge deck nearly a half mile long. There was no percentage worrying about him.

A pair of chatting pedestrians moved aside as he ran past them, one exclaiming something he didn't catch.

Sixty yards ahead, at the exit to the Mississippi River Museum, another guard stepped out of the stairwell.

This time, a weapon was already drawn as Bob

approached. The door opened, and two more came out, both with weapons drawn.

He was losing free space. He had to make a decision.

You can't shoot civilians, Bob. But he couldn't turn and face the other man without moving into easy range, being caught dead to rights.

"HALT! SECURITY. HALT!" The guards ahead yelled. They would've had to be supernatural to hit him moving at that range, he knew; he zigzagged another twenty feet, the guards taking wild shots.

Bob pulled the smoke grenade from his pocket in flight, tossing it overhand.

The guards scrambled, panicking. The smoker blew twenty yards ahead of them, clouds of white haze filling the center of the walkway.

Bob slowed his pace as he entered the fog, squinting against the sting of the acrid cloud. He listened carefully, but could hear no footfalls approaching. They were holding their position.

Damn it. In the smoke, he could've taken them out at close range. Without its cover, he'd emerge a sitting duck. He looked around the long bridge, the haze obscuring his options. He ran over to the side. *How far down...?*

More than a hundred feet.

Diving into the river wasn't an option. He heard footsteps, heels on the concrete behind him. In moments, he knew, he'd be trapped on both sides.

Bob climbed over the right-hand rail. He used the bars to lower himself down until he was hanging from the piping along the rail's bottom edge.

He could see clearly under the bridge. Pipework flanked each side of the dual monorail lines, the cars hanging beneath them, gondola style. He moved carefully hand over hand, then swung slightly outwards, then in, then out again, letting his momentum build. When his body was up to near ninety degrees from the pipe hold, he swung down and out, letting go with his right hand, reaching out and grasping the inner pipe. He pulled hard on it as he let go with his left, giving him the split second of weight differential to grasp the new handhold.

He could see the monorail car ahead, approaching. It had a raised metal guard separating its metal fly wheel and the track from the car's frame. It was a handhold, albeit not a great one.

Insane, he briefly thought. *You're insane. Time this wrong and you're dead meat.*

The car's flywheel squealed as it approached, the sound near deafening. Bob swung his body outwards slightly, letting his return movement carry him towards the monorail line.

He let go of the pipe.

28

The slight drop was momentary, but terrifying, the ground one hundred and eighty-seven feet below.

His hand found the metal edge of the cabling frame. He pulled hard, straining against his own weight with every muscle available as he hung, resting against the carriage's side windows, swinging his left hand quickly around to get a better grip.

The carriages were both empty, the monorail evidently not the draw it perhaps had once been.

But he had more to worry about than being seen. His hands were supporting most of his weight, his toes scrambling frantically to find an edge. The station was just ahead, arms burning, triceps going numb...

His fingers began to slip.

First, it was his left index, then the left middle finger. He hugged the glass of the window. His right index finger slipped off, hands becoming greasy with sweat. His index finger gave... then his ring finger, his body swinging away from the carriage, his left hand unable to take the fullness of his weight as it also slid free, his body falling backwards...

He slammed, back-first, into the concrete at the very end of the station.

By the time the smoke cleared, they would've found the bridge deck empty, likely assumed he jumped over the side, and that no one could survive such a fall. But police would already be on their way.

BOB THREW the door to the stairwell open. He ducked into cover against the wall, a guard walking through the doorway a split second later.

The man spotted him from the corner of his eye and turned, letting off two shots from his pistol. Bob heard the slide click back, the gun's chamber empty. He hurled himself at the man, body weight slamming into the security guard, driving him into the ground, knocking the wind out of him.

The man tried to struggle to his feet; Bob rose quicker, hitting him once with a short, hard shot to the chin, followed by an elbow strike. The guard went down.

He collected the man's pistol, a Smith and Wesson M&P9 in 9mm. He secured it in his left pocket, a good gun that could come in handy if numbers got out of hand.

Bob took the stairs two at a time. They exited into a small parklike area, shade trees surrounding benches, an interpretive wood carving of the site nearby. If he was lucky, the guards on the deck level would already have called police and been told not to engage.

He scanned the area; a few parents were walking with their kids; a man was eating a sandwich on one of the benches. Beyond the park, a building identified itself as the

Memphis Yacht Club. Beside it was a massive display of the river and the states it affected, a giant horizontal map of the Mississippi, carved from wood.

He headed towards it; it made sense that the marina was adjacent.

The movement from the corner of his left eye was barely perceptible, a slip of motion blurring past. Bob's instincts kicked in, and he threw himself into cover, behind another tree's trunk, just as the pistol crack sounded, bullets sinking into the massive map display of the river.

He drew the FN 5.7 and leaned around the tree to return fire but moved back into cover immediately, a bullet taking a two-inch-square chunk of wood out of the trunk of the tree.

From the corner of his eye, he saw civilians running, fleeing the scene, adults yanking the children along so forcefully their feet practically left the ground. The man he'd just seen eating a sandwich sprinted past, using one hand to hold his ball cap on, a terrified expression on his face as he looked over his shoulder.

The noise was a problem. Bob knew he had ten minutes, max, before law enforcement showed. If they were carrying anything heavier than a pistol, he'd be in deep trouble.

The shaded park was circular, with no ability to cover all sides.

But maybe...

Maybe it's one gun. If it were the Russians, I'd know already. They'd be making a ruckus, trying to flank me.

"You know, we could do this all day," he called out. "There's only two of us. We've both got cover. I'm guessing we've both got extra ammo..."

There was no reply.

Okay, so a pro, not a security guard. He thinks his position might be unknown still. Time to divest him of the notion. He turned the other way, around the other side of the trunk, and waited a split second longer before pulling the trigger. The other man popped a few inches out of cover.

Bob took the shot quickly, the report lessened outdoors, his hearing not totally gone.

"HNNNH!" He could hear the other man gritting his teeth about something. "MOTHERFUCKER!"

"Did I wing you?" Bob yelled back. "Sounds like it."

"Splinters," his opponent called back. "You're going to pay for that, Singleton."

He knows my name.

Shit.

That meant either Jerry Perry had friends in town or...

"So who are you supposed to be? Let me guess: you have a funky code name, maybe a Greek letter?"

No answer.

"So not the team. A merc, then? A freelancer?"

Bob snuck a quick peek around the tree. A faint ricochet sound echoed from some distance behind him, and a shot rang out. He ducked back into cover.

The ambush must have been last minute. The gunman probably knew he was headed for the marina. There was no advantage to be gained from trying to outmaneuver or outflank each other. They would, in all likelihood, empty pistols at each other until one party bolted.

He poked a toe out, just enough to catch the guy's line of sight. A single shot sounded.

Yep, that's a pro. The movement caught him out, but he had the discipline to save his ammo.

"We could do this all day," Bob yelled. "Or..."

More silence, for a moment.

Then the voice answered, "Or?"

"Or we toss our pieces out at the same time, and you show me what a big, bad boy you are," Bob suggested. "Come on... I'm supposed to be some sort of legend, according to you people. Tell me you don't want a shot at the brass ring."

A pistol slid across the hard-packed dirt of the seating area.

29

Bob took the guard's Smith and Wesson out of his left pocket. He copied the move.

"Step out on one, okay?" the voice yelled back.

"Okay." Bob drew the FN from his other pocket. He stepped around the opposite side of the tree again and came face-to-face with his target, both men yanking the triggers of their backup weapons as they dove back into cover.

Worth a shot.

He tried to gauge what gun the other man was using. Normally, in the closed environs of a building or shooting range, he'd be able to see it. Or the gun's report would be familiar, narrowing down a maker or model, giving him an idea of how many bullets the man had left.

But his hearing had dulled again, his right ear feeling thick from repeatedly close small explosions, sound from that side reduced to a muffled warble.

"We're going to have company in short order," Bob yelled.

No answer. Bob jutted his pistol out of cover for just a moment. He could hear distant sirens.

No gunshot.

Has he...

"You still there, big man?"

No answer.

He's either moving, trying to get a better angle without me seeing it somehow, or he's backed off. He's gone.

Or...

Or maybe he's just very, very patient.

He had to be careful. This man was wily, looking for advantages. Between crossing the bridge and being caught in a standoff, nearly twenty minutes had passed since he'd left his car. The boat would be long gone, he suspected. But it wouldn't mean anything if he stepped out of cover and someone blew his head off.

Options, Bob. Find another way.

The FN had stopping power, even if it was only a .28 bullet. They used center-fire cartridges, like a rifle, and the muzzle velocity could punch through Kevlar.

How thick is that tree?

It had to be two feet or more, greater than the penetration of the FN slug against a soft target. It was designed to "tumble," end over end, on impact, doing more damage en route, its answer to a soft point. But that wouldn't help against a hard target.

Except...

The tree trunk was a circle. So whenever his opponent ducked around the tree, he moved from its widest point to...

Bob ducked around the tree and fired two bullets into its center. Then he paused and stayed in place, shifting his aim seven inches to the left. A split second later, the shooter glanced around the edge of the tree.

Bob pulled the trigger quickly and smoothly, the FN barely kicking, bullets obliterating the tree's outside edge. He saw an arm fly up, the edge of the man's torso as he staggered backwards and fell over.

He left cover and walked over. The man was lying on his back. He had aviator shades on, a garish shirt, a ball cap a few feet from his head, cargo shorts.

He had three bullet wounds, one to his shoulder, two just above the U neck of his Kevlar vest. He was coughing blood already, a lung punctured or damaged by the tumbling .28 slug.

"You're done," Bob said. "I can finish it quick or leave you for the cops. They might save you, but I doubt it. Probably just a few more hours of pain before you go."

The man tried to talk, coughing his throat clear of blood, a trickle running from the corner of his mouth. He was reaching sideways, blindly, his hand trying to find his pistol.

"D-do it," he muttered.

Bob stood over him. "First, tell me who you are."

"Monroe... Freelance."

"Really? I hate to end things on a sour note, but you're number three this year. Bad career choice." He crouched and looked down at the man's vest, to the dime-sized lens in black plastic clipped to its shoulder strap. "I assume you're his handler, and you're watching this live, whoever you are. Tell Eddie Stone this is never going to end well. We can do this over and over, and it'll end the same way. Just let me be and he has nothing to worry about. Anyone else he sends? Well..."

He rose and shot the man twice in the head. He pocketed

the pistol, turned, and headed cautiously towards the marina.

It was empty. The gunfire was close enough that anyone working there would have scattered or hidden inside, he realized.

It was early evening. Traffic on Memphis's streets would have slowed, the road by the park more passable. The sirens were loud now, getting close.

He heard a car door slam shut, then another. They'd be there imminently.

Bob scanned the row of expensive power boats and larger cabin cruisers. A ski boat with a 175 hp Evinrude outboard motor was bobbing in the shallows at the end of the boat ramp. Whoever had lowered it in from a trailer had obviously taken cover.

"MEMPHIS POLICE!" a voice yelled. "STOP!"

Bob bolted down the ramp. He stripped off his jacket while running, yanking off his shoes by the water's edge. He shouldered his kit bag, then dove into the Mississippi, a strong crawl leading him to the boat's gunwales in a few seconds.

A bullet sliced through the water near him. He looked back as he clambered on board. There were at least eight police officers, crouched, taking aim.

He stayed low as another bullet lodged, with an arrow-like thump, into fiberglass. He crawled to the dash and pilot seat, using a lever to lower the motor, then hitting the ignition. The motor roared, momentarily silencing the crack of pistol shots.

Bob threw the throttle forward. The boat's bow reared up as it sped out of the harbor, towards the Mississippi River.

30

He didn't have long, he knew. The police boat that patrolled the Memphis periphery of the Mississippi would be there soon. The Coast Guard would be alerted to stop him beyond that. Then there was the police chopper to worry about.

At the island's point, he threw the wheel to the right, turning upstream, then gunned the engine, gradually pushing the throttle forward to "full." The wind rippled through his hair, and the hull bounced on whitecaps from its own wake, the boat flying down the murky waterway.

The sun was almost down, visibility decreasing slightly on the vast river ahead.

Downstream, towards the Gulf of Mexico, there were no major tributaries for hundreds of miles.

The Russian would go where he could best hide.

But Bob knew he had one advantage: it was unlikely the bulky cabin cruiser could get above thirty knots. The big Evinrude outboard was paired with an ultralight hull designed to cut through the water at up to fifty knots — fifty-five miles per hour.

A lot depended on Victor Malyuchenko. If he'd taken Jerry Perry's warnings to heart and bolted downstream in the cabin cruiser, he could be a half hour ahead, difficult to catch. If he'd arrogantly spared the engines and cruised off for a few quiet days, Bob knew he still had a chance.

The police chopper picked up his tail just past the city limits.

Bob glanced over his shoulder, the helicopter staying abnormally low and close.

Eurocopter, lower noise from the Fenestron tail rotor.

The chopper could be ignored, for now. It meant eventually he'd need to find an escape route. But for now, it was not a threat. The police loaned it to other agencies, but they weren't going to start shooting at boaters from a moving helicopter.

Ahead, a sweeping curve shifted the river to the northwest, its open surface narrowed by long rock berms jutting out from shore. Boaters had spotted the chopper before it reached them, realized a chase was occurring and had moved off closer to each riverbank.

He turned the boat starboard, towards the southern shore. Ahead, a series of finger-thin islands divided the river into a pair of thinner tendrils.

The boat came into view as he rounded the southernmost island's tip. It was less than a mile ahead, he guessed, but too far to make out the name. Its height suggested a cabin cruiser. The speedboat was gaining quickly, which meant they hadn't seen him yet.

Above, a muffled roar sounded from the chopper's loudspeaker, police commanding him to pull over, as far as he could tell.

Bob ignored him. They weren't going to fire on him with no one else aboard and no one at risk.

"PULL OVER!" the loudspeaker demanded.

Ahead, on the cabin cruiser, a figure moved to the rear lower deck.

He didn't have more than a split second to react. The shoulder-mounted rocket roared off the deck of the cabin cruiser before he could blink.

Bob threw the wheel over to the left, the boat carving a hard turn, kicking up a wall of water in its wake, like some kind of manic surfer. The grenade flew past, exploding somewhere behind him, water spraying a circular shower for hundreds of feet.

To his left, he saw a second boat coming up fast, from behind the island, gaining on the big yacht. It had a gray hull and looked part inflatable until it got closer, its profile low to the water, the bow's edges rounded to cut water resistance.

Transportable Port Security Boat, maybe thirty-five feet stem to stern.

An array of radar antennae and satellite dishes sat atop the cabin.

It was trying to keep pace with him as its crew tried to yell at him to slow down. *They're maxed on speed.* Both vessels were gaining quickly on the cabin cruiser, but the security boat couldn't reach Bob's craft or cut him off, nor could the powerboat outpace it, not by enough to make a difference.

The sun dropped below the horizon, evening settling in. A flash of orange light ahead of him told him the RPG launcher had been fired again, and he swerved suddenly, taking something off the throttle, the Coast Guard pursuer rocketing ahead, Bob's boat pulling in behind it as the grenade blew another geyser of water into the air.

On the Coast Guard vessel, he could see a man at the stern aiming a deck gun towards the larger vessel downstream.

They were too far away for effective return of fire.

The Coast Guard vessel stayed just ahead of him. They couldn't slow down, he knew, without risking a collision. They had no speed to spare, and a vessel ahead of them launching attacks.

"STAND DOWN!" the speaker on the Coast Guard TPSB blared towards the big yacht. "DISENGAGE YOUR MOTOR, STAND DOWN AND SURRENDER YOUR VESSEL!"

Bob threw the wheel to the right and gunned the motor again, slamming the throttle ahead. The speedboat shot forward, drawing even with, then passing the Coast Guard vessel. He hadn't shown a weapon or shot at them, and the agent on the prow, kneeling, pistol at the ready, was showing considerable restraint.

The cabin cruiser was losing ground quickly, perhaps just a hundred meters ahead. He could see a figure near the stern, followed by a staccato muzzle flash in the evening gloom. Bullets raked the water around him, and Bob ducked low as one smashed through the bow storage. There was no percentage in firing back, just wasted ammunition.

He stayed in a low crouch as he steered, not worrying about the water ahead, trying to concentrate on his balance as the boat bounced off rough wake. He made sure he steered the rudder wide as the speedboat reached and began to pass the cabin cruiser.

A man in a black suit appeared at the rail, swinging the muzzle of an MP5 his way.

Bob braced the FN 5.7 against the center speed console, using it as a makeshift tripod, keeping his aim steady even as the boat bounced along. He timed his shot to the bounces, firing twice as the boat came down, aiming center mass, the first halting the man's progress, the second blowing off his right ear, the gunman pirouetting to the lower deck in a spastic collapse, clutching the wound.

Another gunman appeared in his place. Bob fired twice, the man ducking out of sight almost immediately.

Along the lower cabin of the cruiser, just above the waterline, Bob saw a curtain slide back, Malyuchenko's face visible for just a moment.

That answers whether he's on board.

It also made his options easier to parse. He didn't need to shoot Malyuchenko to get the job done.

"SURRENDER YOUR VESSEL, OR WE WILL OPEN FIRE!" The security boat had drawn even with the other side of the cabin cruiser. They had a second machine gun mounted to the front of the boat. The RPG had been a step too far.

He heard automatic weapons, someone on the top deck firing over the other side of the cruiser, towards the Coast Guard pursuer. The Coast Guard's big gun answered back, 105mm shells perforating the upper cabin, a body tumbling to the lower deck.

The Russian was in trouble, Bob realized. *Does he know it? Will he try to get out somehow?*

That couldn't be allowed to happen.

IN THE LUXURY cabin of the Galeon 640 *Spirit of Memphis*,

Victor Malyuchenko was quickly losing what little grasp on sanity he retained.

He paced the cabin, a Glock 19 gripped in his right hand.

Where is Jerry Perry? Why are police all over us? Where is Jerry Perry!? Why is everything going wrong?!

It was the girl's fault.

It had to be.

Ever since he had taken her in, like a lost bird that needed his love, she had been conspiring against him, he realized. She had pushed Alexi to madness, so that he could not accept them together. She had warped his friend's mind. Then she had done the same to him. It was the only possible solution. It could not be his own decisions, he knew, because he was a self-made man, a success, a powerful leader and a genius.

It had to be deception. Betrayal.

That was it, wasn't it? *They are all out to betray you, to take your money, to rob you of your power and reputation.*

The cabin galley door burst open, Artur running in, his shirtsleeves rolled up, breathless.

"Boss, we have to—" He was cut off, both men ducking to the floor as machine-gun fire raked the cabin, bullets perforating the walls high up, near the ceiling, in a jagged line.

"Boss, we have to get out of here! We have to run, try to escape the Coast Guard!"

Victor saw the look of fear on the man's face, eyes full of panic. He felt a surge of disgust well up within him. He pushed himself to his feet and shot Artur twice in the chest.

The henchman lay on his back, moaning, clutching at the wounds. "Boss... you... you shot me..."

"You are despicable worm, Artur. You work with them, probably, to take me down, *da*? We are powerful, strong. We have RPG, we have many guns, and you wish to run like coward..."

"We are overwhelmed..." Artur sputtered.

"WE ARE STRONG!" Victor bellowed. "I am Victor Ivanovich Malyuchenko, son of Ivan Feodorovich Malyuchenko, A COLONEL IN THE KGB, AND GRANDSON OF PIOTR IVANOVICH MALYUCHENKO, HERO OF THE PEOPLE'S REVOLUTION!"

He took a deep breath in, calming himself momentarily. "And you are nothing but dog."

He shot Artur through the chest once more, then walked to the cabin door, the bounce on the choppy river water momentarily wobbling his gait. "If you want something done right, old rule is correct: do it yourself."

He pushed through the galley doors, river spray hitting him as he walked out into the open air. He mounted the red-carpeted steps to the deck carefully. Ahead and to his left, his bodyguard and occasional driver, Tony K, had the RPG on his shoulder, about to fire off another shot.

Victor strode over to him. "Give me that," he demanded.

He turned quickly and knelt in one smooth motion, the RPG balanced on his shoulder. He used the long sight, the trigger depressed as soon as he was on target, the grenade streaking off, its rocket driving it into the pursuing chopper. The pilot must have seen the grenade flare, as he was already backing off the copter's collective, tilting the blades back to catch air, pulling it up and away from the boat.

But it was too late.

The grenade slammed into the cockpit bubble, driving through it at 964 feet per second, exploding a split second later from contact, the craft's fuel blowing with it, a gigantic fireball lighting the night, debris raining down behind them and across the blackness of the Mississippi.

BOB SAW the rocket streak outward from the boat, Malyuchenko's face illuminated for a bare moment in the orange flow of its jet flame, the Russian grinning maniacally. The chopper crew had no chance, the grenade blowing it from the air like an overcooked firework, the explosion fifty yards behind them but the heat palpable.

Debris from the chopper rained down.

The police officers in that chopper had nothing to do with their fight, Bob knew, no stakes except trying to keep the peace.

This can't go on. This has to end, now.

He used one hand to brace himself against the center console, counteracting the turbulent river; he reached down as the boat bounced along, and rummaged in the kit bag until he found Ramirez's little present.

The old claymore mine was about the size of a baseball base, wrapped in a small rusting metal frame, a round metal pad on one side connected to the container by a short coil of thick wire.

He pulled the boat closer to the Cruiser, staying low as one of the Russian's men opened fire once more. He overhanded the mine, aiming for the cabin entrance, their combined momentum shearing it in an arc, the mine thudding to the lower deck.

But it didn't blow.

Damn it.

Ramirez had warned him that its stubby pressure plate attachment might be defunct. It was a forty-year-old relic from Southeast Asia, after all. He'd been sure the charge was good, though.

The boat bounced hard, twice.

Nothing.

Damn it. It's a dud.

Bob looked up and saw the sandbar ahead. He yanked the wheel of the powerboat to port, the vessel cutting in hard again behind the cruiser. Bullets shattered the windshield, and he ducked.

The Coast Guard had not given up. "CREW OF THE *SPIRIT OF MEMPHIS*, TURN OFF YOUR ENGINE AND SURRENDER YOUR VESSEL!" the loudspeaker ordered. The boat's machine gun raked the cruiser's hull one more time, a spotlight illuminating the target vessel's deck. The men shooting at Bob turned their attention to their right, firing back at the government craft.

Bob rose, standing side on, bracing the FN against the windshield support strut as his other hand guided the throttle, keeping him two boat lengths behind the *Spirit of Memphis*. He aimed for the mine on the deck, the first bullet pinging wide, the second long. The vessel bounced on the third shot, and it went wide.

This is impossible, damn it! Come on, Bob, get it right, damn you...

On the cabin cruiser's deck, Malyuchenko strode towards the port rail, ignoring the Coast Guard's barrage as if invincible. He had a second RPG on his shoulder.

If he fires on them from there...

The RPG would blow the patrol boat out of the water at less than thirty feet, Bob knew, killing its crew.

He turned his fire on Malyuchenko, squeezing off four more rounds in quick succession.

The Russian realized he was being flanked and dropped back to one knee, for balance.

Bob ejected the magazine, reaching down into the kit bag for a spare, finding only one remaining.

Last twenty. Law of numbers, make 'em count. He turned his aim back to the claymore, unloading the clip towards it, missing again and again and...

A bullet hit the old landmine, the blast immediate and ferocious, a ball of orange flame spreading outwards; the boat's fuel tanks caught, its ballast tanks immediately superheated to hundreds of degrees, the pressure ripping its hull apart, Victor Malyuchenko roasted alive on the lower deck before he even had time to scream.

Bob had underestimated the explosion, a corridor of orange flame shooting backwards towards his vessel. He threw himself sideways, just clearing the boat's hull, as he plunged into the murky Mississippi.

31

The river water was cold, impenetrably dark, a rumble from the surface above echoing around him as something else blew up.

Bob jammed the pistol into his belt and kicked off, aiming towards what felt like the direction of the shore.

He could feel the heat from the burning debris as he neared the surface, even dozens of yards away.

He popped above the water and looked around quickly. Thankfully, he was closer to shore. There was smoke, burning wood and the now upended frame of the cruiser, slowly sinking beneath the waves.

There was no sign of the speedboat. He assumed it had blown right after the cruiser, the sound he'd heard under water. The Coast Guard vessel had slowed to a slow drift, its spotlight tracing careful paths across the surface as the crew searched for survivors. Judging by the debris and burning oil, Bob thought, there was nothing left of the smaller vessel.

A spotlight swung across the debris pile and towards his position. He took a deep breath and ducked below the water again, using a breaststroke to head for shore, surfacing every fifteen or twenty strokes for air.

The riverbed seemed to rush towards him as the water shallowed, reeds and rushes crowding the water's edge. He crawled up the muddy bank and lay on his back, letting the cool night air refresh him, his muscles and joints aching, adrenaline giving way to raw fatigue.

The cicadas in the nearby trees trilled loudly, drawing attention away from the fainter sounds of the Coast Guard boat's engine.

He felt small pricks of pain on his back and legs. He righted himself and rose to his knees. He pulled the leeches off quickly, chucking them to one side.

The spotlight hit the shore, thirty feet or so to his left. Bob scrambled away from the bank, finding cover behind a bush.

Ahead of him, fields of crops led towards a horizon speckled by the odd light from homes. Wherever he was, it was well out of the city. He stayed low as he headed towards the field. Soybeans maybe?

The soil under his feet mushed between his toes.

He knew he had a difficult night ahead.

Police would have a description of him, at the least, from the cameras around Mud Island Park. His wallet and keys had been in his jacket, which had gone down with his kit bag, along with his shoes.

He had a few hundred dollars stored in the motel room, two hundred stashed in his belt's secret pocket.

No jacket, no shoes, no reservations.

He'd need to find and boost a car, get back to Memphis quickly.

He half expected Alexi to renege on their deal, try to kill

both him and Norm O'Hearn. The man's insane gambit at the house had nearly killed Ellie Grainger. Any number of civilians could have been killed, and he hadn't hesitated.

He would try to honor the bargain, exchange Norm for the girl.

But he suspected that, like Victor Malyuchenko, Alexi's time had come.

32

The Dorchester Club was quiet. Monday nights were always slow, with fewer customers and staff. But the balcony that overlooked DC was inviting, bathed in a warm breeze and soft light.

CIA Deputy Director Andrew Kennedy sat in a padded deck chair, its back slightly reclined. He gripped the Cuban Cohiba cigar between his lips. He flicked his diamond-studded Colibri cigar lighter, the spark insufficient to the task in the evening breeze.

"Damn it," he muttered. His favorite Cognac, Remy Martin 1874, just wasn't the same without a good cigar.

A hand extended past him, striking a match on the wooden armrest of his chair. The match sparked to life, and the hand guided it over, holding it next to the fat cylinder of dark tobacco. He puffed hard, the tip catching, tobacco turning to embers.

"You never know when you'll need someone to have your back," Eddie Stone said as he shook the life out of the match and tossed the matchstick into the ashtray next to Kennedy. "I've always subscribed to that theory."

He walked past Kennedy and leaned against the balcony rail, looking out at the lights of the Capitol buildings, the pale glow of the Washington Monument, its pyramid tip reaching high into the night sky. "I've also always been sure we had each other's backs."

They both knew that wasn't true, not completely. But an agreement of sorts? Mutual aid and appreciation? Sure.

"You know I always will," Kennedy said, and they knew that was a lie, also.

"Then please… tell me what's going on."

"Specifically?"

"Andrew…"

Kennedy took another puff on the cigar, then wiggled it between his middle and ring fingers, admiring the cherry glow. "We had a short window…"

"We agreed that the Team was my domain, my responsibility. We agreed that you would remain hands off. The political rationale, in terms of deniability, hasn't changed. And my advice to you was that we let Bob Singleton go, that he wouldn't be a problem. That he just wants out."

"Your conclusion?" Kennedy asked, knowing Stone would share it either way.

"Singleton has you scared of something. Something bigger than the botched Iran missions. That information… it's been out there in one form or another for fifteen years."

"Not that we knew. We thought it was contained."

"A handful of dead agents and the legacy of a blown mission do not equate to the kind of 'crisis' that requires risking Team Seven's operational status…" Stone crossed his arms, his expression stern.

"Which is why I used a single operative in Memphis."

"He's dead."

Kennedy hung his head, contemplating the news for a moment. "When?"

"About an hour ago. Singleton sent us a message via Monroe's body armor."

"He would; he always had a flair for the dramatic."

"He told me he'll kill anyone we send after him but that we have nothing to fear from him if we leave him alone."

"And you believe that?"

"I do," Stone said. "Bob's nothing if not honorable. He's draped in the shit, to the point that pragmatism can take a back seat."

"And yet you promoted him to Alpha," Kennedy said, regaining a measure of control in the discussion.

"That was a long time ago. Andrew, Earl Monroe was one of the nastiest mercs we had on call."

"He failed," Kennedy interrupted bluntly.

"He was destined to!" Stone retorted. "Yet you ordered me to send him anyway. That was foolish. You know how resourceful Singleton is, how many times he's faced down someone trying to kill him…"

Kennedy got up from his chair and wandered over to the rail, standing just a few inches from his colleague. "Eddie, I've never had to remind you that, ultimately, I make the final call. If you don't like the game…"

"Don't change the rules midway…"

"… then we'll respect the fact that you're past retirement age and working on extension, and find someone who—"

Stone shoved the older man in the shoulder. "Will you shut the fuck up! We've had each other's backs for four decades. You're no more getting rid of me — with what I know — than I could survive without you. But it works best when you don't hand me a line of bullshit, when you keep me in the loop. Singleton is an enormous pain in both our asses, and a potential problem for any number of reasons I already know about. But there's something else going on here..."

"There is nothing else going on. I just don't want the team's reputation so thoroughly dragged through the mud that it can't survive. Am I clear? We need to take him down eventually, whether we do it with a single operative..."

"That went well."

"Or the whole team."

"Also a bad idea. I propose a third option."

That was why Kennedy liked Stone so much. Even when he wasn't offering sober judgment, his tactical sense was second to none.

"Go ahead."

"A freelancer, sure. But a pricey one, a real hitter, not a merc or former agent."

"An assassin."

"Someone who doesn't fail. I'm talking dozens of title defenses, no defeats."

"Hmm. Expensive," Kennedy said. "Risky. Outsiders knowing agency business..."

"We'd hire him through a front. I have a guy in mind already. We've used him before, in Panama..."

Kennedy's eyes narrowed as he cast his mind back to the nineties. "The South African, Van Kamp?"

"The very same."

"He was a convenience back then, already in-country and closest to the target."

"He's run up an impressive CV since. A couple of heads of state, numerous political opposition leaders."

"What's his thing again? Stiletto?"

"Garrote. He had a necklace he used to use, some weird fucking backstory about his policeman father strangling his mother with it when he was five."

"Yeah, that guy. Charming. Jesus H..."

"He's still batting a thousand, though, Andrew."

"I assume he charges a fortune."

"Two million, most expensive on the planet. But he claims he can hit anyone."

Kennedy shut his eyes tight so that he could massage the bridge of his nose with his thumb and forefinger. Two million dollars probably didn't seem like much to the average government military procurement agent; but when a covert department branch spent it without explanation, even people who looked the other way got nervous.

"That's a lot of money. That's the sort of payment that makes congressional committee members ask questions."

"Like I said, we'll hide it. A front company, something offshore in the Channel Islands or Panama."

"And where do we tell him to start? Memphis?"

Stone shook his head. "No. No, not Memphis. Whatever he's up to there, the whole gangster thing seems a sideline, the kind of idiot task Singleton gets caught up in because of his white knight syndrome."

"Then where?"

"That's the million-dollar question. Where is he going? What is he up to? Is he on a specific mission? Or is he just doing what he said and going to ground? If we project that he's moving west after something, maybe we can figure out what, and where. As far as we know, his direct family are all dead."

"Dig deeper. If there's someone there he needs to visit or see and we make it ahead of him, or without him knowing he's still a target..."

"Oh... Singleton will always expect the worst and plan for it," Stone said.

"Then give it to him. Contact your cleaner and put him on alert. On past evidence, he won't stay in Memphis long. But eventually, he'll surface again."

KENNEDY TOOK the elevator from the Dorchester Club on the eighth floor, down to the street, where his limousine was waiting.

Or, where it had been waiting. When the building's automatic doors slid open, his car was gone.

In its place was a stretch Lincoln, also black.

The back door opened.

Kennedy approached the car and peered inside.

"We need to have a quick talk, I understand. I sent your driver home."

Benjamin Usmanov was eighty, at least. The political fixer was tall and thin, with heavyset features and a crown of dark gray hair. A young, beefy bodyguard occupied the jump seat ahead of him. Usmanov patted the bench. "Come, Andrew, sit and talk."

Kennedy checked the street twice. Even though it was nearly eleven, being seen with Usmanov had potential ramifications. He climbed in quickly, and the bodyguard shut the door behind him.

"As delightful as it always is to chat with you, Benjamin,

your reputation these days should preclude this sort of public get-together…"

"We have no clear past history, and I am well known for lobbying the intelligence industry…" Usmanov suggested.

"You are well known in the Beltway for advancing Russian interests here. In the old days, we had a different word for it…"

"And yet 'spy' is so inelegant and inexact," Usmanov replied.

"I'd suggest you're lucky to have so many friends in DC, but I'm sure luck has nothing to do with it. Not when leverage and charm are available."

The businessman smiled at that. "You are always refreshingly direct, Andrew. It saves time. I'm hearing rumors that old business has reared its head. That mess with Kenneth Dahlen…"

"Gerald. Ken was his father."

Usmanov's eyes flitted about momentarily, a slight embarrassment at the mix-up. "Of course. Names… you know, at my age… Still… that did not go well."

"It was a blackmail gambit by one of his former employees," Kennedy lied. "Dahlen told them he was 'Brighteyes' and made his first fortune by betraying his country. The man tried to leverage it, and Dahlen killed him. There wasn't much else Eddie could do but try to arrest him."

"Hmm. Be that as it may… I would feel most assured to know that no one out of our collective past will be making any more surprise appearances."

"I think you can be confident," Kennedy said. "You know me: always bluntly realistic."

"I certainly hope so. Tehran brought us together and made us both a lot of money. The fruits of our working relationship have extended to a world of positive political changes around the globe. You're helping us to reshape the world in the manner it should be. You're helping to keep the right people in control."

Kennedy smiled politely but said nothing. His gaze drifted to the crystal brandy decanter in the center console, the bottle of century-old Laphroaig in the ice bucket, Usmanov's platinum-and-diamond pinkie ring. They were the trappings of wealth, not devotion to a social cause; of greed and venality, not selflessness and public service.

But Kennedy also knew he liked the soft Italian cowhide seats, the suits that cost more than a kid's college fund. That kind of life, that comfort, could make any man a little flexible when it came to how the good fight was fought.

He wanted a better world. He just wanted to get and stay as rich as possible while doing it.

Usmanov knew way too much but was also powerful, connected to Russian politicians, military men and organized crime figures. Eventually, he might have to treat him with the same care and attention as Singleton... and take him off the board.

But for now, no one who knew anything had any vested interest in talking about the past.

The limo finished the short journey to Kennedy's luxury condo building. It came to a halt at the curb. "Don't be a stranger, Andrew," the Russian businessman advised, as his man opened the car's back door.

33

Bob drove cautiously, keeping to the speed limit, signaling properly, doing nothing that might arouse police attention.

The stolen car had been liberated from a driveway in Dixonville, a hamlet twenty minutes out of town. There was no reason to think it would be missed until morning, and it was nearly eleven o'clock at night. He'd leave a hundred dollars under the driver's side visor, in the pocket with its insurance papers.

At Riverside Drive, he discovered the Ford had been towed away. That wasn't surprising, given the traffic jam it had caused. He'd have to get it back for Margie, he knew, or at least pay her back the fees.

He stopped at a Walmart, getting stares from the "greeter" at his disheveled condition. "Men's clothes?"

She pointed him to a back corner of the store. A T-shirt and sneakers would suffice for now, he decided.

He left the stolen car in the store's lot and hiked the

remaining two blocks to the hospital. A police cruiser was parked outside the emergency unit's main doors.

There was no one in the cruiser, which meant they were inside.

Damn it. They're here to question Margie about Ellie.

As far as he knew, his real identity was unknown to the Memphis Police Department. Unlike New Orleans, where he'd been singled out by civilians as present, the gangsters he'd been facing had no real interest in talking to police.

But his description was out there from the shoot-out at the park. There would be another description offered by officers after the boat chase. If he just walked in, he knew, there was a high chance one of the officers in the hospital would match it with the image they'd broadcast.

Outside the ICU doors, a man was about to enter. He looked nondescript in a tan jacket and Detroit Tigers ball cap. He was carrying a bouquet of wildflowers.

Bob hailed him with a raised hand. "Hey! My apologies and all that stuff... You visiting family?"

The man sighed a little. "Sure, technically..."

"Technically?"

"My mother-in-law had an emergency appendectomy. So..."

"Your wife's in there, expecting you to come back with flowers."

"Yeah..." His expression shifted to suspicion. "Look... I have to go..."

"Just... hang on a sec there," Bob asked. "I'll make you an offer for the flowers and your hat."

The man squinted at him. "My... I mean, they're not for me, like I said, they're..."

"Yeah, yeah, but you can get more if I give you enough cash, right? You just have to walk back to whatever store..."

"Just the grocery store down the street. I mean... I guess..." The line about cash had him intrigued.

"Here." Bob handed him a hundred dollars from his belt stash. "I'll give you a hundred bucks for both."

"Sold," the man said, taking the damp cash without hesitation. Then he paused warily. "You know... you could just go down the street yourself. I didn't see any ball caps, but they definitely had more flowers..."

"That's fine. It's sort of a timing thing," Bob said.

The man shrugged. "It's your money."

Bob handed it over. The man passed him the Tigers cap and the flowers.

"Pleasure doing business with you... I guess," the man said. "I... have to go get more flowers..." He turned back towards the lot and headed that way.

Bob put the ball cap on, pulling the brim down as low as it would comfortably go. If he kept his head down, it would trick people out of matching his facial shape and general similarity to the artist's rendition.

He walked into the Emergency unit through the sliding doors. Its waiting area was three-quarters full. The faces were nervous and tired, families waiting to hear word. Near the corridor to the unit proper, a man sat with his arm suspended, held aloft by his other hand, the limb covered in cuts and embedded pieces of glass.

Bob headed to the nurses' station. "Ellie Grainger's room?" he asked.

The nurse scribbled something on the document she was reading, then looked up. "Sir... it's eleven thirty at night. Visiting hours were over at nine..."

"I'm not staying," Bob said. "I just need to drop off these flowers and some keys to one of her family members who's waiting for word from surgery."

She checked her registry patient sheet. "Mrs. Grainger is out of surgery and resting in room two-twenty-nine of the ICU. You can leave those here, and we'll make sure…"

"Nope," Bob said, standing up straight and shaking his head. "I don't get paid for the delivery unless I hand it to Mr. Grainger in person," he said. "Look, I can't afford to eat the cost of this. I have rent to pay. It'll be twenty seconds of interaction, I promise…"

The nurse looked annoyed. "As I said, sir, if you just leave them, I promise…"

"No!" he interjected. "Uh-uh. I'll lose my job. All deliveries in person, no excuses. It's a guarantee."

She glared at him grimly. But she leaned to her right and stared down the corridor, perhaps determining if there was anyone present who was likely to get her into trouble. "Okay, just a minute. I'm watching the clock," she ordered, pointing to the wall clock with her pencil.

Bob hurried down the hall. He turned right, following the wall chart and arrows pointing to her room.

He stopped dead. Outside the room, a police officer was questioning Margie, jotting down her responses in a palm-sized notepad. His back was to Bob.

Shit.

Just past them, a man sat with a morose expression. Bob waved at him to approach, then ducked back around the corner of the corridor.

A moment later, the morose man appeared. "Were you trying to signal me…"

"Are you Mike?"

The man nodded.

"I'm Bob."

He nodded again. "I figured. Are you the cause of all of this?"

"I'm sorry for what happened to your wife."

Mike shot him an angry look. "You're SORRY?! Ellie is clinging to life, and I can't even see her..."

"I told them to stay away, to not engage the guy who took Norm."

He looked Bob up and down, his trousers muddy, a jacket zipped almost all the way up but a clump of chest hair suggesting he had no shirt on underneath. "Jesus... what happened to you, anyway? You look like shit."

"I had an incident in the river."

"An... Never mind, I don't care. Better you'd drowned. You're the reason they took him in the first place, according to Margie. Why should I believe a goddamned word you tell me? In fact, maybe you'd better tell me why I shouldn't go right around that corner and grab that officer and tell him he needs to arrest someone."

"Because if you do that, Norm is dead. Period. End of."

He looked away, clearly trying to restrain his temper.

"What do you want, Bob? You didn't just stop by for a visit because you're a caring individual."

"I need you to pass a message to Margie." Bob outlined what had happened to the car. "I expect police are going to assume it was tied to the shooting there. I ditched it some ways from the intersection, so it's unlikely any traffic cameras have a clear image. Her best bet is going to be telling them she fled when she heard gunshots. It's what a civilian might do."

"Okay. What about the guy who hurt Ellie?" Mike asked.

"What happens to him? Tell me what you're doing about him."

"First, I source a new set of wheels. Then I go after him."

He thought about that for a minute. "Norm and Margie are salt of the earth. They didn't deserve any of this. If you hadn't visited…"

"I know."

"So get him back. Take care of this guy, sure, whatever. I don't care about a bunch of criminals I don't even know, Bob. I do want my wife back, and my friend."

"I'll do what I can."

"No, do more than you can if that's what it takes. Do whatever impossible version of a hundred and ten percent is required to fix this. Then fuck off out of all of our lives. That's what I'd like, 'Bob.'"

The contempt in his voice stung. "I didn't intend for any of this," Bob tried to explain. "I just stopped in town to pick up something…"

"Ellie… my wife, she's always been the most evenhanded, sensible woman I ever knew. We have grown kids, you know, and she made sure they were going to be successful and happy no matter what the world threw at us. She'd probably tell you to just let it go, Bob, let this dude have his gang war, let the police find Norm. She'd see you as some sort of victim in this, because she thinks the best of everybody."

"Mike…"

"Look where it got her, being charitable towards you. She always avoided trouble, selfish choices. So it's not like she'd be speaking from experience. I was the one who got in trouble when we were young, and my instinct? My instinct says you're as much of a dick as they are. It also says you should find the guy who took Norm and hurt my wife. You should find him, and you should fucking kill him. Am I clear on where I stand?"

"You are."

"You said you need wheels." Mike dug into his pocket and withdrew a set of keys. "It's a black BMW in section GG, plate DDC 1213. Try not to destroy it… and go fix this before your selfish bullshit gets any more good people hurt."

34

June-Marie lay on the bed, despondent, chest down, her chin propped up by her left arm as she watched TV.

The movie was garbage, another "modern" western more concerned with whom the characters were sleeping with than any kind of story or tension.

She turned her head left to look at the old-fashioned digital alarm clock by the bed.

11:45 at night, and still no sign of this dude.

Why? What did I do to scare him off? I was polite. I was open. I was six damn degrees of desperate. But instead, I'm chained to this damn bed...

She shook the wrist restraint again, the thick, rubbery plastic turning slightly on the bed frame but in no danger of freeing her. "Damn it."

She thought back to when he'd left. What had he said? *If I let you go and I'm wrong...* something about hedging his bets.

Bastard. I appealed to his decency. He ignored me completely, just like Victor.

At least he hadn't taken her money. That meant he didn't know for sure; he didn't know that the trap had been her idea, that Alexi would've still been staying there if she hadn't warned him.

She'd watched Bob pack his kit bag carefully, to make sure he wasn't trying to sneak anything by her. But there'd been no sign of her money, which meant, she assumed, it was still in the bathroom, in her case.

Instead, he'd stuffed a few items into the bag she didn't recognize and what looked like some pistol magazines. He'd left a few things on top of the bureau: a map of Austin, Texas, a black baseball cap. Then he'd...

She paused. He'd done something else. What was it?

She retraced Bob's steps when he'd arrived. He'd bent down on walking into the room.

He bent down, and... he opened the bottom drawer of the bureau.

He'd stored something, she realized.

June-Marie turned her head the other way, towards the chest of drawers along the far wall, about six feet away. She peered down at the drawer he'd opened.

It seemed out of reach. She looked down at her right arm cuffed to the bed frame, trying to imagine, if she could turn around and face the other way, how far her left arm could stretch...

It wouldn't be easy, but...

She scrambled to her knees and shuffled to the end of the bed, turning a half circle to face the other way as she climbed over the footboard. She reached her left hand out towards the low-slung drawer knob.

June-Marie stretched as hard as she could, until her right shoulder felt like it might dislocate from the joint. Her fingertips were just about there, just grazing the knob, feather touches.

She took a break, relaxing, exhaling heavily.

Don't give up, June-Marie. You can do this, girl...

She reached out again, leaning as far left as she could, then pushing hard, middle finger reaching the knob's upper edge, dragging at it, trying to get enough purchase to move it...

Her finger slipped off, the sudden lack of resistance prompting her to slap the floor, short of her target.

"FUCK!"

There has to be a way...

Her right shoulder ached. She tilted her head and studied the knob again. It protruded a solid half inch from the wood behind it. June-Marie shifted from her knees to her backside, shunting herself to the left until her right arm was at full stretch once more. But instead of her left arm, she leaned back, using her weight shift to balance her core, extending her left leg out towards the knob.

Her toe found the space behind it. She pulled back gradually, expecting the sudden jump as it first began to slide open. She drew her knee up and in, giving her enough room to pull the drawer free from its slides.

It thumped onto the carpet, bottom first.

At the back end of the drawer, she could see a black object. She squinted to get better focus, cursing her vanity towards wearing glasses.

Is that...

Is that a gun!?

Had he found it while hunting for his friend? Was he holding it for someone?

It didn't really matter. June-Marie knew what she needed to do.

She stretched her leg out again, catching the top edge of the drawer's side panel. She dragged it back towards her slowly.

The drawer caught on the carpet. She strained to move it, but it wouldn't give. June-Marie kicked down hard with her heel, the drawer's far end bouncing up off the carpet. She was breathing hard, the effort considerable. She kicked down again, trying to pin the side of the drawer to the carpet. It flipped directly onto its side, spilling the gun out onto the soft surface.

From outside, she heard a car door slam.

No!

Not now, not when I'm this close...

She stretched out again with her socked foot, the material making it hard to grip the smooth metal of the pistol, her foot just sliding over it again and again. "NO!"

She wanted to cry. *I'm so close...*

She heard footsteps on the concrete walkway outside the room door. June-Marie stretched one more time, her big toe finding the trigger guard. She yanked her foot back furiously, not wanting to risk losing her grip. The Colt 1911 pistol skipped backwards, bouncing to just within reach.

Keys entered the door lock.

Her hand found the grip.

The door swung open.

June-Marie swung the pistol around.

"Shit," Bob said.

"Damn straight," June-Marie said.

35

Bob began to turn back towards the door. The key was not to do anything too surprising.

"DON'T YOU MOVE!" June-Marie yelled. She looked him up and down. He was bedraggled, shirt gone, trousers smeared with dirt. "Shit... You look like shit. DON'T MOVE!"

He froze in place. "Fine. What next?"

"Undo these goddamn cuffs right goddamn now!"

He walked over and crouched.

"Slowly!" she cautioned. "If you try anything weird, I will shoot you, I swear to God."

"Have you ever shot anyone before?" Bob asked.

"No."

"It's not that easy."

She reached out and raised the gun to his head height. "My understanding is that if I point it at your face and pull the trigger repeatedly, that'll do it. So... also not that complicated."

He took his keys out of his jacket pocket and undid the

cuffs. "That's a Colt 1911 in .45 caliber," Bob said as he undid the cuff latches. "Just watch out when you pull that trigger, as it'll be tighter than you expect and the kick... well... you're not a big person."

She shook the cuff off her right arm and crept backwards off the bed, keeping him in front of her the entire time. "Don't try to follow me!" she commanded.

June-Marie ran over to the door, opened it and ran out.

Bob didn't move.

A few moments later, as expected, she ran back into the room.

"MY FUCKING KEYS!" she bellowed. "Where are my fucking car keys?!"

He nodded towards the dresser. She looked that way. A set of keys sat atop it, next to the television. She scrambled over to it, snatched them, then backed away to the door. She paused there for a moment, an angry snarl on her face, looking at Bob as if she might shoot him just out of spite.

Then she turned and ran out of the room.

Bob stood there, unmoving. "Five, four, three, two..."

The door flew open, and she ran back inside. "My money," she said. "Get it from the bathroom."

He walked over and retrieved the suitcase from under the sink. He took it into the other room.

"Ah! Just... just put it down a few feet ahead; then y'all scoot over by the bed there."

She kept her eyes on him throughout as she retrieved the suitcase. "You'd better not have..."

"I don't want your money," he said bluntly.

She turned and fled the room.

Bob gave her a five count to get into the car. He picked up his soft-sided travel bag from the bureau, jogged to the door and out into the lot. He got into the BMW and started the engine, eyes on the Dodge Shadow's taillights as it left the property.

He stepped on the gas lightly, making sure he was on Kentucky Street in time to see her car's lights turn right at the next intersection.

The key to following someone without support vehicles was not to stand out. That meant a minimum of lane changing, instead letting the distance between both cars increase and decrease smoothly, as if paying no attention to her speed or heading. If the Team had been tracking her, they'd have used three or four cars, he knew, traded off, sped ahead of her to make it clear they were unconnected, even as another trailer picked up her tail.

But he had no such luxury. The BMW, however, was unknown to her, a boxy black sedan. And he doubted she was paying any attention; as far as June-Marie was concerned, she'd cleverly turned the tables on him by freeing herself with a carelessly stored weapon.

It had occurred to him that afternoon that she hadn't asked about Alexi. If she didn't know about the booby trap, she couldn't have known if he was home or not when the house blew. She'd already confirmed that address was where he was supposedly staying, after all.

She'd claimed she wanted Alexi dead, but when he'd returned to the motel and told her the house had blown up, she hadn't even asked if Alexi survived.

That meant she knew he wouldn't be in the house, and that meant they'd planned it together.

They'd taken out most of his men, and in the event Victor had been wise enough to stay back, they had Bob to blackmail into doing the deed.

But that also meant Norm wasn't in the house, either.

They had him somewhere else. If June-Marie knew the whole thing was a setup... she probably also knew where Alexi was. That indicated they were still a couple; she loved him and wouldn't have betrayed his location.

Not unless she thought she was free and clear.

He'd emptied the pipe and magazine on the Colt before storing it. It had been a risk; if she'd taken a shot, angered, the ruse would've been up.

But she hadn't, as he'd expected.

Now, the question was whether she would run right back to Alexi.

She steered the car away from downtown, heading east towards The Heights. The Dodge Shadow exited Jackson Avenue, and Bob slowed the BMW slightly, keeping her in view throughout. Following someone was meticulous work, requiring concentration, and he emptied his mind of any other matters.

Three blocks into a residential neighborhood, she pulled the car over in front of a house on Hudson Street.

Bob flicked on his turn signal and took the next right. He made sure the street was empty before pulling a U-turn, turning back onto Hudson just as she got out of the car.

He parked three blocks away from the Dodge and watched as she followed the gap between two homes.

She wasn't carrying her suitcase. *Doesn't want to share with Alexi?* Maybe she wasn't as crazy about the Russian as he'd thought. *Or she is, but doesn't trust him completely.* That fit the profile.

He saw a back door swing open for a moment, just visible beyond the left rear corner of a house, then close again.

Bob counted off two minutes before getting out of the car. He followed the sidewalk to the next corner of the block and turned south until he reached the entrance to the lane behind the row of homes.

There were back porch lights on, back rooms lit. It was nearly midnight, but people were still awake. He followed the lane casually, hands in both jacket pockets like any citizen out for a stroll.

At the house she'd entered, he moved close to the fence so that he could try the gate latch. It was open. A light was on upstairs but none downstairs. A transom window at ground level suggested the basement was in use, too.

The yard was empty, the flower boxes overgrown with weeds. A trash can sat just behind the gate. Bob lifted the lid and took a look inside. Bags from fast-food restaurants, a couple of empty Pepsi bottles — *in a Coca-Cola town, no less.* An empty vodka bottle was propped next to the can, perhaps left for a bottle picker to claim the refund.

Hmm... I wonder...

He checked inside one of the fast-food bags.

Yep. This is it.

The back door looked weak, easily pried open if necessary. There was a window halfway up the side of the house — a downstairs bathroom probably.

If you do this now, you go in with the girl there. That's two on one, to begin with; then there's the fact that you might have to kill her to get out of there.

He had no idea what he was dealing with, and no idea how culpable she really was. He had his suspicions, but... Then there were the intangibles. For all he was aware, Alexi could have partners or heavy weaponry. He could've booby-trapped the place to kingdom come.

I would.

He headed back to the car. He'd spotted a phone store on the way there. His burner had gone down with the boat — not that it mattered immediately. They'd risked killing him with the house explosion. That kind of ruthlessness suggested Alexi might renege on their deal. When he called him to discuss Victor, he wanted to be near the Russian, able to act if it was clear Norm was in trouble.

The phone store would likely be open by eight in the morning, nine at the latest.

He's not going anywhere, not right away.

He rummaged through his soft-sided travel bag on the passenger's seat, pulling out the folder Alexi had given him and noting the man's phone number again. In the morning, he could get a new phone, have a little chat with the Russian.

In the meantime... I'll take a little nap. He locked the car doors and put the keys in his pocket. The chances of being bothered while sitting in his car on a private west end street were pretty low, he figured, and he needed a few hours of shut-eye.

He rummaged through the remaining box of ammo.

Twenty bullets, enough for one mag.

Still... more than enough for a guy like Alexi.

36

He woke at four, before dawn.

Bob took a white T-shirt from his bag and used it to cover the passenger seat. He stripped the FN 5.7 down on it. He released the magazine and pulled the slide back to ensure the chamber was empty. He shifted the slide release on the stock, just ahead of the trigger guard, and the barrel and slide assembly came clear. Inside the housing, he pulled the barrel forward slightly to release it, then pulled it out, spring included.

He applied some gun oil to the moving parts and used a thread-free cloth to wipe it down before reassembling it.

At five, he used the early morning light to read through Alexi's file on Victor again, trying to get a sense of the man's level of preparedness, his eye for detail.

He seemed... pragmatic. The notes were devoid of emotion but also light on extraneous detail, things he assumed were valueless but could have helped, like the layout of the mansion's back windows.

So... he's goal-oriented and practical but not particularly clever.

That matched what he'd seen in Iraq. The man knew he had no shot at survival, so he'd hidden himself away. But he'd done it by huddling behind a truck tire rather than trying to use the shadows of the village fence to slink off.

The house? *I wonder if that was June-Marie's idea.* Given how she'd led him back to Alexi, she wasn't winning any Nobel prizes any time soon, it had to be said. So...

Don't underestimate them. Follow the plan; get her out of there; isolate him. He knew he had to compartmentalize his growing disgust with the deadly couple, store it away until business was dealt with. Norm's safety was the priority, not teaching two lowlifes a lesson.

From six until eight, he listened to the radio sporadically, getting updates on the dramatic shoot-out and explosion on the Mississippi.

Police were concluding that the lone gunman involved in another shooting nearby just moments earlier had probably been on the destroyed cabin cruiser when it left the dock. A third boat commandeered by another individual was stolen, and the individual was believed to have been a member of the public "recklessly attempting to catch an armed criminal, which police do not recommend. There has been no sign of him since the explosions, and police fear his body may never be recovered."

Okay, that helps. It wouldn't buy him much time, he knew. Whoever sent the shooter at the dock after him — he had to assume Eddie Stone — wouldn't give up, no matter how sincere Bob's warning. He needed to deal with Alexi and get out of town.

But first, he had to make a call.

. . .

Just after eight, Bob walked to the phone store and bought a burner with a month of unlimited use. He took it back to the car and dialed Alexi's number. He ended it on the third ring, then immediately dialed back.

"Go for Alexi!"

"You seem chipper this morning."

"Bob! I am just waking up; my girl makes me avocado toast; my radio is telling me sources say Victor Malyuchenko is believed to be man killed in big explosion on river. So Alexi has many reasons to be happy. And I presume you are mystery citizen who heroically gave life to save cops, yes?"

"It's a narrative. It helps them explain some things more easily, while bits and pieces of people and boats and a chopper will take months to sort out."

"So... you must be happy too, my friend. This is almost over, and we never have to see each other again."

"Almost? Your guy is dead. Let Norm go."

"Ah! Yes, yes, of course. I will release your friend. When I am sure you have left town."

"That's not going to happen, and that wasn't the deal. I kill your guy; you free mine. That was the deal. If I leave town, you'll put a bullet in Norm's head the second you think I'm gone. He's a witness. He's probably seen your face, since you don't seem like the cautious type, which means he can identify you if you get linked to any of this other shit."

"Tsk..." Alexi tutted. "Is shame you don't trust Alexi. I mean, if I am in your boots, I would not trust me either. Has not worked out so good for others, is true..."

"Let him go."

"Leave city. I let him go."

"I'll have to come and get him if you don't."

"You won't find me."

"I already have."

There was a pause on the line. Then Alexi sniffed loudly. "Yeah... I don't think so. If you know where I was, you would come for me. It would not help you, as your friend is not here, but you would come anyway, try to take me at gunpoint, force me to reveal his location."

"Just the same, I'd tell your girlfriend to clear out before I come around for our little chat. I followed her there from the motel last night. She's not exactly what you'd call tactically astute. If she gets anywhere near being in the way, I will shoot her."

He didn't like that. He sniffed again, loudly. "If you ever were to harm hair on her perfect head, I WOULD DESTROY YOU!" he barked. "I WOULD DESTROY YOU, YOUR FAMILY, EVERYTHING YOU LOVE!"

Oh my. He has it bad.

I doubt she feels as strongly.

"It does not matter, as she would not go," Alexi said. "She loves Alexi so much, she would rather fight and die with me than go."

"Tell her that. Tell her I'm on my way over, and before I get there, she needs to get the rest of her bags out of her car, because you're going to be there for a while. See how she reacts to that."

Alexi fell silent for a moment. Bob could practically see him, eyes flitting side to side as he tried to parse the possibilities.

"What are you playing at, American? You are trying to trick Alexi..."

"Nah. I just want to see how she reacts to the notion of being your wingman, comrade."

"Comrade? Oh, so little ethnic political dig now? Small, Bob, too small for man like you. I try. We see."

He ended the call.

Bob put the phone in his pocket and kept his eyes on the Dodge Shadow two blocks ahead.

After less than three minutes, June-Marie appeared, bolting from the back door and running to the car. His hand drifted to the FN 5.7, anticipating Alexi possibly chasing after her.

But the Russian was at least disciplined enough not to do that. A few seconds later, the Dodge pulled away from the curb, tires kicking up dust as she stepped on the gas.

His phone rang.

"You are satisfied? She run like little child," Alexi said sullenly. "How you know?"

"Alexi..." Bob really didn't feel like explaining arrested emotional development to a self-pitying sociopath, or how it was behind most shitty human behavior. "Let's put it this way: if you were in the middle of a shoot-out, and the other guy had one bullet left, and you had the chance to either take that bullet in the chest, or pull her in front of you..."

The Russian sighed. "So... I see. It is... what's the word in English..."

"Just say it in Russian."

"You speak Russian?" he scoffed. "I am not surprised, I guess. *Ona byla prachmatina.*"

"She was being pragmatic. Yeah, exactly. Just like you wouldn't take that bullet for her, she decided she wasn't going to help you fight me."

"I still have your friend. He is... in a safe place."

"Uh-huh."

"So... if I don't show and make sure he has air, he dies."

"Yeah... maybe. Or maybe you're just full of shit."

That was the last straw for the Russian. *"Chert tebya poderi! Prikhodi za mnoy! Pokazhi mne, chto u tebya yest', d'yavol!"* Damn you! Come after me! Show me what you've got, devil!

He cut off the call.

Bob allowed himself a small smile. Alexi was rattled, angry, feeling like he had a score to settle.

He'd be at his most careless.

It was almost time to stop by for a visit.

37

Bob watched for a half hour as people left their homes on the way to work. Occasionally one would glance at the BMW long enough to seem a little curious. But after forty minutes, it had quieted to just the odd passing car.

He drew his binoculars from the travel bag and propped an elbow against the door.

The house was well-chosen, doubtless a short-term online rental. It had no front balconies; the roof was a good twenty-five feet above ground level; the front yard was shallow, just a strip of grass before the path, steps and front door.

Anyone approaching from there would be seen instantly. He might've put USB cameras on the front windows, allowing him to monitor remotely.

The side window was six feet off the ground, complicating a break-in there. Even if he could use it, it would likely lead to a downstairs bathroom, an enclosed box of a room with no cover or space to maneuver. An automatic weapon could perforate it so thoroughly in seconds that no one inside could survive.

That left the back door, the same door June-Marie had used.

Which means it has to be booby-trapped and guarded somehow. It was tactically difficult, with Norm in the potential crossfire and ruling out going in heavy. It was a serious choke point.

So how do I unchoke it?

Triggering whatever defenses Alexi had in place was an option. If he could breach the door without putting himself in the firing line, he knew, he could exhaust half of whatever tricks the Russian had up his sleeve before putting a foot inside.

He put the binoculars back in the bag. The Russian could be reckless, that much was obvious. He'd likely had June-Marie's help with the exploding house gambit. But he was also ex-military, smart enough to know he couldn't bunker down without defending his perimeter.

So how far would he go? Shotguns rigged to fire on opening the door? Probably. Low-grade explosives? If he has Norm in the basement, sure. Can't risk losing his one piece of leverage; that's his last line of defense.

A thought occurred. Maybe it was like the night at the mansion. Maybe it wasn't so much a matter of opportunity as one of means.

He took out his phone. A quick flick through Alexi's folder produced the number he needed.

It rang through to voicemail. Before the message could fully engage, he ended it and tried again.

This time, it took two rings to get an answer.

"Who is this?"

"Jerry Perry! How is the bureau's best and brightest on this fine Tuesday morning?"

"YOU PRICK!"

"Now, Jerry…"

"YOU MIDWEST, PODUNK, SOLDIER-FIELD-FUCKING, BRATWURST-EATING PRICK! If we ever meet in person again…"

"Jerry… now you're just being silly. I've had practice dummies that would give me more of a workout."

"Three years of undercover work, and now I'll BE LUCKY IF BRIGHTON BEACH DOESN'T PUT A HIT ON ME, LET ALONE KEEP ME IN THE FAMILY, YOU USELESS COCKSUCKAH!"

Evidently, he'd been betting on Victor. His Jersey accent had slipped back in, flattening his *r*'s.

"HEY!" Bob yelled back, slipping into the role. "You made your own bed; now you get to lie in it. Do you want to know why I'm calling? Because I'm damn sure losing any incentive to help your useless ass… all right, SIMON? Yeah, I know who you are, too."

The agent didn't deserve a break, Bob knew. He'd put multiple members of the public at risk. Worse, he'd protected Malyuchenko for most of three years, allowing who knew how many others to be hurt by the sociopathic Russian. For what? A possible route into another potentially bigger bust, in a city far away. Glory for the bureau?

But then, helping him wasn't really the point of the call.

"So say what you've got to say," Perry demanded.

"You can still pin all of this on someone tangible, someone Brighton Beach can understand: Alexi Pushkin. I know where he is. You just have to go and get him."

"I don't have any men. I have Martin, the driver. That's it."

"It's one guy. You have two guys. The odds are in your favor, big man."

There was a pause as the bureau man thought it over. "You're a deceitful fucker, Singleton, you really are. You just want me to go do your dirty work for you."

"NO, big guy! I want you to go do my dirty work for *us*. Listen... you want to breathe a few last breaths into that dying cow you call a career, I'm more than happy to oblige. Plus, we're sort of supposed to be on the same side. Sort of."

"Yeah... I trust you like I trust a Nigerian prince."

"Do you want the address or not?" Bob demanded. "It's in the west end somewhere. Or maybe east. I'm still not real solid on Memphis geography."

"Go on then."

He gave him the address on Hudson Street. "He's renting it, and my source says he's paid for one more day, which means it's probably today or nothing. Given what went down last night, probably the earlier, the better. He's a skittish sort of fellow."

"Die in a fire, Singleton. Seriously..."

"Okay, yeah, this has been sweet for me too. Later, cupcake."

Bob ended the call.

Now... time to buy a coffee, a breakfast sandwich and have a pee. Then grab a front-row seat.

IT TOOK another forty minutes for the Black Mercedes to slowly creep its way to the curb, across the street from Alexi's rented home.

Bob knew he had to time things carefully.

The moment they breached that back door, something was going to happen: a gunshot, a shotgun blast, an explosion. After that, the situation would escalate quickly. If Alexi took out either Perry or his henchman at the door, he would try to finish the other off.

Then you step in to mop up.

It was all fine in theory. But he'd seen missions planned intricately by tactical pros go sideways in an instant. This situation was even more fluid. If Alexi hadn't stashed Norm in the basement, as was most tactically sound — or in the bedrooms at the very least — the potential for a SNAFU grew exponentially.

This would be easier if you had a shot of courage in you. Just one little shot of vodka, help calm the nerves...

"Oh, would you shut the fuck up!?" he said out loud. "It's official: you're talking to yourself. You've snapped, Bobby."

Down the street, Martin the driver got out of the Mercedes. He walked around to the trunk and opened it, taking out a single-barrel pump shotgun. Then he walked around to the passenger side, working the shotgun's action with one hand en route, chambering a shell.

Jerry Perry got out of the car. He had a black suit on with a gray shirt and the usual aviators, his gray-black hair moussed to a motionless crown. *Looking every bit the next boss*, Bob thought. *I wonder if he even knows where the line is anymore...*

The two men crossed the street, furtively checking each direction for witnesses. Martin went for the front gate, but Perry stopped him at the last moment and directed them down the side path, between the two houses.

Good going, Jerry. All that undercover work certainly hasn't dulled that keen tactical edge the bureau teaches you guys.

There was always a risk, of course, that Perry would put a brave or tough face on and go in first. But that wasn't likely, Bob knew. Instead, he'd send in Martin, one of the thugs he'd knocked cold behind BB King's, just off Beale Street. He'd do that because Perry was at least smart enough to stay alive.

Bob wasn't that concerned either way. The agent's first reaction on bumping into him had been to call Washington. He'd had no trouble with Bob getting picked off and removed from the equation, or June-Marie for that matter. As treacherous as she was, she was still a civilian, one of the people he was supposed to protect.

Betting he's wearing a vest, too.

The pair disappeared behind the house.

Bob retrieved the FN 5.7 and chambered the first round, his finger resting lightly on the safety, just above the trigger. It was one more reason why he liked the accurate law-enforcement weapon: the safety position encouraged trigger discipline.

He opened the car door and got out.

Across the street, he saw a flash of movement. Someone diving clear…?

The explosion blew the back door off its hinges, splinters and chunks of wood flying outwards in concert with the plume of gray smoke.

Hand grenade? The size of the blast seemed about right.

Bob sprinted for the path to the back door.

38

He reached the back corner of the house. Jerry Perry was lying a few feet away, a massive splinter — the corner of the door, it appeared — sticking through the top of his thigh. He was grimacing, gritting his teeth, flat on his back.

Bob ignored him. Just in front of the steps to the house, Martin's body lay faceup. The driver had taken the blast point blank and was dead, his face and hands scorched and burned, flesh torn away in chunks.

He crouched low, staying left of the door slightly as he approached it, keeping an advantageous angle on anyone exiting. The smoke hadn't cleared, making seeing past the entryway impossible. He stayed wide until he reached the side of the steps.

Bob peeked around the corner. The smoke from the blast was beginning to dissipate, but the interior hall wall was smoldering, the blast having torn away chunks, the inner framework exposed.

At the far end of the hall, about twenty-five feet away, was a door — a bathroom, perhaps. A few feet prior to it, the hall branched off to the right.

He entered the main corridor, crouching low to lower his target profile, moving slowly towards the far door and the other hall.

He peered through a hole in the adjacent wall, to his right; it appeared to be an empty room, the light out.

He crept forward methodically.

Alexi leaned around the far corner, low, a shotgun in hand. Bob dove back and to the right, towards the damaged wall, letting it cut off some of the angle as the shell blasted a hole in the drywall to his left.

He landed on his back. He leaned up and swapped the FN to his left hand with a half-toss, raising it in the same single motion, firing down the length of the wall, squeezing the trigger twice as the Russian dove back around the corner, into cover.

"Standoff," Bob said. "I know my ammo will cut through that drywall like it's nothing. But I don't know where you're standing…"

"And if you shoot me through wall, you give away position, and this will most definitely put hole through wall, as you already see, so…"

"You could just give up," Bob said. "Save us both the hassle."

"Ha! You still have sense of humor, Bob. This is good."

"Can't survive in this business without it." Bob leaned his back against the wall for a moment, letting the immediate tension slip away. It felt momentarily calming, as if years of fatigue were going with it. He wondered if Alexi was doing the same.

Maybe the whole ordeal had to come down to this, he

thought. They were both dead men, in a sense. Neither had accepted it yet. Whoever walked away was probably just delaying the inevitable.

"You still there, Bob?" the Russian called out.

"I am."

"I wonder, sometimes, what it's like when you die. I was sure in Iraq you would kill me, you know. So scared. I shake uncontrollably, my heart pounding. I think if I even tried to raise pistol, I would drop it, my hands shake so much. It was worst moment of my life. It's a terrible thing, caring if you live. After that, I let go. I had to not care, throw myself at what I wanted. That fear, it is worse than the act, yes?"

"Maybe."

"No! Not maybe! Is true. When we were in Iraq and you kill my friends, you also kill someone very special to me. You shot Yuri through the back of the head as he tried to get up, beside the truck."

"I remember the shot, I think. He didn't freeze, when so many of the others did. He was brave."

"He was my younger brother, my only family left on Earth. I keep his ashes around my neck, to remind me of him every day."

Of course he was, and of course you do. Things were never uncomplicated, it seemed. "So this was never going to end well, then."

"No. I admit... it is not fear, but... I do not want my life to end. I also cannot let you live, for Yuri."

"I've never feared dying," Bob said. "Never even occurred to me to be worth it. You won't care when you're gone, right?"

Alexi scoffed. "Come on! Even man who is dead inside has things about life he enjoys, people he will miss..."

"Sure. And they'll die, too. Everything does. But we're all

just bit players in an endless game, Alexi. We can build ourselves up in this life, seek fame, fortune, power... but in a hundred years, few will remember and even fewer will care. Even those who find immortality are tainted by bad memories, biases, social change. No one escapes pure. No one's legacy is magical or perfect. And in the end, it's usually better when we're eventually forgotten."

The Russian was silent for ten or fifteen seconds. Bob wondered briefly if he'd winged him and Alexi had lost consciousness. "You still there?"

"Yes. I... I feel pity for you, Bob. I know you loathe me and do not want this. But... as bad man as I am, maybe, at least I still feel for myself. At least I feel I matter. At least I can feel enough to love, to fall in love with June-Marie, my angel. My downfall. At least I can hate. To... to hate you for killing my brother. You are just... nihilist, lost in darkness, stumbling towards the edge of a cliff. Is... Is sad, to hear great warrior so humbled."

It should have riled him, irritated him at least that the Russian was looking down on him, pitying his lack of identity, his absence of desire.

If it had, Bob supposed, it wouldn't have been true.

Pull it together. He's in your head.

But you're working, and Norm's life is at stake.

That's something. Helping others is something, right?

"Only one of us can walk out, Bob. And you do not care if you live or die. But... I wonder why you do this now, here. Why? If you do not care, why do you fight so goddamned hard for this man... these people?"

"Because... when I do go, I want to leave something behind that mattered. If that something is someone else having a long life, having kids, having happiness... well...

then it mattered. It mattered that I was here. It mattered, even though I'm not even a memory."

Alexi was silent again for a few moments. When he did speak, he sounded tired. "This is... noble reason, I suppose. But... it is not what I mean, really. I just want to know why HERE. I tell you what will happen to your friend, that he is buried, and yet still you come..."

That snapped him back to attention. For all his banter, Alexi was deader inside, Bob knew, than he could ever be. "And I don't believe you," Bob said.

"Is awful risk to take."

"Not if I'm sure."

"Or perhaps you care so little about your own life that you do not pay attention to how it hurts others."

The MK3A2 concussion grenade ricocheted off the wall ten feet ahead of him. Bob scrambled backwards and threw himself, headfirst, towards the back door, covering up.

The grenade blew, the hallway showered with shrapnel, chunks of drywall and wood, the light fixture crashing to the ground behind it.

Bob rolled over, the debris sliding off him. The explosion had been loud enough to blunt his already damaged left-side hearing to a squealed whine. He felt a sudden rush of heat, his ankle scalding.

He looked down. His pant cuff and sneaker were both on fire. He rolled over, turning the leg rapidly back and forth against the ground. He shook his foot frantically, the flame petering out. He felt a pain in his thigh, a burning sensation. A piece of jagged metal from the grenade's casing was embedded. He was lucky, he knew, that he'd flatted outside the concussion grenade's six-foot kill zone. It was in less than a half centimeter. He pulled it out, the small gash bleeding slightly.

If that's a pineapple instead of a concussion blast, you're a dead man. Take the advantage. Move while he's still wondering if you're alive.

Bob righted himself quickly and clambered to his feet, turning and sprinting for the corner, ignoring the wobbly sensation of his brain bouncing around in his skull. He rounded the turn, aiming down the hall and firing twice blindly, his feet barely able to keep balanced.

He saw Alexi lean out of the far-left doorway and adjusted his aim, a third shot taken just as the Russian yanked the shotgun trigger again. Bob dove to his right, into the first room, the shell wreaking further havoc on the hallway.

It was dark, a kitchen, just a slight glow of natural light through the damaged walls. He leaned against the ajar door and quickly checked the corridor again. He saw Alexi peek around a doorframe across and down the hall, then go back into cover.

"You have lots of bullets, yes?" Alexi yelled. "Because I have many shells. We can do this for a while, yes? Perhaps one of us gets lucky, hits the other. Perhaps not."

He seemed to be about to pitch some sort of bargain, one in which Bob had no interest. "So... I take it you're out of grenades," he replied instead.

"Ha!" Alexi sounded deeply amused. "I swear, Bob, if you weren't such a fucker, I would buy you beer and forget whole thing. You got style, my man. So... we do this, then?"

"Yeah... no time like the present, I guess..." Bob dropped low and leaned around the corner into the hallway at waist height.

Alexi darted out of the room, the shotgun exchanged for an H&K MP5, his torso naked other than a Kevlar vest. "Body armor, motherfucker!" he snarled. He raised the submachine gun to aim down the metal sight.

Bob shot him twice in the chest before he could complete the move, the SS190 "blacktip" ammo slicing through the Kevlar like it was tissue paper.

Alexi stumbled backwards, falling onto his backside, the gun flying from his grip. He leaned back, one hand on his chest wounds, the other reaching for the MP5, behind him, as Bob closed on him at a walk.

His fingers were brushing the grip when Bob shot him through the chest again.

Alexi gave up his efforts and slumped to a motionless fetal position. A trickle of blood ran from the corner of his mouth. He gurgled slightly as he tried to speak. "How..."

"Armor-piercing rounds," Bob said.

"Huh... Ex... ex-expensive. Rare in Memphis."

"Why would you run from cover like that?"

"Thought... you would protect your friend. Thought... you bluff Alexi." He giggled slightly, then wheezed and coughed, blood spattering his face around his lips. "I lie to you, I admit... but... how you know... I tell you is buried alive, but you attack me anyway..."

Bob shook his head. "Despite your suggestion he was in a hole somewhere, I was sure he was here. And that meant he wasn't at immediate risk of running out of air."

"Not possible. When I move... is middle of night, no one around. I would notice. How...?"

"Hot sauce," Bob said.

"Hot... sauce?" The dying Russian was obviously puzzled.

"Hot sauce. You hate it. You mentioned it in the diner. But Norm? Norm eats that shit like it was the air we need to breathe. And the brown paper bags in the trash behind your house are full of empty packets of hot sauce."

"Hot sauce," Alexi bemoaned. "Fucking Memphis."

"You got that right." Bob shot him through the head.

The smoke was beginning to build, visibility beginning to decrease. He felt a sting in his sinuses and tickle in his throat.

The house is on fire.

The drywall and wooden framing in the main hallway had been burning when he'd rounded the corner. But that didn't matter in the moment: he needed to find Norm. Bob tried the two doorways immediately adjacent. One led to a bedroom.

The door at the end of the hall fronted stairs down to the basement.

He took them two at a time.

Norm was seated near the boiler, his legs tied to a chair, his hands manacled together with handcuffs.

"BOB!"

For a man who'd been captive for two days, he didn't sound put out. Bob made his way over to him. "Sorry I took so long. Shit: handcuffs."

"The key's on that loop by the dryer," he said, nodding across the wide-open room.

Bob jogged over and retrieved it. "Margie's going to be happy to see you," he said. "She's the reason I found you, you know."

Norm smiled at that, and a tear rolled down his cheek. He wiped it away and looked away, blushing. "Ah geez... that's..."

"It's okay," Bob said, clapping the older man on the back. "It's just the smoke, I bet. Now... let's get the hell out of here before this whole place goes up."

THEY WERE ten feet out the back door, just passing Martin's dead body, when Bob realized Jerry Perry's figure was no longer prone by the side fence.

He put a gentle hand up to Norm's chest height. "Stay here."

Bob moved cautiously to the side of the house and peered around the corner.

"D-d-don't you FUCKING MOVE!" the undercover agent spat.

He was lying on his back, the large piece of wood still jutting out of his leg, a trail of blood leading back to the fence line. He had a Glock 19 in his right hand, his left elbow supporting him as he tried to stay in a seated position.

The hand was shaking, wobbling from side to side, his increasingly weak state unable to properly balance the pistol's weight.

"Jerry, if you try to shoot me, the way you're jerking about, you're liable to kill someone in one of the houses behind us. Just... put it down, big guy, okay?"

"I... I should... should fucking kill you, Singleton..."

"But you won't, because you know I could've killed you any number of times and didn't. Because we're supposed to be on the same side."

"Should... should..." His eyes were flitting about, blood loss obviously dazing him. "Where...?" The gun hand slumped down beside him, and he lowered himself ungracefully to the ground, lying on his back.

Bob crouched beside him, found the man's phone in his pocket and dialed 911.

"911 Emergency, go ahead, please..."

"Yeah... you'll have fire and police headed to a house on Winter Harbor Lane already. You're going to need to send an ambulance, too. Guy has a bad leg wound; he could bleed out. No, that's it, bye." He hung up the call and tossed the phone down next to Perry. "They're on their way. I'm going to be leaving, too, Jerry. We won't see each other again unless you choose to make an issue of it. I wouldn't recommend it."

He rejoined Norm. The two men were halfway across the road when Perry called out after him, "This isn't over, Singleton. Not... by a long shot."

Bob helped Norm to the car. By the time they got there, two days of stiffness had subsided enough for him to climb into the passenger seat unassisted.

The distant sirens grew louder as the BMW sped away.

IN THE TINY front garden of their home, Margie was weeping, hugging her husband so tight he begged off.

"Hon... hon, I can't breathe..." he said.

She relaxed slightly but didn't let him go. "I was so scared, Normie. So scared you'd die and we'd never talk again, and I'd never see you again..."

Bob watched them from by the gate. He'd stayed near the car so as not to intrude on the moment.

He heard movement behind him. He turned. Across the road, Mike Grainger had taken a seat on one of the wicker porch chairs and was looking his way. Bob half-raised his hand to wave hello, but Grainger turned his attention deliberately to a magazine.

Ouch. But you had to expect that, Bobby. His wife is alive, but it's no thanks to you.

Margie led Norm into the house. Bob had turned back towards the car and was walking that way when her voice sounded sharply behind him.

"HEY!"

He faced the house. She was steaming up the path at a race-walker clip.

"I figured you wouldn't want me to stick around..." Bob said.

She stopped on the other side of the gate and crossed her arms. She looked incensed. "So you drop my husband off and just go, without offering us a word of apology? Is that it?"

"I'm sorry, I didn't mean to..."

"You're SORRY?! You're fucking SORRY?! You didn't mean... what, to have my husband nearly killed, to put my best friend in a hospital, clinging to life?"

"Look, Margie, I didn't intend..."

"Oh, fuck right off with your good intentions! I don't give two goddamned shits what y'all intended. You're involved with dangerous people, murderous criminals, criminals right here in my hometown. And yet you think it's okay to accept my husband's kind hospitality..."

"I didn't know Alexi was here. I swear..."

"And what happens if it's not over?"

"They're both dead. You're safe..."

"And I'm sure you figured that was true when you came to stay, too. But y'all missed a few possibilities, clearly. What if they have more friends y'all don't know about, other criminals who want you dead? Are they going to show up at our door and try to hurt us? Are y'all going to ride to the rescue again from wherever you've disappeared to?"

She was beet-red and had bunched her hands into fists, spitting mad. She looked like she might lean over the gate and punch him.

"I can't do anything to change what happened," Bob tried. "I can only apologize and promise..."

"DON'T PROMISE ME SHIT!" Margie bellowed. "JUST... just get the fuck off our street and out of our lives! Don't come visit Norm again! Don't bring your shitty criminal world around us again! I'm going to be opening the front door for God knows how long with Normie's Colt in my hand, because now I can't sleep at night, and I can't function, and I can't do anything without worrying if someone is going to invade our home..."

Bob hung his head, the venom cutting deeply.

"And you know what? Y'all had better never be standing on the other side of that door, Bob, because I swear to God, I will shoot you myself."

"Margie..."

"GO! Just... just go. Go play hero for someone else. Go convince yourself you're a good guy somewhere else."

She turned on her heel and strode back to the house, slamming the front door behind her.

Bob walked back to the car in shock. He asked himself how else she should've reacted. Once again, he'd been nothing but trouble.

He took out his phone and ordered a hire car. He needed to grab a few things and a bus ticket before stopping by the bank.

Then he could put Memphis behind him.

The feeling was clearly mutual.

39

The bank vault was bright and wide, lined on each side with four-by-four-inch metal drawers set into the walls and protected by tiny steel doors.

The bank clerk seemed pleased to see him. "Usually, it's just the seniors needing help with bills who come into the branch these days. Everyone does their banking by ATM," she said, unlocking the safe-deposit box and pulling it from its slot. "I don't begrudge them it, though. Lord willing I'll still be able to walk to the bank at their age…"

She placed it on the countertop dividing the room into two. "There you go, sir. I'll just leave you to it. Give us a call if you need any help."

Bob gave her a smile, then waited until she'd left before placing his soft-sided bag on the table. He needed to act quickly; his bus out of town was forty-five minutes away, and a not-entirely-terrible artist's rendition of him was circulating on the TV news.

He lifted the metal lid.

The box was lined with stacks of bills.

He counted the rows and layers and did some mental math.

Fifty thousand, all there...

The exit plan had been his former teammate Jon Rice's idea. He'd planned on doing the same, not trusting their bosses at the agency to let any of them walk away from the Team.

But it was obvious, first from New Orleans and then Memphis, that retreading old turf was dangerous to others. He'd intended on revisiting regrets from the past, and instead had brought pain and suffering down on two separate families.

He had to go somewhere unfamiliar, full of unfamiliar faces. No ties to his dangerous past, no risk to others.

He was halfway down the broad stone steps to the sidewalk when a familiar voice ahead caught his attention.

"So that's it? You were just going to drop me off at home and then leave, after everything?"

Norm O'Hearn sounded hurt. He stood at the foot of the steps, hands in the pockets of his bomber jacket as a light rain drizzled down.

Bob wasn't surprised. He'd expected Norm to be upset.

He'd also expected to get out of town before it became an issue. There was no percentage in telling his old friend what Margie had said to him earlier, no good in driving any wedges between them — or worse, finding out that Norm agreed.

"I thought I'd done enough harm already," he said. "I thought the quicker and farther I got away, the less you'd have to relive any of this, the less chance some friend of Victor or Alexi comes looking for me."

Norm nodded. "I sort of figured." He gestured toward the street. "Walk with me to the club?"

"Okay. Sure."

Norm kept a languid pace, traffic along Overton Park Avenue sparse on an early Tuesday afternoon. "Margie... I ain't seen her so happy since I got back from 'Nam. But... she's... she's not real fond of you right now, Bob. She kind of agreed with your suggestion that your choices haven't gone too well for others."

"It's not really a debate," Bob said. "It's the abject reality."

"She's not always right, though," Norm said.

"She is in this case. I mean... this is what I do, Norm. It's why you shouldn't be around me. People get hurt, then I hurt people... then people get hurt, and it just goes on. So do yourself a favor: listen to your wife."

He took a deep breath in at that, like he didn't like being told what his conclusion should be before he'd reached it himself.

"You know, it's one thing to spend your time wandering around the country, trying to make up for whatever you done that's got you all squirrelly. But if you then continue to beat yourself up despite trying to pay your dues... well... pay your dues, or moan about it and feel guilty. But don't do both. That's just unnecessary."

"It feels very necessary. It feels like I always just make things worse."

"It feels that way because you've got losses you haven't really come to terms with, a past you can't let go of. I get that. Can I tell you a little story? It's one of the few benefits of age, having stories."

"Shoot."

"I grew up in Asbury Park, New Jersey. Tough neighborhood, but a tight one. My best friend growing up was this kid Lee Kenner. Tough as nails, great at stickball, maybe could've had a future as a ball player if he hadn't wanted to join the army so bad. He was eager to go to 'Nam, eager to do his bit to spread democracy."

"This kind of story never ends well," Bob said.

"Just so. So I'll skip you the speeches he made about changing the world, because we already know where this is headed..."

"How long?"

"One day. He'd been in-country for one day when a sniper shot him through the head while he was walking from his barracks to the latrines. Didn't even spot the Cong what done it. Didn't spend a day in combat. Didn't achieve anything. I'd regretted how into army life he'd become when we were in high school. But I had two more years over there, fighting my damnedest just to stay alive, to regret not telling him how I felt, not even trying to change his mind."

Bob stopped walking. "You can't possibly blame yourself for that..."

"I know it's not reasonable," Norm said, "but it's how it feels. How it feels to have your buddy just die, for nothing, while you're sleeping thirty yards away in a cot, unable to do a damn thing. And he was only the first of many. That's a hard row to hoe, my friend. But I put it behind me because it wasn't fair to me, and it wasn't fair to Margie either."

Norm had learned the most painful lesson, Bob figured: that killing for something you believe in is still killing; that dead is still dead. And that some pain never goes away. "She's pretty special, Norm, no doubt."

"That she is. When I got back from 'Nam... well, I can admit it, Bob, I was pretty messed up. I was a kid, just twenty-three. She knew how bad I was, the nightmares, the sense of loneliness, cut off from my squad. But it never gave her pause. She never doubted me; despite everything she'd been through, growing up with the colonel as her father, she never did anything but love me."

"Yeah... Yeah, I knew someone like that once..." Bob said, though it came out a half-whisper.

"At night, the terrors... I'd see things in my sleep worse even than what really happened, men destroying each other, eating each other, burning alive. And she'd stay up with me. She'd hold me. 'I knew you'd always come back to me,' she'd say. Then she'd pour us each a shot of courage and sit up with me 'til dawn, even though she was working a solid eight."

"I had to get better, for her. That's the whole point, being there for others, having them be there for you. If you never put your mistakes behind you, or even the things that you just wish you'd done different... it won't be fair to you or the people who care about you, Bob. Because it'll just be a never-ending cycle of you walking out, without even saying goodbye; walking away and figuring you never done no good for nobody."

Norm resumed his leisurely pace, the club at the end of the block.

"There's one significant difference between our stories, though, Norm..." Bob stopped walking for a moment. "You're not the one who shot your buddy. I'm the guy who usually pulled the trigger. That's why guys like Alexi hate me. And when I wasn't, I was in charge of the guys getting shot. Either way, I'm still a killer. You're not."

Norm hung his head slightly, uncomfortable at the bluntness of it. "Yeah... yeah, she brought that up too. I don't expect she'll ever feel comfortable around you again. Staying at the house is..."

"Out of the question. Yeah... I get that."

They began walking again.

"There are things I still have to figure out," Bob said. "Things I need to know before I can get peace of mind. I know what you're saying is true. I was just following orders pretty much all of the time. Hopefully, at some point, I can stop running from the men who gave those orders and figure out how much blame I truly hold, come to terms with being me. I mean... if I even can. There are some bad people who really don't want me alive, Norm. And there are good people out there I'd like to help. It's hard pursuing that, though, when your past is on your tail."

"Fuck 'em," Norm said. "Living is the best revenge. Maybe if you want to stop running, the key is... to stop running."

That was worth considering. Bob knew he'd probably never find out every detail of the betrayal that led to his being burned by the agency. That meant the survivors of his dead squad mates, the few family they left behind, probably wouldn't either.

But maybe that was how it had to be. Maybe the fact that they hadn't been to blame for its failure meant he should let their memories rest. Could he have changed anything that had happened?

Maybe, but probably not. Except for Maggie.

His ex-fiancée had been angry when she'd split, but he hadn't stopped her, though he'd known she could be careless behind the wheel even when she wasn't hotheaded.

That pain — that shame — was never going away, he figured.

They reached the club.

"Well... here we are," Bob said. He took his bag off his shoulder and took out the thick brown envelope. "Here."

"What's this?" Norm asked.

"That's some money to help the folks hurt by this crap."

"I can't take this," Norm said. "I can't take your—"

"It's not mine," Bob interrupted. "It belonged to one of the criminals who started this whole mess. If you don't want any of it, give it all to Mike and Ellie, or the guy next door to the house that blew up. I know you'll make the right choices with it."

"Fine. How much is it?"

"Twenty-five grand."

Norm's eyes widened. "Yowza. Lot of cash. Hey... you know, the one thing you probably CAN tell me is what the hell that guy Alexi was so upset about in the first place," he said as he pocketed it. "You never explained it to me."

Bob filled him in about Iraq. "I didn't think he even really held it against me, until he explained that one of the men I'd killed was his younger brother. I was a bad memory until I walked past him, at which point I became an opportunity. Alexi was just that kind of guy."

"Maybe what he hated deep down is you were the hero in that story, the guy who saved the village from the evil Russkies tormenting their sons and daughters."

Bob winced a little at that. "Alexi thought something similar. But... you know what a war zone can be like. Things... they didn't really go down like that. Look... I've got a bus heading out in a half hour." Bob pointed a thumb over his shoulder. "I need to hit the road. Margie's friend Ellie..."

"She'll be okay, I'm sure. Some stitches, some bed rest,

some physio. She has one last surgery this morning; then she's past the worst of it. We'll be there for her."

"That's good. Give them my love, okay, Norm? And again, I'm sorry…"

"Don't be. I'm good. We're good." Norm extended a hand, and they shook. "Just maybe skip Memphis the next time you're heading across country. I'm not sure my marriage could take it."

Norm headed inside. Bob began walking towards the bus station, pulling his ball cap down, the soft case over his shoulder holding a few new changes of clothes, a couple of books for the trip, and a pile of cash.

Hero? No. Iraq had never been like that, no matter how successful the mission.

He'd never felt like he did a damn bit of good.

40

Bob watched the Ural-4320's red taillights disappear into the distance, the cloud of dust behind it obscuring the glow long before darkness took over.

Letting the Russian go went against his better instincts, his training and his orders. They were all supposed to die. But he hoped that by sending a stronger message — one whimpering about his dead friends — maybe the Ferak Group would look elsewhere for their fun. The villagers didn't look like warriors.

He turned back to the gate. In the village beyond, a few lights came on.

He looked around at the scene. The Ferak Group usually came pretty lean, not carrying much more than their weapons and rations. But the villagers would pick them clean in short order, he imagined. Their lives were already difficult and harsh, sustenance existence in a desert climate. It wasn't about disrespect, just about waste and provision.

"*Madha faealat!?*" *What have you done!?* The village's burly chieftain was striding over, his white-and-blue robes billowing in the evening air. He had both hands in the air and was gesticulating feverishly. *"Laqad qataltna jmyean 'ayuha al'ahmaqu!"* Fool! You have killed all of us!

Bob replied in Arabic. "These men were raiding your village on a false pretext, raping your daughters, assaulting your sons, stealing from you..."

"You told us to stay indoors for a day and everything would be solved! That is what you claimed. But this... this is a slaughter!"

A small crowd of villagers had begun to gather behind the chief.

None looked happy.

"They were coming back. They were going to keep coming back..." Bob began to say.

"And you expect what? Us to fight their friends when they come for revenge? With what? Our good intentions?" The chief's words stung with contempt. "You do not think every heart breaks in this village when they approach? But no one fights for us! No one will come here and defend us. We are farmers! So we give them what they want and no more, and they leave. We have no value except as bait for them... and they for the likes of you. But where will you be tomorrow, American? Or the day after? The likes of them, the jackals of this world... they never leave."

And with that, the chief spat on Bob's boots. "Go on, leave us to die! That is what your orders are, I assume? Come here, kill all of these men for the glory of your country's leaders, then fuck off back to wherever you are from? Well?"

He wasn't sure what he'd expected, but it hadn't been that. Bob felt a moment of profound emptiness, like something had broken. Then it was replaced by rage, anger at the man and his village... even though he understood that every word was true.

He turned back towards the road in, his jeep just a half-klick off. "I have to go," he said.

"Of course you do," the chieftain spat. "I doubt, should you ever return, that we will still be here. They will return soon enough, and next time they will bring more men and more guns, and one man will be able to do nothing — if he were even here. Go home, American. Give some of your own kind a reason to wish your death. Go be a hero, bathed in the blood of the righteous."

A small stone flew past his head, then another. A third hit him in the back.

He ignored them. Within a few seconds he'd be out of range anyway, out of their world, just as they'd expected.

There would be a new target, a new community soon enough.

A new reason for someone to want him dead.

41

It had been an hour-long wait for his bus to depart, and Bob had begun to stew a little.

He'd been considering Margie's diatribe, the anger from Ellie's husband, Mike. Maybe Norm was right: maybe he'd played everything as straight as he could. Maybe they were angry at the circumstances, and he just happened to be the person they could most easily blame.

Maybe this was Al-Mazrae all over again, the people he'd saved somehow seeing him as the problem.

You didn't flag down Alexi Pushkin, or get involved in Victor Malyuchenko's business. All you tried to do was help.

For once, his inner monologue was giving him good advice instead of trying to get him to take a drink. So he'd taken it. Instead of buying a ticket to a smaller, out-of-the-way location, he'd booked a ride on the next bus to San Diego. It was the last known residence of the family of Ellery Azadi, a Team Seven member killed on the Iraq mission.

Maybe there was something he could tell them, something that would make them feel better about his death.

Maybe Norm was right about the past, too. Maybe the shame he felt over his career and the deaths of his fiancée and colleagues was just anger; anger that his life hadn't turned out well, that he wasn't one of the normal people, enjoying their time on this Earth.

Maybe finding somewhere quiet to settle down wasn't necessary. He'd told Dawn Ellis that there were always other people who needed him. Could he fulfill that role while hunkered down in some small town or city, avoiding Team Seven and the hitmen Andrew Kennedy sent after him?

On a TV suspended from the upper corner of the ceiling, the midday news had just come on. It was a follow-up story to the house explosion on Monday, cameras capturing neighbors cleaning up. There was a brief interview with a florid-faced, flustered man identified as the owner of the rental home.

Then another picture, a still headshot, flashed up on the screen.

It was Ellie.

"Hey!" Bob called out to the man at the nearest ticket counter. "Can you turn that up real quick?"

The clerk looked annoyed but grabbed a remote from the end of his counter, swiveled on his stool and did as asked.

"... died this morning due to complications arising from surgery. Mrs. Grainger was fifty-eight years old and leaves behind a husband and two adult children."

Bob slumped back into his chair, his onrush of optimism gone in an instant.

But... Norm said she was going to be okay.
She had nothing to do with it.
Nothing.

He said she was going to make it.

Bob knew he'd let them get involved. When Margie had called him and said she was tracking Alexi's car, he could've warned them off, he knew, scared them even.

Could have? Should have. You should've made sure they were nowhere damn near any of it. Instead, you got caught up in the mission.

And you ignored the risk of collateral.

Again.

The image of Mike Grainger sitting on his porch, forlornly waiting for a wife who would never return...

He hadn't cried in a long time, not since Maggie. But now, Bob couldn't help it. Tears ran freely as he felt his internal, gnawing emptiness grow.

He thought back to the cop who'd died in DC, Sgt. Edward Purcell, a man who'd done nothing more than follow Bob into a blocked tunnel — a tunnel he'd caused to be blocked to trap a target.

You've done it again.

It's the dead cop all over again.

Only this time, it's a wife and mother. A complete innocent.

He pulled the bus ticket out of his pocket. *San Diego, to be a hero? What is wrong with me that I can't just let the past die?*

Bob rose and walked over to the ticket counter.

The clerk looked up from his terminal. "How can I help you today?"

"I'd like to cash this ticket in, if possible, switch to another route."

The man took a look at it. "I can only exchange it for equivalent fare or less, sir... this is all the way to San Diego..."

"What about Tucson, Arizona?"

The clerk nodded. "That should be... yes, it's cheaper by nearly sixty dollars."

Bob collected his new ticket and went back to his seat. *Back to the original plan. Lie low. Find somewhere you don't matter, and stick to it.*

EPILOGUE

As Air Canada Flight 633 to Sydney, Australia, taxied down the runway, June-Marie realized she was actually safe.

The flight was sparsely populated, business class mostly empty.

She looked around to make sure no one was paying her attention. She retrieved the soft-sided overnight case from under the chair ahead of her and unzipped it, propping it on her lap.

Under the top layer of clothes lay the cash.

She lifted a few of the little piles, scarcely able to believe she'd pulled it off.

It had been after a year with Alexi that she'd realized his boss was staring, that a few flirtatious comments might be all it took to set them against each other.

She'd believed in Alexi, believed he'd eventually kill Victor and take over his business.

Then she'd planned to fleece him out of every dime she

could get. It was the least he deserved for all the pawing he'd done over the prior two years.

But it had all gotten out of hand. By the time she'd taken up with Victor, she'd overstimulated his desire to protect his interests, turned his dislike of his former gunman into antipathy, hatred even. She'd expected them to fight it out, man-to-man, and instead, Victor had sent half of Memphis after the other Russian.

She lifted an end stack, feeling the heft of the piles, three bundles of...

Something felt wrong.

The stack is top heavy, as if the bills on top weigh more than...

A rapid sense of shock set in. She lifted the first two piles away.

A pair of twenties drifted loose. They'd been disguising the plastic-wrapped travel packs of Kleenex occupying the space that had once been home to her purloined cash. She pulled the rest of the stacks apart, more packets of Kleenex visible under the top layer of cash.

There was a note, on a square white Post-it.

Took $25K to cover the damage you've caused. Good luck. You're going to need it. -Bob

Her hand slumped to her lap.

All but twenty grand... gone.

He left you enough to start over. Maybe just... keep your cool, June-Marie. Y'all know things could be worse.

"Ma'am?" a flight attendant asked gently. "Ma'am? If you could store your... cash under the seat ahead of you..."

June-Marie glared at the flight attendant but did as requested.

"Is there anything else I can help you with?" the woman offered.

"Got a time machine? Then no." She smirked acidly at the airline employee, hoping she'd take the hint.

The woman walked back down the aisle.

It was okay, June-Marie figured. She knew Australians liked to party; she'd met a few. And she knew they spoke English, sort of. She could find someone gullible, a real dope.

A nagging thought occurred: whether real life or TV, she'd never seen someone take a bag of cash through an airport. *Can I just take that much cash on me through customs?*

It had to be fine, she figured. Money always talked loudest.

THE GREYHOUND COACH ROLLED WEST, the land flat, the view in any direction from the highway fields of soybeans and corn stretching off to the horizon.

Bob checked his phone. GPS said they were in Plum Bayou, Arkansas.

It was a long trip to Tucson, twenty hours of listening to siblings squabbling and other people's phones. Someone was already smoking illegally out a window, the fumes drifting back towards him. They had stops in Texarkana and Dallas where they'd be able to stretch legs; but otherwise, it was going to be a while.

In the row beside him, an elderly man in a short-sleeved dress shirt opened a plastic container and took out one of two egg-salad sandwiches. He saw Bob notice his efforts and offered the other.

"Sure, thanks. Much appreciated."

The senior nodded towards his arm, the tattoo near his wrist. "Thanks for your service, son. You headed to El Paso?"

"Arizona."

"Ah! Long-haul man, huh?" He reached over with a hand to shake. "Tom Kamanis."

"Bob Welling. You're heading home, Tom?"

"I am indeed."

"Almost cheaper to fly these days."

"Never cared for it," said the senior. "Came up to Memphis to visit the grandkids last week. We went to a soccer match. It was better than I'd expected. What about you, Bob? What's your story?"

It was a great question.

"Not sure," Bob answered. "I guess I'm still figuring that out."

The money would make it easier, allow him to settle down for a while, rent a place, maybe find somewhere quiet to work. Helping people didn't have to mean reopening old wounds; maybe it was just being there for them when needed.

Maybe it was just finding something low-key to do for a living, being a good worker, being value for money.

He had plenty of time to think about it — twenty hours, at least.

It was going to be a long ride.

ABOUT THE AUTHOR

Did you enjoy *Dead Drop*? Please consider leaving a review on Amazon to help other readers discover the book.

Ian Loome writes thrillers and mysteries. His books have been downloaded more than a half-million times on Amazon.com and have regularly featured on the Kindle best-seller lists for more than a decade. For 24 years, Ian was a multi-award-winning newspaper reporter, editor and columnist in Canada. When he's not figuring out innovative ways to snuff his characters, he plays blues guitar and occasionally fronts bands. He lives in Sherwood Park, Alberta, with his partner Lori, a pugnacious bulldog named Ferdinand, a confused mostly Great Dane puppy named Ollie, and some cats for good measure.

ALSO BY IAN LOOME

A Rogue Warrior Thriller Series

Code Red

Blood Debt

Dead Drop

Hell Bent

Hard Country

Snake Eyes

Printed in Great Britain
by Amazon